MURDER BY SUNLIGHT

This Large Print Book carries the
Seal of Approval of N.A.V.H.

A QUILTED MYSTERY

MURDER BY SUNLIGHT

THE CHARITY QUILT

BARBARA GRAHAM

WHEELER PUBLISHING

A part of Gale, Cengage Learning

Detroit • New York • San Francisco • New Haven, Conn • Waterville, Maine • London

GALE
CENGAGE Learning

LIBRARY OF CONGRESS CATALOGING-IN-PUBLICATION DATA

Graham, Barbara, 1948–
　　Murder by sunlight : the charity quilt / Barbara Graham.
　　　pages (large print) cm. — (A quilted mystery) (Wheeler Publishing large print cozy mystery)
　　ISBN-13: 978-1-4104-6557-3 (softcover.)
　　ISBN-10: 1-4104-6557-8 (softcover)
　　1. Sheriffs—Fiction. 2. Quilting—Fiction. 3. Tennessee—Fiction. 4. Large type books. I. Title.
　　PS3607.R336M875 2013
　　813'.6—dc23　　　　　　　　　　　　　　　2013047189

Published in 2014 by arrangement with Barbara Graham

Printed in the United States of America
1 2 3 4 5　　　18 17 16 15 14

Mom, you are gone but not forgotten.

ACKNOWLEDGMENTS

Numerous people have cheered me on, corrected my work, tolerated my mental excursions, and answered, more or less politely, any number of odd, inane, and frankly murderous questions. Thank you, all of you. I'm not naming names here — you know who you are. While you might have been tempted to cover my errors, pointing them out to me is a greater kindness.

Ones I must mention by name are:

Michelle Quick, for testing yet another mystery quilt for me. In spite of not enjoying mystery quilts, or maybe because of it, she does a wonderful job.

My husband for a bit of proofreading, a large dose of reality, and the willingness to play dead on command (the dogs won't cooperate). My request usually begins with "you don't need to know why, but . . ."

Alice Duncan, of course, editor extraordinaire, who sees what is invisible to me and encourages me to fix it. Now.

The Charity Quilt
A Mystery Quilt by Theo Abernathy
The First Body of Clues

Finished size is approximately 49 by 61 inches. Fabric requirements given are generous and based on useable fabric widths of 40 inches. (The useable amount seems to have been shrinking.) This pattern assumes familiarity with basic quilt construction, quilting terms, rotary cutting skills, and an accurate 1/4" seam throughout.

Fabric A — this fabric should be a non-directional print created with at least three colors.
  2 yards.

Fabric B — a complementary contrast to A — it can be one of the less used colors in print A.
  1 1/2 yards.

Fabric C — a blending fabric with A — for example, if A is a red/green/blue print, C might be a different blue print.
  5/8 yards.

Fabric D — a high contrast to A — reads solid from a distance.

1/4 yard or a fat quarter will work.

Cutting — be sure to label each with color letter and size.

From Fabric A:
   Cut four 5″ strips the LOF (length of fabric).

From remainder of A:
   Cut 4 pieces 9 1/2″ by remaining WOF (width of fabric).
   Cut 2 pieces 3 1/2″ by remaining WOF.
   Cut 4 pieces 2″ by remaining WOF.
   Cut 8 squares 3 1/4″ inches.
   Cut 16 squares 2 7/8″. Cut 4 squares 2 1/2″.

From Fabric B:
   Cut 8 strips 2 1/2″ by LOF.

From remainder of B:
   Cut 2 strips 3 1/2″ by remaining WOF.
   Cut 12 strips 2″ by remaining WOF.
   Cut 4 squares 5″.

From Fabric C:
   Cut 2 strips 6 1/2″ by WOF.
   Cut 8 squares 2 7/8″.

From Fabric D:
Cut 8 squares 3 1/4".
Cut 10 squares 2 7/8".

CHAPTER ONE

Sheriff Tony Abernathy opened the door of his wife's quilt shop and stepped outside into the summer sunshine. East Tennessee was enjoying a brilliant clear sky with only the normal blue haze over the Smoky Mountains, and no rain in the forecast. Late morning and it was already hot, the expected temperature for almost the Fourth of July, but not blistering. Maybe he could get home in time to do a little yard work. Then Tony remembered his wife had hired some help, freeing him to finish painting the new room built for the baby girls. He took a deep breath and sighed, savoring the moment. The smallest county in the state seemed pretty calm for tourist season.

"Say there, Sheriff." A familiar, nasal voice addressed his left shoulder blade. "I voted for you and I could use a little of your time and help."

Feeling a bit like he'd jinxed himself, Tony

turned and looked down into the face of Clyde Finster. The middle-aged man peered up at him through water-spotted glasses, and a frown line creased his forehead.

"What's up?" Tony said.

"You might not remember my prize fish." Mr. Finster spread his hands far enough apart to indicate a small whale. "It's in danger."

Intrigued in spite of his better judgment, Tony pulled his notebook and a pen from his pocket. "Tell me." He thought Finster's name was appropriate for a dedicated fisherman.

"After we, me'n the fish, won the big fish contest, I had it stuffed and mounted and hung it over my television." Mr. Finster waved his arms about, almost hitting Tony in the face. "I had to move. Rent was too high on the house, and my friend Duke and his wife moved into my old place. They said I could leave just the fish on the wall until I was settled, and can you believe it? A few minutes ago I drove past and saw it out on the burn pile. What's the matter with people?"

Wondering how the man could see anything through those spotted glasses, Tony jotted down the address. "How long did they keep it?"

There was a brief pause while the man worked out the mental math. "Not more'n five, maybe six, years." Mr. Finster turned his head and wiped his dripping nose on the sleeve of his t-shirt.

Tony thought five days of staring at someone else's prize catch might be long enough for him but didn't say anything. "I'll drive out and see what I can learn. If they've already burned it, there isn't anything I can do. Five years might qualify as abandonment."

Knowing his deputy, Wade Claybough, would never forgive him if Tony left him out of a sensational stuffed fish hunt, Tony radioed for him to meet at the address in question. Sure enough, when they arrived, about as far from town as possible and still within Park County, there was a large fish, mounted on a wooden background complete with a brass plate identifying the date it was caught and its size and the fisherman by name. Other than being big, although perhaps a bit smaller than the proud fisherman had indicated, it was an ugly, miserable-looking fish. Tony didn't know if it had been deformed when it was pulled from the water, or if the taxidermist was an amateur and had altered it. In Tony's favorite scenario, it had seen a reflection of itself, had a stroke, and accidently swallowed a hook with its last gasp.

A glance in Wade's direction showed his deputy, staring, apparently mesmerized by the fish and the way its eyes were skewed at an unpleasant angle. The gaping mouth faced the viewer instead of a fake bug, and Tony thought the fish looked as though it had fangs. A vampire fish?

The nasty-looking fish trophy topped a mixed trash pile of dry brush, papers, and miscellaneous yard and kitchen garbage. Standing next to the pile was a tired-looking young woman in jeans and an oversized t-shirt celebrating chocolate. Dark circles rimmed her eyes and more mouse-brown hair had escaped the ponytail clasp than remained in it. She clutched a box of wooden matches in one hand and held an unlit match in the other. Tony recognized her from the grocery store where she was a checker. Her name was Beth and one of her sons played on his older son's baseball team.

"I've gotten a complaint." Tony didn't get further before Beth waved the matches under his nose, stopping him.

"You think you've heard a complaint. I'll give you another one. I'll bet it's about fish." The fatigue in her face and posture vanished in a heartbeat, replaced by a fighting stance. She looked ready to take on any challengers. "That's the ugliest thing I've ever seen, and I've looked at it every day since Duke and I moved in here. The kids are scared of it, and it takes a lot to scare my brood of boys. Even the cat won't stay in the same room with it."

When Beth paused to inhale, Tony said, "Why not call Finster and have him come get it, or at least put it out of sight in the garage?"

"Duke said every time he tried to talk about it, Clyde Finster was on his way somewhere and would be by in a few days. Well, his time is up." She scraped the head of the match on the box and smiled at the flame. "Unless you want it."

Tony did not want the grotesque fish. It was revolting to look at, but he decided to take it to its rightful owner. Being the sheriff in Tennessee's smallest county often required him to do more "serving" than "protecting." Even as he deposited the plaque and fish in the back of the Blazer, Tony felt nothing but sympathy for the woman and her family. The more he looked at the prize, the worse it appeared. He thought Beth deserved an award for keeping it so long.

"I hope there aren't others like this one in the lake," said Wade. "It's simply hideous. I can see a possible headline now: *Mutant Fish Eats Skunk.*"

Wade's muttered comment echoed Tony's feelings about the trophy.

"Keep an eye on the fire." Tony smiled at Beth as he climbed in the vehicle. "It's been a little dry lately."

"Don't worry. I won't turn my back on it. This is not my first trash burn." Beth pointed to a garden hose near her feet. Water ran from it, soaking a nearby shrub. "Thank you for taking the ugly thing away."

The mayor and undertaker, Calvin Cash-dollar, tiptoed into Tony's office. He was dressed for a funeral. Tony could tell, because the man wore the same suit for every such occasion and it was beginning to look a little worn. Calvin's broad smile indicated his lack of personal involvement with the deceased.

"Can I talk to you for a minute?" said Calvin.

Tony tried to come up with a reason the mayor couldn't, and failed. "Have a seat."

Calvin settled into the chair across from the desk, his tall, skinny frame folding in stages until he finally finished, sitting with his knees near his chest and his big feet neatly placed side by side on the floor. A few strands of wheat-colored hair dangled across one eye. He reminded Tony of a vulture sitting on a branch.

Calvin launched right into his topic. "It's about security for the car convention."

"Is our county big enough to handle a convention?" Tony had lurid visions of intoxicated people in party hats, raccoon caps, or clown wigs, staggering through the quiet streets of Silersville, throwing up on the sidewalks.

"Only small ones." The mayor released his pent-up breath in a big sigh. "Nothing the national media would find interesting." He looked both disappointed and resigned.

"I've been to a few conventions." Tony pretended he hadn't heard Calvin. "The attendees and their spouses often have separate needs. What about this group?"

"According to my contacts, the members and their spouses all drive vintage cars — some are really old. They will need to be allowed to drive slower than the normal traffic. We also hope you can provide some extra security for the cars when they're parked overnight at the motels."

"My staff is going to be stretched pretty thin as it is. There are always problems with fireworks and partiers on the Fourth." Tony was already dreading the increased workload, and the mayor's expression told him there was more to come. "What else?"

"We are inviting them to participate in the parade. I'm sure you and your staff will do the best you can." Calvin unfolded and stood up and looked directly into Tony's eyes. "And here it is, election year already." He said no more but gave Tony a small salute as he left.

Not amused by the mayor's less than subtle message, Tony began reworking his deputies' schedules. He could use a much larger staff in the summer months than they needed in the winter, but there was no money to make it happen. At least, he thought, antique car lovers could be a fairly sedate group, especially if they were the same vintage as their vehicles. He could dream.

Theo wasn't surprised to see her husband wander into her workroom for the second time in one day. Her quilt shop wasn't far from the Law Enforcement Center and he had been a most welcome sight when their twin girls were newborns. He'd helped with their frequent feedings. Now they were on something of a schedule and he often dropped by, maybe to help, but more often to take a break from his paperwork and watch little Lizzie and Kara explore their toes.

She smiled as Tony applauded Lizzie's attempt to crawl. Balanced on her hands and knees, Lizzie held her feet off the floor and rocked back and forth before collapsing onto her face. Her shocked cry was a good excuse to lift her high and kiss her neck.

"How are you going to manage to work up here once they start walking and climbing?" Tony seemed fascinated by her assortment of scissors, razor-sharp rotary cutters, and innumerable pins, needles, and seam rippers. Any could be dangerous in the wrong hands.

Theo deflected the question. "Just like you'll keep them away from guns, knives, and most of the things hanging on your belt." He was interrupting her work and her impatience must have shown because he quickly changed the subject.

"I'm actually checking with the business owners about the parade route. Do you see a problem with closing the street to parking, beginning on the evening of the third instead of the morning of the Fourth?"

"Not really." Theo considered the question and whether the closing would affect her business. "It might even be better. People will be wandering all over downtown and it would be less congested."

Tony put Lizzie back next to her twin and headed for the door. "I'll leave you to your work."

Silence returned, Theo stared at the mess on her worktable. There was no reason the mystery quilt pattern should not work, but it didn't. She had sketched the thing out and was sure she'd counted the right number of pieces when she'd cut them. Zoe, the shop cat, sat on the corner of the oversized cutting table carefully inspecting one tiny black paw. Theo thought the feline's expression reeked of disdain, as if she'd never make such an error. The haughty expression in her amber eyes gave nothing away.

"Did you steal a square like this?" Theo picked up a small piece of blue fabric and waved it in the cat's direction.

The cat refused to discuss the problem and jumped from the table to the floor and stalked away. The very tip of her tail flicked once, snubbing Theo. Thankfully, she left behind the missing piece of fabric. Theo retrieved it and hurried to sew it into place before she misplaced it again.

At the end of the day, on his way home,

Tony stopped by the hardware store to pick up another gallon of paint. The brand-new addition to their house, built as a gift from his brother, Caesar Augustus, and his rich wife, Catherine, had not included the paint. Tony had underestimated the amount of pale yellow he'd need to finish a second coat in the new bedroom for his twin girls. The babies needed to move soon; their current nursery was smaller than a closet.

"Sheriff?" Duke McMahon greeted him from behind the counter. "Need some help?"

"Another gallon of the yellow paint." Tony reached for his wallet.

"Is it going on okay for you? Not splotchy or anything? You know the key is even application." The owner of the hardware store seemed skeptical of Tony's abilities.

Thinking the man was not far off the mark, Tony answered honestly. "Yes. It's just not going as far as I expected. It's like the walls are absorbing it."

Nodding his understanding, Duke ambled from the register to the paint department, peered at his records, and pried the lid off a new can of base paint. He glanced up at Tony. "I got a call from Beth."

Tony grinned. "I delivered the rescued fish. Finster said to tell you thanks for keeping it, although he did seem a bit put out by the situation and not particularly thrilled to have it back. I'm pretty sure he's going to have trouble getting his wife to allow him to hang it in their house."

Duke's lower lip moved forward in a pout. "Women don't seem to like a lot of things. It's not just the fish, I have a poster my wife won't let me hang either. Bought it at a motorcycle rally. Cute chick and hot bike." His expression resembled that of an overgrown eight-year-old, except for the mustache and beard.

Tony couldn't help but envy the man's long, thick, chestnut-brown hair, combed straight back from his forehead and hanging down to his collar like a mane, but he managed to keep himself from whining about his baldness. He guessed Duke's disgruntled expression might have more to do with being barely over thirty and having three boys, one almost twelve, than being married to a woman who didn't want her home to resemble a men's locker room. Whatever Duke thought he'd be doing at thirty, it was probably not running his family hardware store. Being sheriff gave Tony information about people he'd often rather not know. In this case, it was Duke's spending more time drinking at The Spa, a local bar, than he did at home. Tony decided on a change of subject. Baseball. "The boys have their first tournament game tomorrow evening."

"That's right. Your oldest and my youngest are on the same team." Duke studied Tony's bald scalp as if he were trying to calculate the difference in their own ages.

Tony thought about telling Duke he was almost forty to the hardware man's thirty but decided not to waste his breath. Duke had finally poured the color packet into the base paint and was starting the paint-mixing machine. It made such a racket, no one could talk about anything and be heard. Tony suspected the machine might need an overhaul. Above the chugga-chugga sound was the whine of metal grinding against metal. It made Tony's teeth ache, so he moved to the far side of the hardware store and studied the garden tools. They reminded him to get some cash to pay young Alvin Tibbles. The teenager had recently become the Abernathy yard and garden assistant. The boy mowed and weeded and trimmed for cash, but he seemed to enjoy the work immensely.

Alvin was not alone in the yard when Theo got home. His mother, Candy, who did less to raise the boy than anyone else in town, had parked her car at an angle so it blocked the new driveway, leading to the new garage. Theo parked in the street rather than create a fuss. Theo didn't know if she ought to interrupt the parent and teenager discussion or not. While she considered it, she managed to pull the infant seats out of the SUV without disturbing either sleeping baby. Her triumph did not prevent Theo from thinking that Candy on a good day was what Theo's grandmother would have referred to as "trashy." It wasn't a nice term, and it was one Theo rarely even used in her thoughts, but Candy was not as sweet as her name.

Candy grew up in a nice home. If her parents were not rich or exciting people, they were at least normal people and caring parents. They clothed her, fed her, took her to church, went to parent/teacher conferences, and did all the usual family things. Candy had decent clothes and spending money. Somehow, though, she never quite grew up. She was unambitious, unremarkable, and lived only for herself. Toward the end of her time in high school, she developed an unfortunate tendency to party. There was talk that she would do anything for a beer. Before graduation, she produced

Alvin, and to everyone's surprise, he was a perfectly normal baby boy.

Theo assumed not even Candy could be sure why she picked the name Alvin. Like the identity of the father, everyone assumed her reason was lost in the murky reaches of her mind.

Alvin and his mom lived out of town a few miles, in the same house where Candy was raised. Candy had never lived anywhere except with her parents. Theo guessed she continued to live with them because doing so was easy and free. And, except that it meant they would lose Alvin, her folks might have thrown her out at some point. Candy's mom worked at the school cafeteria, and her dad did odd jobs like shoveling snow and mending fences. They raised Alvin.

At least they had until one day when Alvin was about twelve and they were killed in a traffic accident. The bottom fell out of his world. He lost his real family. His mom was worse than useless. Theo thought Candy simply lacked certain qualities most people take for granted. Candy didn't have what it took to take care of herself, much less her son. So Alvin was moved in and out of different temporary foster homes. None had worked out well.

27

On the opposite end of the energy and respectability spectrum from his mother, Alvin worked from the day he was big enough to deliver a paper or carry trash or mow lawns. Frequently, or so Theo had heard, Candy stole the money from Alvin and stayed out all night, leaving him alone. He'd had a bad relationship with the former sheriff but liked Tony, maybe because Tony saw to it the boy had a bountiful supply of food. He could eat in the jail kitchen any time he was hungry, without his mom's interference.

The schools had instituted a program to supply all children who ate two meals free at school, including teenagers, with bags of food to take home on Fridays so they would have something to eat on the weekends. Candy stole Alvin's, more, Theo suspected, from laziness than money problems. It was easier to steal than cook.

Recently Alvin had achieved legal emancipation. He now had his own apartment. His own bank account his mother could not access. A locked door to protect his privacy and his food.

As Theo approached, she heard Alvin say to his mother, "I'm leaving tomorrow for botany camp, but I'll be by to see you, or I'll call Sunday morning as usual and we can talk about it then."

"You're going to miss the fireworks." Looking almost panicky, Candy grasped his arm. "You love the fireworks."

Alvin patted his mother's back. "Botany camp is special. You know I'm excited about it, and while I'll miss watching the fireworks with you, camp's only for a couple of weeks. Will you remember to water my garden? I drew you a map of where to set the hoses. Did you get it?"

Theo watched Candy nod and had to force herself not to interfere. She could tell there was no way Candy was going to help him.

"Just in case, I'll ask around and see if I can get someone to do it instead. You won't have to worry about it." Alvin glanced up and gave Theo a half smile. "I'll be done here soon."

Candy wailed, "I need my baby to come home."

Theo saw Alvin wince, but he said nothing, just turned back to his yard work. Theo guessed he'd had long practice dealing with his mother's melodramatic behavior, and she studied her appearance. Candy looked terrible, worse than usual. Dirty strings of mud-brown hair hung across her face. Bloodshot blue eyes peeked through the resulting curtain. A fair number of her teeth were missing, and her skin looked gray with blotchy red spots. Younger than Theo, she looked almost as old as Tony's mother, a woman who mysteriously never aged, in spite of annual birthday celebrations.

Tony arrived, and after parking the official Park County sheriff's vehicle behind Theo's SUV, he climbed out, paint can in hand. He stopped and nodded to Candy.

Not surprisingly, Candy abandoned her car and scuttled away, walking diagonally across the park that their house faced. She didn't even look back at Alvin, who had returned to his yard work.

Without looking at his wife, Tony said to Theo, "I presume you know where our boys are?"

"Yes. Nina said she'd drop them off at practice. Remember, Chris has a game this evening." Theo watched Tony as he continued to watch Candy. "Did you stop at the bank for me?"

He didn't change his focus but reached into his pocket and pulled out some cash and handed it to her. Still studying Candy, he shifted the paint can and reached for the handle on the nearest infant carrier and lifted it.

Relieved she wouldn't need to get some

money herself, Theo stuffed the cash into her pocket and, grabbing the remaining baby carrier, walked past her husband and into the house. She couldn't help but wonder what he found so fascinating about Candy. The last time she looked, he still hadn't moved.

When Candy was out of sight, Tony turned to Alvin. "Will she come back for her car?"

Alvin gave a slight shrug. "If she remembers where she left it. Luckily it's only four miles out to the house, and she walks home unless she gets a ride when she drinks too much."

Tony looked at the car blocking his driveway. The brown sedan was as disreputable in appearance as its owner. The keys were in the ignition. "Shall we take it out to her?"

Alvin hesitated. "Sure. Give me a head start. I'll leave it in the garage for her. While I'm out there, I'll check on the plants in my garden."

Chapter Two

Theo followed the smell of fresh paint and found Tony in the girls' new room. She chattered away, talking to him about the upcoming town events and household schedule. "There's going to be a picnic, games, and fireworks to celebrate the Fourth of July. And of course there's the parade. You won't want to miss it. The girls are going to be peas in a pod. The boys came up with the idea."

Tony kept his eyes on the paint-laden roller as he moved it across the slightly pebbled surface of the nursery wall, turning it the color of sunshine. "Uhm-hm." So far nothing Theo said was cause for alarm. Unfortunately he'd had enough experience in the years they'd been married that he was able to guess word of an impending calamity was coming. He could sense it building like a thunderstorm. Theo didn't tiptoe around a subject unless she was trying to be diplomatic. Diplomacy was a feat she was not good at. It wasn't that she didn't try, but Theo's childhood with the "old people" had required her to be silent or absolutely honest. Her current attempt at tact could only mean one thing. Disaster brewing. "What kind of celebration is my mom planning?"

Surprise lit Theo's green-gold hazel eyes and she ran her fingers through her blond hair — now grown back after a shorter cut to the natural curls they both preferred. "I'm not sure of the details. When she told me to reserve the date, she mentioned a few things."

"More flying vegetables?" Tony exhaled sharply, wondering if you ever really outgrew the parent-child relationship. His mom could push his buttons faster than a catapult could launch a squash. "The ramp festival was chaos."

"Everyone enjoyed the vegetable weapons though." Theo didn't dispute the "chaos" part of the comment but mumbled, "I really don't know what's planned. When do you think we can move the girls in here?"

Tony wasn't sure if this was his wife's way of changing the subject or simple curiosity, but he followed her lead. "Once the paint is absolutely dry, like tomorrow morning, we can hang the curtains and put in the rugs. At least it's warm enough to have the windows open, so the room can air out completely." He wiped the sweat off his bare arms with a rag, spreading a glob of yellow paint up to his shoulder.

Theo began laughing. "It's July. With the outside temperature today it's warm enough to bake a potato in here. I'm more concerned about finding a way to cool it off."

Since he was sweating like crazy in his cutoff jeans and a t-shirt with the neckband and sleeves removed, Tony admitted to the same concern. "Gus said the portable air conditioner he supplied would be able to handle cooling the girls' room and my new office."

"You didn't want to use it while you paint?" Theo wandered around the room, the expression of joy on her face having nothing to do with his painting and everything to do with a room large enough for their infant twin girls to share through high school.

"Truth? It didn't occur to me." Still wondering how he and Theo would ever be able to repay Catherine and Gus for the amazing addition, Tony rolled more paint, hoping the mundane chore would ease some of the concern he felt, which had nothing to do with his mom's celebration and everything to do with Alvin's mother. Candy Tibbles had a long history with the Park County sheriff's office, but something in her expression made him think they didn't have as much information about her as needed. Or, more specifically, the people she hung out with. Candy couldn't organize the items in an empty box without help.

Tony stood in the dugout watching the baseball game when his cell phone began vibrating. Chris's team was playing hard and held the lead going into the bottom of the last inning, but they had lost games on the last play in the past. No lead was large enough for this team. Tony reached for the phone. Caller ID showed the dispatch desk. One person handled calls for the sheriff's office, fire department, and search and rescue. This call was for him.

"Sheriff, I hate to bother you," dispatcher Karen Claybough stated briskly. "We have a situation." Wade's sister sounded intrigued more than concerned.

Tony wondered if he'd still hear those words in his head after he retired. When he agreed to run for sheriff, he didn't expect to have a nine-to-five job and weekends free, and he didn't. He'd also learned "a situation" could be anything from a lost cat to a bank robbery or murder. "And?"

"Well, sir, Sheila's found a dead body. In a tree."

At least this call showed some originality. "Is it a possum or a raccoon?"

"Oh, no, sir, it's a man. Human," Karen said. "Near the old underpass."

Tony heard a great cheer behind him and turned just in time to see Chris make a diving catch to end the game. The whoop he made into the phone probably rendered Karen deaf. "Sorry."

"No problem, sir." Karen's voice sounded a bit strained.

Tony caught Chris's attention and grinned and pumped his fist showing his excitement to his son. He paused as he walked past Theo. "Tell him great play!"

Theo nodded.

"Where's the tree?" Tony listened to the address and talked to Theo at the same time. "I have to go. Are you getting ice cream?"

Theo gave him the "Are you kidding? Of course we're getting ice cream" look and sent him away with a nod and the wave of a hand.

By the time he arrived at the address, the ball game excitement had diminished somewhat, and his curiosity had heightened. How did a body get into a tree? How did Sheila find it? A small group of people had gathered on one side of the road, watching his only female deputy stringing yellow tape. It was early evening and still almost as hot as it had been in the afternoon. Sheila's face was scarlet, and sweat dripped off it like rain. Her neatly braided blond hair appeared much darker than its usual color, when it was dry. The audience was sweating too, but most of them were dressed in shorts and t-shirts, while Sheila wore her brown uniform shirt over a protective vest, khakis, and a heavy utility belt. Tony had seen her look happier.

He parked the Blazer between Sheila and the audience, and flipped on every light he had that could flash. He waved a couple of volunteers toward him and sent them off with "road closed" signs before approaching his cranky-looking deputy.

Sheila didn't say a word, just pointed above her head.

She needn't have bothered with the hand signal. Tony could smell it. Rank, rancid, and rotting were the first three words to enter his head. He accepted the flashlight she offered and looked up. There was no doubt about what was lodged in the branch.

A human, male, deceased for some time. The legs dangled on one side of the sturdy branch and the head and arms on the other. The sound of the flies buzzing about the body was almost deafening. He said to Sheila, "Have Karen call out the doctor and tell her to bring her husband."

"Doc Nash is still on vacation?" Sheila reached for her radio.

"Yep, so our Grace is the physician on call." Tony hoped this wasn't going to cause her to rethink marrying Wade and moving to Silersville. If she decided against life here, Wade would follow her anywhere, even to the moon. A good doctor and a good deputy had options. In fact, Tony knew Wade had turned down offers from some federal agencies, but he could still change his mind. "Oh, and tell Karen to send some trucks with tall ladders."

With the barrier tape in place and the doctor on the way, Tony suggested Sheila take a break. "How did someone find this?" He nodded toward the tree.

Sheila wiped her face with a handkerchief. "There were some kids riding their bikes around here." She pointed to a section of the road with a fairly steep drop and a yellow speed hump. "They love to pedal downhill super-fast and use that smooth edge on the hump to launch their bikes into the air."

Tony studied the hump. Sure enough there was a spot on one side, smoother than the rest of it. He guessed it would allow the bikes to take flight rather than be stopped when the wheels rolled into it.

The fire truck arrived first. Tony had it park well back from the branch and extend the ladder to just below the body. Wade and Grace got there in time to watch it settle in place. A second ladder lined up next to it.

Dr. Grace Claybough was not quite as attractive as her absurdly handsome husband but lovely nonetheless. She glanced at the tree branch and exhaled sharply. Grace, a recent bride and their new doctor, turned and smiled at Tony as she walked toward him. "Doc Nash did warn me."

Tony relaxed. So far, Grace didn't look like a woman about to throw in the towel. She also didn't look at her husband, who was quietly throwing up into a shrub. "Shall we climb?" Tony asked and gestured toward the ladders.

With a nod, Grace accepted a helping hand from the fireman nearest her and headed up the ladder with her medical bag slung over her shoulder. Tony moved up the other ladder while holding a flashlight and carried a larger light on his back. There was still daylight left, but he guessed this would not be a quick examination, and it was much darker under the canopy of leaves. "Take all the time you need, Doc."

Grace gave him a saucy smile. "He's definitely dead. Let's see what else we can learn." Disturbing the buzzing insects, she stood on the ladder and studied the body by the light she took from Tony. For what seemed like a long time, she was silent and intent but didn't touch anything with her gloved hands. When she was apparently satisfied by what she observed, she reached out and, gently but firmly, checked the body and measured the liver temperature. "Sheriff, can you lift him, just a bit, right here?"

Following her precise instructions and trying not to breathe in, Tony lifted. It wasn't easy, as the body seemed to be stuck on something and gravity was working against them. The way the legs dangled on one side and the shoulders and arms on the other, it could probably withstand gale-force winds without falling out.

"Stop." Grace shone the light under the body while Tony held it. "Okay, you can let go. I've seen something like this before. We had a rash of these kinds of things in Georgia when I was doing my internship. This is the first time I've had one die in a tree though." She backed down the ladder to the ground and waited for Tony. Wade and Sheila joined them immediately. Grace glanced up again. "I'll want to examine the body once it's down, of course, but I think this guy might have been car surfing."

"Surfing?" Sheila frowned. "On a mountain road?"

Grace nodded. "I didn't say he was smart or sober. I'd say he was standing on the roof of a car or pickup when he hit the branch and was impaled. It's possible he might even have survived with immediate, proper medical treatment."

Tony shook his head, denying what she told him. "So the driver just left him up there?"

Ignoring his question, Grace pointed to the body. "I need the measurement from that limb to the ground. Then we'll be able to figure the height of what he was standing on."

Wade pulled a measuring tape and markers and the camera out of his investigation kit. He took pictures from all directions and then measured the height his wife requested. Tony and Sheila walked along the road, searching for anything that might have fallen off the body. The only thing they picked up was a half-full can of malt liquor.

"I'll bet this can has got some interesting fingerprints on it," said Sheila, holding it with her gloved little finger inside the can.

Tony agreed. "Driver, or surfer, or neither?"

"Loser buys pie?" Sheila suggested. "I'll say surfer."

"You're on. I'll take driver." Tony saw the ambulance waiting and waved it closer. "Let's get this guy down and give him to Grace."

Getting the body off the branch and into the ambulance proved more difficult than originally thought. They ended up cutting the branch from the tree with a chain saw. By the time the body and a significant section of the tree were loaded into the ambulance, most of the crowd had dispersed. Tony made sure Sheila got names and addresses for everyone watching. He was almost certain one of them had been driving the surfer.

The surfer's wallet was in his pocket. Grace held it open so Tony could get the dead man's name and address before she placed it in the bag with the body. The license photograph matched their body.

Grace rolled her shoulders and loosened her neck. "I'll go with it. I'm sure there needs to be an autopsy and I can't do it, you know. I'll let you know what's happening."

Half wishing their county's coroner hadn't taken off on a well-deserved vacation, Tony saw nothing else he could do here. He turned to Sheila, "I'm going home to change my clothes before we call on the family." The absolutely worst part of his job was death notification, and doing it alone was not a good idea.

"I'll meet you there." Sheila glanced up from her notebook. "Fifteen minutes? That will give me enough time to at least wash my face and hands."

It didn't take him long to change his clothes and drive to the address on their body's driver's license. He didn't know the man, Miles Curry, which rather surprised him, since he would guess it had taken a lot of alcohol to inspire surfing on a moving vehicle. Many of the county's heavy drinkers had passed through his jail or at least their names showed up on reports. He wasn't sure he could drink enough to give him the artificial courage to do it.

He was startled by a tap on the passenger side window. Sheila.

"I left my car on the side street." She gestured in the general direction.

"Okay, let's do it, it's not going to get any easier the longer we wait." He followed Sheila up the sidewalk. The door opened at almost the same time as Sheila rang the bell. Tony thought either someone was expected or the resident was on her way out.

A pleasant-looking woman, maybe in her mid-forties, held the door wide. Tony knew her professionally. Her name was Paula and she worked as the guidance counselor at the high school. It was inevitable their paths were bound to cross many times. He knew little about her personal life.

"Miles Curry lives here?" Tony had no idea what their relationship might be. As Paula stared at the badge on his chest, the expression on her face changed abruptly from welcome to dismay.

"May we come in?" Tony didn't really give her a chance to say anything. Sheila walked in and Tony followed, shutting the door behind himself. "This *is* the residence of Miles Curry?"

Paula nodded. Finally responding to ·Tony's question.

"Are you his wife?"

Paula shook her head. "No, we're not married." Her breathing changed, increasing until she was almost panting. "What's happened? Is he dead?"

Sheila took her arm and gently steered Paula to a comfortable chair and finally got her seated. "Yes, I'm afraid so. It looks like he was involved in an accident."

"I'm afraid we need to ask you some questions." Tony sat across from her. "Does Mr. Curry have family?"

"They hate me." Paula's voice was low but intense.

"We need to contact them." Tony took out his notebook and pen. Usually the sight of the items inspired people to at least give him an address or a name.

Instead of cooperating, she pressed her lips tighter.

"Let's start with some simple questions." Tony waited until she nodded. "What is your full name?"

"Paula Louise Merkel Smith." She stared at the floor.

"Thank you, Paula." Hers had been one of the names Alvin Tibbles mentioned as references during his emancipation hearing. Tony had to ask questions he already knew the answers to. "I believe you still work in the high school counseling office."

Paula nodded. Sudden tears ran unchecked down her face and her nose started to drip.

Sheila offered water and headed for the

45

kitchen, returning seconds later with a full glass and a box of tissues she'd found somewhere.

Tony waited until Paula sipped a bit of water and blew her nose. He tried again. "Where is Miles's family?"

"Kentucky." Much calmer now, she stared at the wall behind him. "He's from Louisville or Lexington, I'm not sure which one, just that it's one of the 'L' cities." She paused. "He moved here about a year ago and works as a janitor at the middle school."

It surprised Tony to hear the Curry family disapproved of Miles's and Paula's relationship. He thought she seemed very nice; she certainly had worked hard to help Alvin. "Do you have any idea why his family objected to you?"

"I'm divorced. They consider me a fallen woman. Plus, I'm quite a bit older than Miles. Six years." She pulled a few more tissues from the box and wiped her eyes. "We want . . ." she hesitated on the word. "We wanted to marry and hoped his family would come around, but they seemed to find the idea of his marrying me embarrassing."

Tony shook his head in sympathy and managed to keep his words to himself. He couldn't help thinking that if it was determined their son Miles actually died while surfing on a car, and most likely while under the influence of a great deal of alcohol, his family might not be too proud of *him* either.

They talked for a while, but Tony didn't learn anything particularly useful. He guessed the family would take over planning the funeral and all Paula would have left would be her sorrow. While they chatted, Sheila worked on finding the right family in Kentucky, and she finally did. Once Tony talked to the family on the telephone, they prepared to leave. Paula would be alone.

"She didn't want us to call a friend or a neighbor, but . . ." Tony hesitated on the porch. "Can you stay with her for a bit?"

Sheila nodded. "I'll see if she'll tell me if this was regular behavior for Miles."

"Maybe when she calms down she'll know who else might have been with him." Tony didn't understand what drove people to do such potentially self-destructive things. Standing on a moving car? Allowing someone else to do it? There were enough ways to get hurt that it didn't seem necessary to go hunting for more.

CHAPTER THREE

Theo was surprised to find Blossom Flowers waiting for her when she arrived at her quilt shop the following morning. The generously proportioned cook had been Tony's "admirer" and pie supplier for years. Blossom had always tolerated Theo, but had never shown any interest in being friends. Even though Blossom now had a fiancé and would become a stepmother when she married, Theo doubted Blossom's adoration of Tony would cease.

Twenty years earlier while Tony was home on leave from the Navy, he had stopped a couple of sixteen-year-old boys from tormenting the chubby ten-year-old. The boys had grown into frequent guests of the county jail and Blossom remained Tony's most ardent admirer.

Theo hauled the babies up the stairs and Blossom trotted behind her, a pie clutched in both chubby hands. It was not the apple pie Tony preferred; this one was coconut cream, Theo's personal favorite. The woman knew her pies and her customers. The diamond flashed on Blossom's ring finger, making Theo think the engagement was still on. At least one good sign.

"Can we talk?" Blossom panted from her exertion on the stairs. "This is for you."

Still reeling from surprise, Theo managed a weak, "Of course" before setting the girls, still sound asleep in their car seats, in the kids' end of her workroom. When she turned, the pie, tantalizing and fully six inches tall, sat on Theo's cutting table. "You don't have to bring a pie to talk to me."

Blossom blinked back tears in her large, bulbous blue eyes. "It makes me feel good." A couple of tears couldn't be stopped and traced over her chubby cheek, dripping onto her chest.

Discounting the woman's obvious lack of accuracy about baking making her happy, Theo waved Blossom to a chair near the window. Blossom's thin, rust-orange hair looked uncurled and unkempt. Not Blossom's style at all. The plus-size woman always took the time to look her best. "What's wrong?"

"I've got to talk to you." Blossom sniffled into her hand and fell silent.

Hoping there was a tissue in the hand, Theo sat across from her and waited. With the exception of more sniffling, production of the tissue, and loud nose blowing, the conversation had stalled. "What's wrong?"

Blossom seemed to shudder all over. "He's cheating."

"Who? With whom?" Theo asked, assuming Blossom would say it was her fiancé. Theo doubted he was. She'd seen them together recently, and Kenny and his little girls all adored Blossom.

"T-Tony." Blossom's next sob almost knocked her forward and out of the chair.

If Theo ever sat down and tried to imagine the oddest conversation in history, she certainly wouldn't have come up with this one. Tony's groupie crying because he was cheating on his wife. Theo didn't believe it for a second. The cheating part. Even if he wanted to, and she didn't think he did, when would he find the time? "How do you know?"

" 'Cause I saw him, holding her." Blossom rummaged in her bag and came up with a whole box of tissues. She blew her nose about six times, using a fresh tissue each time, and lined the used ones across her lap.

"Who is *her*? And where were you?"

50

"It was Paula Smith. She lives across the way. Me and Kenny was out for a walk with the girls and Miss Cotton — you know, my dog." Theo nodded. "And there he was, going into the woman's house across the way." Blossom shuddered. "She's got a live-in boyfriend, but I saw Tony wrap his arms around her and then they both went inside and he closed the door behind him."

"Oh." Theo wasn't sure what to say. What she learned from gossip, she shared with Tony. What he told her concerning his job, she couldn't talk about. She guessed the whole thing was tied to the man who'd died in a tree. So she patted Blossom again and murmured something inane about it not being a problem, and she already knew about it.

Blossom reared back in her chair. "You knew about his cheating and you don't care?"

"Well, of course I *care*, but what can I do? It's part of his job." Theo heard the way her words sounded but couldn't grab them out of the air and start again.

Hearing Theo's ill-advised statement, Blossom lurched from her chair and waddled toward the stairs, making good time for one her size. A row of balled-up tissues dropped on the floor marked her progress. Theo started after Blossom, hoping to clarify her statement, when both babies began crying and the telephone started to ring. By the time Theo decided to ignore the phone, let the babies cry for a minute, and dashed down the stairs, Blossom was already headed out the front door of the shop. It looked like she was talking to someone on the sidewalk. Her arms waving, fat jiggling, Blossom kept looking back toward Theo's shop. In a town like Silersville, Theo knew the gossip would travel like lightning, and by the time the story got back to her, she hated to think what it would sound like.

Trudging back up the stairs, she soothed the infants' tears and called Tony. As expected, he wasn't amused by Blossom's story. It might have been because Theo mentioned the coconut cream pie several times in passing and he was jealous about the pie, but she suspected he knew there was about to be a firestorm of gossip. About them.

Neither of them really enjoyed being the center of attention.

Tony might have found the story somewhat amusing if two things hadn't just happened to moderate his attitude. He received a preliminary report from the pathologist in Knoxville who was handling the tree victim's autopsy, and the deceased young man's parents wanted to talk to him.

As far as the cause of death, physically it was massive trauma to his heart, liver, lungs, and spleen. Much as Grace had predicted, and estimated with scientific probability, the impact of man and tree took place at something around a hundred miles an hour. Curry's neck suffered whiplash injuries, most likely from the sudden stop. But, there was a chance he might have lived with prompt medical attention. The embedded branch had missed all vital organs.

Tony's department needed to find the driver of the vehicle upon which Miles Curry had been surfing.

In the meantime, his visit with Curry's grieving parents from Kentucky was not going well. Mr. and Mrs. Curry sat in the visitors' chairs in his office, staring at him. They were as stiff-necked and unpleasant as any two people he'd ever met. They didn't seem as concerned about their son dying as they were about word of his drinking being spread about.

Tony, sitting on his side of the desk, was thinking of using the case as a deterrent to both over-imbibing and vehicle surfing. The photographs of the deceased, impaled on a branch, were enough to make him want to throw up in a bucket, like Wade. What a waste of a young man's life. Tony couldn't give the family what they wanted and he had work to do, so he gave the almost-grieving parents directions to reach the Cashdollar Mortuary.

Wade knocked on his door frame as soon as the couple left. "They doing okay?"

"It's hard to tell. They have to be in shock. They'll feel worse when it wears off." Tony shook his head, hoping the couple cared more about their son than was apparent. "What did you learn? Any idea who his companion in the deadly adventure was?"

"I've got a couple of maybes. I did a little survey at both The Okay and The Spa. Found someone who thinks one possible works at the school with him, and another one lives down the block from him." Wade rubbed a thumb up and down the bridge of his nose. "According to my sources, both of them were kind of heavy-drinking guys he liked to hang with, but only occasionally. Curry wasn't a regular."

"How's Grace handling this?" Tony had seen many worse sights than a dead guy in a tree and imagined Grace hadn't gotten through medical school without being involved with even dumber people than this one. Inherently self-destructive people made up a sizeable amount of the population in every state.

Wade finally smiled. "She thinks its sweet you're worried about her. I have to warn you, sir, behind her lovely, gentle manner is a very down to earth, pragmatic, mule-stubborn woman."

The description of Wade's bride made Tony smile. His deputy might have been describing Theo. "I just don't want her running off to a better place — robbing my children of a pediatrician and causing me concern about their health." Tony leaned back in his chair. "Not to mention that it has taken me a long time to train you."

"Yeah, I thought so. I'm not wild about the idea of Grace running off myself. It took me some time to convince her to join me here." Wade shifted position. "Did you manage to finish painting your addition?"

"I did."

Wade's cell phone rang at the same time as both his own cell and his desk phone did. Not a good sign. Tony reached for the desk phone and his antacid supply at the same time.

Dispatcher Rex Satterfield's distinctive voice came through the earpiece. "Sheriff,

55

you're not going to like this."

Tony believed him. He always believed Rex. "What happened?"

"Nothing yet, at least nothing's been reported but I received a nine-one-one call from an obviously intoxicated woman. Emily Austin's the name. She's claiming her cell phone was stolen, the one she's calling me from, and she's chasing the thief, driving down the highway after him."

"Anything else?"

"It sounds like she's waving the phone around and telling someone named Jeff I'm phobic because I knew her name."

"Phobic?"

"I'm guessing she meant psychic. Coming up with any 'p' word's pretty good for someone in her condition."

Tony felt like slamming the receiver on the desk. "Is the moon full? Never mind, have you got any idea where she is? Or where she's headed?"

"I contacted Sheila and Mike, but they're both tied up. Can you send Wade out toward Kwik Kirk's convenience store on the highway? My guess is Emily Austin's driving either a yellow Dodge pickup or a red Subaru sedan. At least those are the vehicles registered in her name." Tony heard a more muffled comment. "I'm not sure I've ever heard someone drunker than she is."

"Heaven help us." Tony lunged toward the door, following Wade. "Once we get to the store, maybe someone will be able to tell us which way she's heading. All we need is a massive accident."

"Still worried Grace might quit?"

"Nope, wondering how I might."

Wade laughed. "You're elected sir, you don't get to quit."

CHAPTER FOUR

Tony couldn't believe his luck. After his and Wade's chase through the entire county, it was his own mother who caught the intoxicated woman — or, rather, her museum did. Jane Abernathy claimed since she survived teaching high school Latin, the death of her husband, raising four children, and opening a museum, dealing with an intoxicated woman driving through one of her fences was nothing. At least that was close to what she told Tony when he drove into the museum parking lot, lights and siren signaling his approach.

"Really, Tony, did you have to make such a ruckus?" As Jane emerged from the office and headed for the next building, she flapped her arms, imitating one of the speckled chickens following her across the grass, squawking and fussing as if she was their leader.

The birds were recent additions to the folk

museum, and it was clear to Tony that they considered her either their mother or their queen. He wasn't quite sure who was imitating who.

"Turn that noise off. Think of your poor old mother." Jane kept up her stream of complaints. "You could give someone a heart attack. Like me."

Tony flipped off his siren and climbed out of the Blazer, but the horn in Mrs. Austin's pickup continued to blare.

Not in the mood for his mom's snarky attitude, Tony walked past her and approached the pickup. Wade wasn't smiling either as he walked to the passenger door. The driver had taken them on a wild pursuit through the county and barely missed killing any number of people. Tony wanted to rip the driver's door off but managed to content himself with tapping on the driver's window.

Emily Austin glanced at him, gave him a little wave, and returned her attention to the cell phone clutched in her right hand.

Tony pulled her door open in time to hear part of the conversation over the blaring horn.

"Got to go, sweetheart. That nice policeman, you know the tall bald one, just asked me to dance." Emily dropped the phone onto the floor and peered at herself in the mirror almost like she was checking her lipstick. Then she gave him a wide smile and threw up on him, coating his uniform with beer, whiskey, and her lunch. A salad of some nature. Lots of greens.

Wade, once he managed to silence the horn, made a sympathetic groaning sound. Tony thought it sounded like one Wade used to mask a laugh.

Probably because he was so relieved and grateful the three of them were all still alive after the chase, Tony felt a bit more philosophical than angry. Emily was not riding to the Law Enforcement Center in his vehicle though. He looked at Wade. "You get to transport her." Tony did gently pull her out of the pickup and slipped handcuffs on her, carefully double-locking them so they couldn't keep tightening around her fragile wrists. "I don't want you to cut your hands off."

"Thank you." Slightly chastened, Emily stood quietly, waiting for instructions until Wade led her away.

Ignoring his mother, Tony stalked back to the museum office building, picked up the garden hose, and turned on the water. The first gush of water came out hot. The more he rinsed, the colder it got. He turned the water off. Without making eye contact with his mother, he went to the Blazer, got in, and drove away. He needed soap and a clean uniform. Lots of soap.

Theo was inundated with calls from the curious, asking about her husband's girlfriend, sympathizing with her while trying to extract a modicum of fresh gossip. Blossom must have told everyone in her huge family what she thought she knew and asked them to tell everyone they knew or encountered. Wildfire would look calm compared to this blazing gossip storm.

There was no place for Theo to hide. The shop was busy with tourists, the locals, and the nosy. Up in her office, Theo still had work to do on the new pattern in progress, and Gretchen, her only full-time employee, was swamped down on the main level. Surrendering to better business practices, Theo pitched in to help. She could hear a clamor of excitement in the classroom, which doubled as the local gather and gossip site.

"Tony is cheating on Theo. Can you believe it?" Betty's voice carried over the din.

Theo approached the speaker, Blind Betty, who was promptly shushed by her sighted companion, the much younger

Dottie. "Believe what?" "Er, hi, Theo." Dottie clamped a hand over Betty's mouth and practically yelled in the woman's ear. "Hush."

With their sweet little drunken speed demon under lock and key, and Tony dressed in a clean uniform, he and Wade returned to their investigation of the surfing incident. "Let's go see what Mom Proffitt can tell us about this situation. I really, really want to find the driver. Even if the men don't drink at her establishment every week, I'll bet she knows them."

Wade agreed.

A short time later, the two of them walked into The Okay Bar and Bait shop. Run by tiny, feisty Caroline Proffitt, the woman everyone in town called Mom, The Okay was more clubhouse than saloon. It hadn't sold bait in ages but the business's full name was still painted on the sign. At this time of day, late afternoon, the regulars were beginning to arrive, looking for a beer or a cold drink and some television or conversation. Mom greeted Tony and Wade from behind her spotless bar.

"I'll have a glass of lemonade, Mom." Tony settled on a stool and relaxed. Next to him, Wade ordered unsweetened iced tea.

"What's up?" Mom asked after delivering their beverages. "I'm guessing this isn't a social call."

"There's a couple of guys whose names have come up in an inquiry, I wonder if you know them." Tony handed her a paper with several names written on it. Only two were ones he didn't know. The last thing he wanted was some set of big ears listening in.

Mom Proffitt studied the list. "This first one comes in occasionally and always with a man from the school. Don't know the next two by name. I don't suppose you have pictures?" She paused.

"Hold on." Wade pulled out his smart phone and tapped on the screen, his fingers flying across the surface, pulling up a driver's license picture. "Here's one of them."

Mom shook her head. "He's never been in here."

Wade went back to his data search and showed her a different face. Their dead surfer. Mr. Curry.

"Yes. He's been in from time to time. He's a nice enough man but simply cannot hold his liquor. He doesn't come in often, but when he does I always have to keep his keys overnight. He was in here the other night for a while. I still have the keys." Mom picked a key ring off her board just as a couple of men walked through the front door and tossed their keys onto her counter. She picked them up and hung them on the board.

"I'll go." Wade took the abandoned keys and headed outside.

"Want to tell me what's going on?" Mom rarely asked Tony any questions when he came on official business.

"There's been an accident." Tony hesitated. "I'd appreciate anything you can tell me about the man who left his keys and the first man on the list."

Mom fielded a few more keys and filled some drink orders while she considered his request. "The one who left his keys — Miles is his name — anyway, he was saying something I thought was odd. He was going out the door and asking if anyone else wanted to go surfing." Mom shook her head. "Since there aren't waves on the lake unless a boat's going too fast, it caught my attention."

Wade returned, sat, and placed the keys on the bar. "The registration matches our guy."

Tony asked again. "And number one. Was he here at the same time?"

"I'm not sure." Mom wiped the bar. "I know number four was. His name is Bart Sullivan, and he's in the game room."

"Let's see if we can learn anything from him." Tony stood. "Maybe he hasn't started playing his game."

Number four, now known as Bart Sullivan, sat watching the others playing the video game with the intensity of a coach watching his team vie for the tie-breaking point to end a championship game. When Tony and Wade failed to gain his attention in any traditional manner, Wade stepped in front of him to block his view.

"Ah, man, move over." Sullivan craned his neck trying to peek around the deputy and see the screen. He finally glanced up, a sullen accusatory expression on his face. "What?"

"You know Miles Curry?"

"Yep." Evidently satisfied by his level of cooperation, Sullivan wiggled around, trying for a different vantage point.

Tony blocked him. "You know what he was doing night before last?"

Sullivan looked up, meeting his eyes. "I know what he was talking about doing. He wanted to surf on the top of my pickup, stand on it while I drove him around." Sullivan shook his head. "Crazy man. I said no way. I walked home, 'cause I only live, like, half a mile from here and I figured Mom wouldn't give me my keys back."

"If you didn't allow him to surf on your truck, do you have any idea who else he might have called on to drive him around?"

"Naw, we ain't close." Sullivan squinted up at them, his gaze shifting back and forth between Wade and Tony. "Why don't you just ask him? Save us all time."

Convinced Sullivan was telling the truth, Tony said, "We think he did find someone who'd drive him. He ended up dead, and we're looking for the driver."

"No way." Sullivan shook his head, actually ignoring the screen, focused on the situation at last. "Well, don't that beat all."

Tony shifted out of Sullivan's line of sight. "Let me know if you hear anything, especially like who did drive?"

"Yessir, I will. I swear, I had no idea." Sullivan watched the game in silence, shaking his head.

Tony returned to talk to Mom while Wade quietly talked to a couple of men waiting to play a car racing video game. Mom went through her entire collection of keys, giving him names and general observations about them. No one sounded like their person of interest.

Wade waved his notebook and led the way outside. "I have an address. A couple of the video-game players came up with the same name. David Logan."

"Let's go pay him a visit." Tony felt more irritation than curiosity. It seemed like people had nothing better to do than try to kill themselves or others, and it was creating lots of work for him and his department.

Unfortunately, finding Logan wasn't as easy as Tony had hoped. The address was a rooming house on the edge of town. The proprietor, one of Blossom's myriad sisters, met them at the front door. Santhe, short for Chrysanthemum, Flowers was a landlady to be reckoned with. Large, like most of her sisters, but more muscular, she dyed her hair a flat black and pulled it into a tight ponytail. And not only did she have more hair than the other sisters, she had colorful tattoo sleeves on her arms. Both of them. Tony thought they resembled holiday hams packaged with labels of large tropical vegetation. Leaves, vines, and flowers complete with a lizard capturing an insect with its tongue covered them from wrist to shoulder. Santhe's eyes spoke of irritation more than a willingness to help when she looked at him.

"Sheriff. Wade." Santhe narrowed her eyes and rested her fists on her wide hips. "What do you want?"

"Have you got a renter by the name of David Logan?"

"Maybe, maybe not."

Tony saw no sign of concern or curiosity on her face. He found her attitude pretty remarkable. The few people he'd encountered who didn't openly wonder why he'd come to question them already knew the answer. He took a step closer. "Which is it?"

Santhe didn't back down. "Why?"

"I don't think that's really any of your business." Tony leaned closer. "Unless you'd care for an obstruction charge." He was bluffing, but he was also intensely irritated.

"Yes. And if it matters, he pays on time." She started to close the door in his face.

Wade jammed a foot in the space, keeping it open.

Tony said, "Is he here?"

"I heard you're cheating on your wife." Santhe glared back. "Blossom told me. My little sister is not happy with you at all, so, neither am I."

"I am not cheating on Theo." Tony shook his head for emphasis. "Blossom witnessed me on a condolence call, added one and one, came up with thirteen, and then created some ridiculous tale and spread it across the county in record time. I am not happy with Blossom."

Wade spoke up. "Sheila was there too. Did Blossom mention her?"

"No. I'm sorry." Santhe looked chastised and convinced, even as she shook her head. She opened the door wide. "I'll tell Blossom to fix it. How can I help you?"

"Is David Logan here?"

"No. He's never here until quite a bit later."

"Will you call my office and let us know when he returns?"

"Absolutely." She raised one hand in the air like she was taking an oath.

The way she agreed so quickly made Tony think Santhe was eager to make amends for her sister's faulty information. He decided she might be a good person to have on his side.

CHAPTER FIVE

Theo wondered why she could go for months without seeing a particular person and then for the next week, she'd run into them everywhere she went. Candy Tibbles was not someone Theo ever expected to see in her quilt shop. The woman had never expressed any interest in quilts or fabric. In fact, if Theo was honest, she wasn't sure Candy was even aware of the things around her now.

Candy stood in the middle of the shop, staring. She showed the same amount of interest in the tools and toys quilters liked as she did the myriad colors of fabric, and as she did the floor. Theo thought she might actually be more interested in the faux wood-patterned flooring than in anything else in the room.

"Do you need something, Candy?" Theo spoke softly, almost tentatively. There was something so . . . so absent in Candy's expression Theo did not want to startle her.

Candy spun around in a circle, stopping where she began. "Where's my boy?"

"Alvin?" Theo asked automatically.

"Do I have others?" Candy's question seemed honest, not flippant. She pressed a clenched fist to her chest and coughed.

"Not that I know of." Theo edged closer, herding Candy out of the center of the shop and closer to the workroom. Was there someone she should call? "Are you feeling ill?"

Ignoring Theo, Candy stopped short of the doorway into the workroom. "What are they doing in there?"

Theo peeked around the taller woman. A small group of elderly women worked together on a colorful quilt stretched on an old-fashioned wooden quilting frame, stitching it by hand. "They are quilting a charity quilt. It will be raffled off to raise money."

"Is my mother in there?"

Theo was seriously concerned now. Candy's parents had been deceased for maybe four years. Four long, emotional, traumatic years for Alvin, during which he lost his beloved grandparents, was taken from his mom, and given to foster family after foster family. He didn't fit in. He was moved. He became an adult in a young body. Theo touched Candy's shoulder. "No Candy, your mother passed away."

"Oh, that's good." Candy gave a little laugh and seemed to relax. "I couldn't find her."

Theo backed up slightly and glanced around to see if anyone else was listening. From the expressions and body language she saw, everyone was listening and pretending not to. No one made eye contact with Candy. "Is there something I can help you with?"

Candy shook her head, giving her lank hair a bit of a toss. "I was just curious." And she left the workroom, passed through the main shop, and opened the door. A second later, she was gone as mysteriously as she arrived.

Theo exchanged puzzled glances with the quilters but there was really nothing to say.

"You do remember this Friday is the Fourth of July?" Theo handed Tony another screw, which he quickly tightened into place. The final curtain rod was almost up in the girls' room.

"I'm trying very hard to forget it." Tony stepped down from the ladder. "Two more screws on the other side, and we can hang those curtains."

Theo's smile was brilliant but she continued on her topic. "The quilt show is always held during the celebration for the Fourth. Can you help us hang quilts on Thursday?"

"As far as I know. What time?" Only half listening to what she told him, Tony focused on the screws. He knew he could depend on Theo to remind him several times before the event. Hanging quilts in their show was not his favorite job or, for that matter, his least favorite. He was part of a small, well-trained crew, mostly husbands, who know how to erect the display system consisting of poles, guy wires, and electrical conduit. The quilters owned the poles but borrowed the conduit from Duke McMahon's hardware store, which helped the ladies and gave Duke free advertising.

Once the big quilts were hung, most of the smaller ones would hang on some collapsible frames. He'd make his escape as soon as the big quilts were up and assumed he'd be as surprised as usual to see it in its much improved final state. He thoroughly enjoyed the quilt show. It wasn't the time and work involved in helping hang it that bothered him, it was his fear he'd accidently ruin a quilt. An action both awkward and unforgivable.

He tightened the last screw. "Ta-da! Grab

those curtains you worked so hard on and let's see how the room looks."

Obligingly, Theo vanished. She returned less than a minute later, her arms filled with white curtains dotted with vivid colored bunnies, butterflies, and caterpillars.

He grasped the rod, sliding one end into the space for it, just below the top edge of the curtains. "Wow, these are heavy."

"That's the blackout fabric lining. It weighs a ton, but without it, this room will light up like a runway the second the sun climbs over the mountains."

Tony immediately realized Theo was right. The twins' current room was small as a closet and only marginally brighter than one. Moving them into an airy, sunlit space would require some adjustment for all of the family. He lifted the curtain-covered rod into place and the sunny room vanished, replaced with, if not total darkness, something close.

Theo pushed the curtains apart, bringing in the light again, and attached the tie backs. "We have some pictures to hang on the walls."

"And the rugs you bought. And the cribs to move." Tony, once again, but surely not for the last time, silently thanked his brother Gus for giving them this room. Theo's excitement made her green-gold eyes sparkle as she walked across the shining wood-grained laminate floor. "There's even room for your old rocking chair."

Theo smiled and nodded but couldn't seem to speak.

With little encouragement from him, she dashed off to gather the rest of the room's décor. He, no less excited than Theo, forced himself to leisurely approach the moving of the cribs. In just a few minutes, Kara and Lizzie would get to move into their space and spread out.

CHAPTER SIX

"Sheriff, you're not going to like this."

Tony imagined the statement would be true, just from dispatcher Flavio Weems's tone of voice. Tony felt a surge of adrenalin and stomach acid at the same time and poured a handful of antacids from the large jar under his desk and dropped most of them into his shirt pocket. He popped the two in his hand into his mouth and started chewing. "What's happening?"

Flavio flipped a switch to let Tony listen in. "It's Sheila. She's looking into a nine-one-one call. Man called about an intruder who attacked him in the shower. Hit him with a wrench or something. She got a little description and gave it to me."

"Ambulance needed. I can't leave him. Backup needed. Now." Sheila's voice was clear and concise. "I have no idea where the attacker is now. I can't reach my weapon and hold this guy. I have to stop the bleeding or we'll lose him."

Tony could hear Sheila trying to calm a man. The sounds were something he'd imagine if two people were trapped in a box with a bear. Growling. Moaning.

Tony said to Flavio, "Tell Sheila I'm on my way too." Tony hurried through the hall, raced outside, climbed into the Blazer, flipped on the light bar, and headed out. The address Sheila had given was just past the intersection where Ruby's Café and the Thomas Brothers Garage sat. It was a major intersection of the highway and the road connecting downtown Silersville to a less-populated residential area. It was possibly the busiest section of road in the entire county. He listened to the radio.

Sheila's voice. "Stay still. You're about to faint. I need to hold this pressed against your wound." Then sounds like a bull thrashing in a stall drowned out Sheila's words.

Tony kept the volume up on the radio and heard bits of the conversation between Sheila and the victim. A man's voice, barely a whisper. "Bob, he kept calling me. Bob. And he said he knew I was there, like we were on a different planet."

"People call you Bob?" Sheila's voice was muffled.

"No. Not Bob, and none of my neighbors is named Bob either." The voice sounded much weaker than it had.

"We need that ambulance." Sheila spoke clearly. "He's out cold now and losing ground fast. So much blood."

"It's on the way. They say five minutes." Flavio knew every deputy's location and what they were doing. "Mike's almost there too."

Tony hoped help would get to the injured man and Sheila in time. He pressed the accelerator a bit more.

Tony heard Flavio talking to Mike. Then there was quiet as Flavio listened to Sheila and relayed the information to everyone on the system, speaking clearly and calmly. "In the neighborhood of the highway and Ruby's Café, be on the lookout for a white male, five foot six, one hundred and forty pounds, thirtyish, close-cropped black hair, last seen wearing a dirty white muscle shirt and jeans. Carrying a claw hammer and a pipe wrench, neither one new, blood on the shirt. On foot when last seen."

Tony watched Mike make the turn ahead of him, his vehicle almost airborne, flying up the road to the next turn and then stopping. Mike jumped out of his vehicle, spotted Tony, and signaled he was going to the back of the property. The ambulance arrived next. Tony held back, staying behind them, and parked just before the ambulance crew headed toward the house. Tony was careful to park well out of its way. He hoped it would leave as quickly as it arrived, with a living patient.

Hurrying out of the Blazer, Tony glanced around, studying the area, hoping to see a medium-sized man in a white t-shirt. All he saw was a quiet neighborhood. Houses, fenced yards, and assorted vehicles. Lots of shrubbery and tall grass. Nothing moving. A couple of dogs barked, but not like they were frantic, guarding homes from strangers. On the radio, Mike told everyone what he could see from the back of the property, which didn't take long. Nothing appeared out of place.

Now running to get ahead of the paramedics, Tony gestured for them to wait for his signal before going into the house.

He moved inside, keeping his heavy semi-automatic raised. He quickly searched for the intruder and found no one. Inside the kitchen, Sheila knelt next to a large, naked man stretched out on the floor. Blood was everywhere, including on Sheila. She pressed a wadded-up piece of fabric, maybe a t-shirt, against the man's neck. Her hands and arms were covered with blood. She didn't look up as she talked. "Sheriff, I'd have chased the attacker, but couldn't leave this guy and risk he'd bleed out."

Thinking she'd done the right thing, Tony stepped out of the way, signaling the ambulance crew inside. They quickly freed Sheila from her life-saving job. Information from Mike was negative. "We'll have to go house to house."

Sheila stepped over to the kitchen sink and scrubbed the blood from her hands with dish soap before she followed Tony outside.

"What happened?" Tony kept his gaze moving, checking for the attacker.

"Poor guy. From what I could understand, he was in the bathroom, taking a shower, you know, when some guy he's never seen before breaks in and starts whacking him with this old pipe wrench and claw hammer. I guess the attacker kept calling him Bob. It's like something out of a movie. All I could get from our victim was that he's Not Bob. Not Bob's got at least one good-sized gash on his head above his ear and a broken cheekbone, but most of the blood was coming from his neck. About here." She touched a place near her windpipe. "Luckily, he made it to the kitchen and got his cell phone."

"You got a pretty good description."

"Maybe." Sheila looked uncertain. "He was all but unconscious when I arrived. I couldn't even get his name from him so I'm not sure how much this guy really saw, and how much he made up to fill in the blanks, you know."

"What do you think he saw?"

"I'll bet he saw the white shirt, the jeans, and maybe dark hair." Sheila shrugged. "Maybe he saw everything he reported. He is a big guy and he was standing up when the attack began, but I'm guessing he got hit several times when he tried to dodge away from the wrench. He was blindsided."

Tony agreed with Sheila. Often people didn't see as much as they thought they did or vice versa; not until everyone calmed down were they able to reconstruct events. "Motive?"

"He said the man was screaming at Bob about payback for his wife," Sheila said. "Our guy's in shock but I've seen him around, usually hanging out at The Okay, or when he's at work. He seems nice enough. Not rich, not mean, not married. Just a guy minding his own business when some whack-job comes into his house and attacks him."

"And his work?" Tony couldn't place him.

"You'll recognize him when you get a chance to really look at him. He works for the county in road maintenance. He's usually shoveling asphalt into potholes when I'm driving through the county." Sheila did smile then. "He wears a battered straw cowboy hat."

"That's why he looked familiar." Tony shook his head. "What a mess. We better find the guy who attacked him before he finds another Bob."

Wade arrived and they divided the street in half. Wade and Tony would work on one side and Mike and Sheila on the other. They'd have to knock on each door and talk to anyone at home, look in every shed, under every tarp, and still watch for suspicious movements. "Sheila, I know you can't do anything about your clothes, but you might want to see if you can get some more of that blood off your arms. Your hands are clean now but you look like you've been swimming in it." He frowned, thinking of all the blood-borne diseases she could have been exposed to. "It's on your face too."

"I've got some heavy-duty antiseptic towelettes." She walked toward her car. "One second."

So the work began. They spent hours tak-

82

ing pictures, talking to the few people who answered their doors, lifting trash-can lids, checking every possible hiding place. No one they talked to saw anything or noticed anything special until the arrival of Sheila's car caught their attention. Then they watched from the windows, curious about the reason for the deputy to stop. No strangers, nothing.

They learned Not Bob was actually named Will Jackson and the neighbors thought he was a quiet, but friendly, addition to the neighborhood. He'd lived in the house for about a year.

By the time Sheila and Mike were almost finished searching their side of the street, Tony walked toward them to compare notes. Sheila was beyond filthy. Dirt mixed with blood coated almost every inch of her. "You looked better when we arrived."

"It can't get worse." She muttered but changed her story when she crawled under a house on a raised foundation. Holding a flashlight and gun didn't allow her a way to cover her nose or mouth. She needed the flashlight and might need the gun. "Oh, nasty. Something died under here."

Mike relayed her message via the radio to Flavio, but omitted some of Sheila's more colorful, extraneous words.

"Please, please, let it be something we don't have to investigate," Tony said. He could happily do without any additional work.

"Next house one of us has to climb under is your turn, Mike." Sheila gasped. "I see what smells so bad. It's okay, sort of. It looks like a possum."

Relieved but sympathetic, Tony and Wade continued their own hunt. They found lots of dirt, some termites, a cranky chicken, and at the end of the road, an even crankier citizen who didn't want them coming into his yard. "I'll shoot you if you come on my property."

"Fine." Tony's patience level dropped from thin to non-existent. He'd had some dealings with the man before. Miller was his name. "Did you happen to threaten anyone else today, Mr. Miller?"

"Yep." Clearly surprised to be addressed by his name, Miller let the barrel on the shotgun waver fractionally. "Just a bit ago. Feller in a white shirt."

"Where'd he go?"

Finally satisfied this particular group came in peace, Miller moved his finger from the trigger and lowered the barrel, pointing it at the ground. "I watched him go between those trees." He nodded at a couple of scraggly dogwoods outside his fence. "I watched him stomp all the way down to the highway. Looked like a plumber with a big old wrench he was swingin' like a club."

"A wrench?" Tony said. "What kind of wrench?"

"It was a pipe wrench. Kinda rusty looking." He frowned, looking thoughtful, "I almost forgot, he had a hammer in his other hand. Looked kinda odd to me."

"The man or the hammer looked odd?"

Mr. Miller chuckled and a gleam of amusement sparkled in his eyes. "Now that you ask, I'd say both of them, but the hammer had a real long claw." He gestured, indicating about six or seven inches.

"You notice anything else?" Tony hoped the now relaxed Mr. Miller might remember seeing someone he recognized give their assailant a ride.

The man nodded. "I might not of seen him at all but for his loud talkin'. He was fussin' at someone who wasn't there and givin' them a real earful. Oo-wee, he was so mad, he was frothin' worse'n a mad dog."

Hoping they hadn't missed anything during their search, and after getting Mr. Miller's contact information, they followed the path their shotgun-wielding witness indicated. It was a fairly decent path down to the edge of the highway, probably often used by the nearby residents. It was not a long walk down, so Mr. Miller might have been able to see any vehicle that stopped to pick their assailant up. If there had been one.

They saw nothing on the shoulder of the highway except an assortment of used fast-food wrappers, cups, beer cans, and a couple of diapers tossed out on the grass by people Tony didn't want to know. Litterbugs and home invaders were not on a par with each other, but Tony didn't like either of them.

CHAPTER SEVEN

"Sheriff?" Deputy Mike Ott and his bloodhound, Dammit, stood in the doorway. "Have you got a minute?"

Tony looked up from his paperwork. Even though it was the bane of his existence, he'd rather do it than have to deliver bad news to another family. "What's up?"

"I need to take Ruby to Knoxville for some medical tests. Sheila and Holt said they wouldn't mind covering my schedule, but I was wondering if Dammit can stay with you. I hate to leave him home alone for very long or maybe overnight."

"Of course I'll keep him." Tony said. "Is there a problem? Do you need extra time off?"

"No. Ruby and the baby are fine."

Tony thought Mike sounded more defiant than assured. "What's going on?"

"They just want to make sure the baby's heart is growing properly." Mike gnawed on his lower lip. "The test is not supposed to take long, and everyone says it's probably just fine. Just a precaution."

"Leave the dog here and go home." Tony leaned forward. "Now. Call me when you know something."

Mike wasted no time following his instructions. Dammit flopped on the rug near the door and stared at Tony, giving him the baleful bloodhound stare, acting as if his life would be a misery if he had to stay with Tony overnight. His homely face with its loose skin was the picture of sorrowful abandonment.

Tony had to laugh. The dog was a fraud. Dammit loved to visit the Abernathy house because Daisy lived there. The bloodhound and golden retriever were great friends and playmates. Together the dogs weighed about two hundred and fifty pounds, and running up and down the stairs made the old house shake.

"The man we think might have been driving the car surfer has turned up." Wade's voice came through the radio. "Should I wait for you, or do you just want me to bring him in?"

"Where are you? I'll come there." Tony wasn't sure he was prepared to learn what happened, and he was sure he wasn't going to like it.

"I'm at Santhe Flowers's home. She called in to let us know our suspect, David Logan, is back," Wade said. He lowered his voice. "She's trying to make up for Blossom's mistake."

A very different Santhe Flowers, having repented her former bad attitude, shepherded them into her rooming house, smiling and chatting with Tony. The large two-story house was at least a hundred years old and in need of some paint. The old white house had a wide front porch that wrapped around to one side, where the door leading into the kitchen was located. They went in through the front door. A staircase was directly in front of them, dividing the lower floor of the house in half. She waved one hand upwards. "There's four bedrooms up there, one bathroom, and four men. No women. Not even visiting. I have my rules and standards."

Tony thought the glare she focused on him would intimidate anyone. "Do you spend any time with the guys, or do they come in and immediately go upstairs?"

"Oh, I see what you want to know." Santhe led them to the left, through the kitchen, and into an alcove. "This refrigerator is theirs to share. They can keep small amounts of food and beverages in it. Same thing with this cupboard. No food is allowed anywhere except in here, in the kitchen, out on the porch, and in the TV room. Make a mess, clean it up." She pointed to a half-closed door. "Television's in there. First man in gets the remote. No fighting. They can bring dates here if they want."

Wade pushed the door open a bit wider. "Looks very pleasant."

Glancing past his deputy, Tony saw a large-screen television, a row of older style but comfortable looking recliners, a video-game system, and a stack of oversized floor pillows. He'd expected a caveman atmosphere, but the room was well lighted and had nice curtains and didn't reek of sweat and tobacco. "Very nice."

At his compliment, Santhe seemed to relax a bit. "My roomers are nice or they leave."

"Tell me about David Logan." Tony shepherded Santhe out onto the shady porch. "How long has he lived here?"

"Hmm." Santhe mimicked her sister Blossom's habit of pressing an index finger to the indentation between chin and lower lip when she was thinking. "I'd say six months, give or take a bit."

"Did he tell you what happened the other night?"

"Not really. When I told him you wanted to talk to him, he said that he was afraid he'd screwed up something and it couldn't be fixed." Santhe's curiosity became visible. "He didn't say what he did."

Tony thought "screwed up" pretty well summed up the drinking and surfing episode culminating with a corpse in a tree. "I need to talk with him."

Santhe stepped aside. "He's upstairs. First room on the left."

Tony and Wade trudged up the stairs. Tony felt the weight of responsibility pressing down on his shoulders. He was certain Logan had done a wrong thing. He was not certain what all the man was legally guilty of doing. At minimum, it was probably reckless endangerment and having an improper rider or some other well-hidden violation. What were the chances he'd intentionally driven down one of the few roads with low branches overhead? There were yellow warning signs clearly indicating the unusually low vertical clearance, but maybe he forgot the height of the man. Or maybe he knew exactly. Accidental or intentional? Dumb or criminal?

Tony knocked on the door and waited. He heard the sounds of someone coming to the door. When the door opened, a tired-looking man in his late twenties, maybe early thirties, stood quietly staring at the space between himself and Wade.

"Sheriff?"

"Can we talk?"

"Sure, sure." Logan backed into the room and waved them inside.

Tony gave the room a quick glance. Messy but not too bad. The bed wasn't made, and there was a stack of clean laundry on a straight-backed chair. "You want to tell us what happened the other night?"

"I, uh . . ." The words stopped. He might have decided confession would be good for the soul but really bad for the rest of him. "No."

Tony traced a line on the floor with his toe. "No?" He shook his head. "Why not?"

"I, uh . . ." A shoulder twitched once and went still. "Dunno."

"Dunno what happened or why you don't want to tell me?" The man had the lost, stunned appearance of an accident victim himself. "Are you all right?"

"I, uh . . . Dunno." Logan blinked rapidly, then stopped. "I don't feel too good."

Thinking their suspect looked like he was

about to lose his lunch, Tony stepped back and glanced down the stairs. He really didn't want another person throwing up on him or his shirt. "Why don't we go outside and sit in the fresh air."

Logan led the way downstairs, practically running until he burst outside onto the porch. Santhe barely stepped out of his way in time. When Logan threw up in one of her flower pots, her expression lost its pleasantness. "You *will* clean that up."

"Yes, ma'am." Logan bobbed his head. "I'll do that in just a minute."

Santhe glared at Tony. "See that he does."

"Yes, ma'am." Tony's own head was bobbing as she stepped back into her house and slammed the screen door behind her. Evidently their truce did not extend to allowing someone to be ill on her premises.

Logan whispered. "She's nice. But. She don't care much for a mess." He struggled to his feet, ambled over to the spigot, and turned the knob. He let it run until it cooled a bit, and ran it over his face, hands, and hair before he filled a watering can and carefully washed the geraniums. When he finished, he sat on the step, his hands clasped together, and started talking to Tony.

"Curry said he'd seen something on the television about car surfing and asked if I'd ever thought about trying it." Logan couldn't seem to stop his head from moving ever so slightly from side to side. "I never heard of such a thing."

"Did you try it or just do the driving?" Wade leaned against the column supporting the porch overhang.

"Oh, I tried it. Curry drove just a little way down the road before I fell off." He lifted the sleeve of his t-shirt exposing a large area covered with myriad small scabs. "I lost a fair amount of skin pretty fast."

"And then?" Tony wanted to ease him into the remainder of the story.

"Some great big dude in a shirt with the sleeves ripped out jumped on the top of my truck and I thought the roof was caving in. He said he wanted to ride next." Anger was filling in some of the places where guilt and fear had been. "He broke it. See? Look at my truck."

Sure enough. The roof on a not new, not old, dark green extended cab pickup showed definite signs of having experienced too much weight.

"Then what happened?" Tony studied the man's face as he stared at his damaged truck. Anger seemed to be pumping some energy into his system.

"I made him get off. There was a bit of a

skirmish and then it was over. The big dude had a monster of a pickup and it was all jacked up high, you know, with way over-sized tires. Practically need a ladder to get into it."

"Go on," Tony suggested. He was appalled and fascinated by the scenario being described by Logan.

"Well, we're zooming around the streets, Curry is standing on the top of the monster truck laughing like crazy, and the big dude is driving. And then, all the sudden" — he paused, breathing heavily — "everything went quiet. Curry was gone. Man, he was just gone. He wasn't on the truck. Wasn't in the bed. We drove up and down looking on the roads, the shoulders, and the ditches. It was like he'd been abducted by aliens."

"Okay." Tony rose, dusting off the seat of his pants. "As they say on television — don't leave town."

Logan's bloodshot eyes watered in the bright sunlight. "What happened to Curry?"

Wade was already on the radio, looking for information about the monster truck when Tony explained the result of the evening's entertainment.

"In a tree? I had no idea. Now I'm sorry I was complaining about a little road rash."

95

■ ■ ■ ■

In a community the size of Silersville, it didn't take long before Tony and Wade located their new surfer dude, or at least his probable vehicle. Logan had not exaggerated the height and size of the dazzling orange truck's tires. Theo would need a full-size ladder just to reach the door handle. He and Wade studied the vehicle from several angles. There were a couple of scratches that looked a bit fresh, but Tony had no way of knowing what caused them. Their dead surfer had been wearing tennis shoes.

The truck's owner, a bleached blond giant, hurried out the front door of his house, letting the door slam behind him. "Did somebody hit my truck? Is she all right?"

"This is yours?" Tony wanted to be sure he was talking to the owner.

"Sure is. Isn't she a beauty?" The giant grinned and patted the tailgate like it was a pet. "Every dime I make goes into maintaining it."

"And your name?" Wade turned to a fresh page in his notebook.

"Uh . . ." The man hesitated. "Everyone calls me L.L. It stands for Larry Lowell."

Tony decided his expression said it all. For whatever reason, L.L. hated his given name. "Where do you work?"

"I, uh, I'm between jobs." The giant looked puzzled. "Say, is there a problem?"

"Do you know Miles Curry?"

Shaggy eyebrows lowered, shielding his eyes. "Don't believe so. He ever use a different name?"

"Okay, skip the name. What were you doing two nights ago?" Tony wouldn't be surprised if none of the men had bothered to introduce themselves to one another.

"Two nights?" L.L. massaged his earlobe with a hand the size of a baseball glove. At length his eyes brightened, the eyebrows raised. "I had dinner over at The Okay, drove around a bit lookin' to see if anyone I knew was out and about, you know, and come back and watched the tube, baseball mostly."

Tony wasn't sure what to believe. He was usually happier when people's stories bore some relationship to each other — not the exact phrasing or word for word, because in most cases that meant they were working from a script — but he did like it when everyone was at least talking about events along the same lines. Tony was positive a minimum of one person was lying about the surfing incident. Lies made him think maybe it hadn't been an accident and the two remaining parties were in collusion.

"Maybe we could ship off the shoes and check for matching prints." Wade climbed onto one of the tires and leaned forward, moving his head to catch a different angle of light on the roof. "Spotless."

The pristine condition of the paint and the damp spots near the tires made Tony think "just washed."

"Say, Sheriff, are you thinking we done somethin' illegal?" L.L. craned his neck, keeping a close eye on Wade. "News to me."

"I'm sure it is illegal to let someone ride, standing or 'surfing' on your moving vehicle. And even more stupid than illegal, if it's possible. I think I'd better consult Archie. Our prosecutor will want to be kept apprised of this one."

Tony punched speed dial. He left a message with Archie's overworked secretary, Clare. She was a force to be dealt with and didn't believe in wasting time. Their conversation lasted less than ten seconds. Clare was approximately a hundred years old and weighed maybe a hundred pounds. Tony suspected she had no home. Why would she need one? She never seemed to leave the office. He'd bet she kept her wardrobe in one of the file drawers.

Tony didn't even have his phone put away when Archie called him back.

"Sheriff, I've got to tell you it ought to be illegal to be that stupid. It's bad enough, what I hear some of the things people will do in the so-called name of fun." Archie sounded like he was jogging as he talked. "Standing on a moving car. That's about the second dumbest thing I've heard of lately."

Tony wasn't sure he could handle hearing about number one, but asked anyway. "What's one?"

"Ghost riding." Now Archie's breaths came in gusts.

"Are you running?" Tony couldn't visualize Archie moving fast enough to muss his hair.

"Late for an appointment." Archie wheezed. "I'm in Atlanta."

"Just give me the short version of the dumbest. What is ghost riding?"

"Well, it's the scariest for the rest of us anyway. The driver climbs out of his own car and onto the roof while it's moving down the road."

"No driver?" Tony remembered seeing something about this on the Internet. He'd chalked it up to stunt drivers.

"You know what they use to stop the car?" Archie's voice was suddenly very loud and easy to understand, making Tony think he'd arrived at his destination.

Tony thought Archie sounded frightened. "A passenger?"

"Nope. It's usually a ditch or a tree or another car." Archie said. "Car surfing or ghost riding falls under the subsection of unlawful riding or towing, I think. Going back to your case, do you think the driver knew the rider was there? If so, everything would change."

"Why?"

" 'Cause he'd be in charge of the vehicle and moving and steering it." Archie started speaking so quickly, it sounded like one long word. "If he didn't know someone was on the truck, the fault falls on the passenger. It wouldn't be as effective a form of suicide as throwing yourself under a train, but . . . well, no matter how this comes out, I'm going to sum it up as criminally stupid." He disconnected.

Tony stared at his cell phone but wasn't really focused on it. This was a mess, and he suspected it was not going to disappear.

Tony was startled when Wade tapped on the door frame. "Come in."

"I've been checking on Not Bob." Wade's expression was serious. "They airlifted him to Knoxville. His condition is considered grave."

Tony felt his eyebrows lift. "Which means?"

"According to Grace, it means he can still go either way. Evidently his blood loss was extraordinary, and there is no way he would have survived if Sheila had arrived a minute later or ran after the assailant. If he lives, she saved his life."

Remembering the condition of the victim, his home, and Sheila, Tony was a bit surprised the man had any blood left in him at all. "And if he lives? Are there likely to be lasting issues?"

"Very possibly not." Wade came into the office and sat down. "Grace says they'll know a lot more in the next few hours. I understand the gash in his neck was closed surgically but will take a while to heal completely."

"I'd like to talk to him, of course." Tony relaxed a bit. "And see what Not Bob might be able to tell us so we can protect Bob."

"If there is a Bob." Wade didn't look convinced. "I think Bob's a figment of the attacker's imagination."

Tony found himself hoping there was a

Bob and, if so, maybe he could point them toward Not Bob's attacker.

CHAPTER EIGHT

Dammit and Daisy made a stunning canine couple. The enormous bloodhound cavorting with the oversized golden retriever threatened to demolish the inside of the Abernathy house. Wrestling and pouncing on each other, Theo thought they had no idea how huge they were and how much damage they could do to the house just running into things. In their world, they were just two little puppies having fun.

Theo opened the kitchen door and sent them down the steps, barking and leaping into the yard. She forgot Alvin was working back there and the sight of the massive dogs charging toward him made him stand up and freeze, an expression of alarm on his face.

Seconds later he was laughing. The canine clowns were putting on quite a display, and except for their passage through the new flowerbed, where they scattered the newly turned earth, there was nothing they could harm.

Alvin waved to attract Theo's attention. "I'm leaving for plant camp in just a few minutes. My ride is picking me up here so is there any special chore you want me to get done first?"

"It looks so much better than it did with all those overgrown vines and shrubs removed." Theo joined him, admiring the changes he'd already made.

"They will take over if you don't stay on top of them." Alvin clipped a few more pieces off the honeysuckle vine and dropped them in a bag. "I've seen small trees choked to death by these things."

"What goes there?" Theo studied a large square wire cage next to their new vegetable garden bed. The raised bed contained soil now but no plants yet. It was well past the normal time to start a garden but they'd be ready for next summer. "Tomatoes?"

"Nope. Compost." Alvin launched into his explanation. "It will turn your food scraps and dry leaves into free plant food. As they decay, they'll give off some heat."

"We've never composted before." Theo studied the cage. "I can put everything in here?"

"Well," Alvin's smile was full of mischief.

"Your husband's pretty big, but I guess if it gets hot enough you could dispose of a body. Personally I don't put meat or bones in my compost. Some people do."

"Thank you." Theo laughed as she handed Alvin his pay. "When will you be back from camp?"

"Not for two weeks. I've arranged for a friend to mow your yard while I'm away."

"Thank you. Be sure to have some fun." Theo called the dogs back into the house so Alvin could finish what he was doing without being knocked over or have the dogs leave massive paw prints in his work.

Tony was awakened in the night by Dammit. Mike's bloodhound was sitting near the window, baying like he'd treed a possum. "Shut up dog," Tony mumbled. As he climbed out of bed, he glanced at the clock. Midnight. The oversized dog stood up, glancing toward Tony before looking back out the bedroom's front window, the one overlooking the park. "Where's Daisy?" The last thing Tony wanted to do in the dark was to trip over his own dog.

Daisy must have heard her name because he heard a soft "woof" from the direction of the boys' room. It was her normal spot to sleep if she wasn't downstairs on the sofa in the parlor. Dammit had grudgingly decided he could sleep in his and Theo's room. At least for a while. Tony made his way to the window and pushed Dammit away, shushing him. Seemingly satisfied by Tony's presence and wide-awake condition, the dog flopped back down on the rug.

Through the open window Tony realized he could hear hushed voices. He climbed out the window and onto the small balcony built long ago by an early one of his wife's relatives. Now he not only heard soft human voices but he could see lights flickering in the park. At first, he thought they looked like fireflies, but then he was able to discern the reflection of light on human faces. Candles? He tried to judge the size of the group. Between the park's lights and the ones being carried, the illusion formed was almost like watching moonlight and ships' running lights reflected on a choppy sea.

He dragged some clothes on, found his cell phone and flashlight, and removed his gun from the safe. Even as he headed out the door he was in contact with dispatch. Wade's sister, Karen, was on duty. "Have you received any calls about activity in the park?"

Karen said, "Not exactly. I did get a call from a woman claiming there was a coven of witches having a meeting tonight. She did not specify a location before she hung up."

Oh good, Tony thought. "Witches?"

"Yessir, she said they were chanting spells outside her bedroom window and trying to lure her into joining them outside. I recognized her voice."

Tony was pretty sure he could guess who made the call. "Mrs. Fairfield?"

"Yessir." Karen laughed. "She was most insistent so I sent J.B. over to check it out. He's calling in now." She flipped the switch allowing Tony to listen in.

J.B. preferred working the night shift. Amusement threaded his voice as he said, "There's a group of twenty young adults having an impromptu memorial service for their recently deceased surfing friend, Miles Curry."

"Do you foresee any problems?" Tony walked briskly through the park, following the group.

"No sir. Some of them have been drinking but they are being well behaved and there's several sober ones as well. I don't think what happened to Mr. Curry is going to create any copycats."

Tony was now fairly close to the group. They were singing softly and several of the

107

young women were crying. His girlfriend was surrounded by friends, standing near the tiny pond. Several picnic tables had been moved closer together. While Tony watched, the mourners formed a line, and one at a time each launched a small, paper boat onto the still water and touched it with the candle to light it on fire. For just a couple of seconds, the pond seemed filled with fireflies.

There seemed to be no reason to interfere with their memorial so he went home and back to bed.

After an interrupted night's sleep, the last person Tony wanted to see at the Law Enforcement Center was Orvan Lundy.

Tony hadn't even sorted through the mail on his desk when Ruth Ann appeared in his doorway. "Mr. Lundy has something he wants to confess."

"Really?" Tony felt acid drip into his stomach as he wondered what he had done to deserve having the old sinner enjoy confessing to him on a regular basis. He might feel differently about it if Orvan would tell him what he really wanted to know. Tony was sure the old guy had killed a number of people, maybe forty years ago, but there was no time limit on murder. "Did he give you any hints?" He wasn't surprised when she shook her head.

"He looks terrible," Ruth Ann whispered.

"Okay, let's get this done." Tony called Wade on his radio. "Orvan's here." He headed for the greenhouse, their interview room, nicknamed for the impressive humidity level achieved by more than two people speaking for any length of time. The tiles and drain in the center only augmented the title but they made it easy to clean.

While Tony waited with Orvan for Wade to arrive and for Ruth Ann to return with some water, Tony studied the old man. Ruth Ann was right. Orvan looked even older than his considerable age, whatever it was, and sort of gray and pasty. Normally he dressed "formally" for his interrogation and confession, clean overalls, the collar on his best long-sleeved flannel shirt buttoned, fresh shoe polish on the top of his snowy hair. Today Orvan was dressed in his work overalls and a ragged shirt with no discernible buttons. His white hair bore signs of staining from various polishes but nothing fresh.

"Everything all right, Orvan?" Tony might not really like the man but he certainly didn't hate him.

Orvan leaned forward and held his head

with both hands, his elbows resting on the table. "Not feelin' so good."

"Do you need a doctor?" Tony thought Dr. Grace, as she had become known, would make an office call. He glanced up at Wade who had just arrived.

Wade pulled out his cell phone, waiting for guidance. "Should I call Grace?"

Orvan just shook his head and moaned. "I saw them. You got to protect me."

In spite of his best intentions, Tony leaned forward, already intrigued. "From whom?"

"They are a-coming for me." Orvan tipped back his head and howled like a coyote. Then he quieted and whispered, "Tell 'em I confessed."

"To what?" Tony thought a little detail would help.

"I seed the river of fire." Tears splashed on his skinny chest. "It were filled with the cries from Hades. I'm doomed."

Before any of them could respond, Orvan passed out, falling onto the floor. "Forget Grace." Tony radioed dispatch. "Get an ambulance."

Wade was doing CPR on the old guy when the paramedics arrived. They checked him over, started an IV, and lifted him onto the gurney. While the paramedics worked, they asked questions about his age and any physical complaints.

Tony answered as well as he could. "He's always seemed strong and active. I've never seen him like this before."

"He have anything health related in particular he complained about? Palpitations? Nausea?"

"Nothing I've heard about. Only his fear of burning in hell." Tony stayed out of the way. "I'm sure he saw the burning paper boats on the pond last night but I can't imagine it was enough to inspire this."

"He seems pretty dehydrated," said one paramedic.

His assistant agreed. "His pulse is thready and the heartbeat's not very strong."

Orvan thrashed a bit on the gurney but didn't open his eyes.

Tony held the doors open as the ambulance crew hustled back to their vehicle with their patient. "Are you taking him to Knoxville?"

"We'll stop first at the clinic and see what Dr. Grace, er Claybough, has to say. It will be her decision. She might just want to keep him in one of the beds there."

"I think the hammer and wrench guy just struck again," Sheila reported. "I'm out on the highway."

Tony thought Sheila's voice held a note of excitement through the radio. He said, "I'd love for you to tell me he's handcuffed in the back of your car and you've got the hammer and wrench neatly sealed in a couple of bags."

"No such luck," Sheila said. "I'm near Ruby's, maybe a half mile from where Not Bob was attacked and I'm waiting for the ambulance again."

"Who was attacked this time?" Tony left his desk and headed for the door.

"A hitchhiker. He's got ID and I ran it through the system. No wants, no warrants. The guy's just a guy trying to catch a ride somewhere. It doesn't look like robbery because he's still got his wallet, some cash, and a duffel bag."

Tony heard Sheila talking to the arriving ambulance crew for a moment. "This man was obviously standing by the highway, I'd guess either he was just dropped off or was hoping for a ride when bam, he's hit from behind. Hard. He was knocked completely cold. I saw him stretched out there on the shoulder, face down in the dirt. Scared me, I thought he was dead."

"Was he able to tell you anything?"

"Nope. I've never seen anyone *that* uncon-scious before. I checked his pulse and called for medical help. I'm afraid this one might have a broken skull or neck." Sheila's voice lowered. "Our attacker has a vicious swing so I'd guess a fair amount of muscle behind it."

"Maybe the assailant lives in the area near Ruby's. Walking distance." Tony closed his eyes, trying to visualize the area. Next to Ruby's was the garage run by the Thomas brothers. A zigzag walking path over a hill ended in downtown Silersville. The cluster of homes they had visited after finding Not Bob was one of several small groupings of houses and there were quite a few homes nearby with no neighbors visible at all. "Let's find him."

CHAPTER NINE

Tony arrived at Sheila's location in minutes. The ambulance bearing the unconscious hitchhiker was just pulling onto the highway, headed for Knoxville. The driver, a man Tony wasn't familiar with, lowered his window. Tony was surprised because he knew he'd get the story from Sheila and the driver was wasting valuable time.

"I forgot to tell Sheila," the driver lifted his sunglasses. "There was nothing in his wallet showing any allergies. If she, or you, finds anything related to his medical history, call us."

Tony cut in. "We know what to do." If Tony weren't so concerned about the second similar vicious crime, he might have given the man a piece of his mind.

With a jaunty wave, the driver drove away, using lights and siren to clear the road.

"I don't like him." Sheila was staring at the back of the ambulance as well. "He's a vacation substitute. He acted like we're all too dumb to read much less to think."

Tony reached for the victim's ID she held in her hand. "Find a relative, if possible. And I don't want anyone giving out any information to anyone else. Not his name. Not where he's from. Nothing."

Sheila's eyebrows rose at his unusual statement, almost like she'd been slapped.

Tony knew his people would maintain the man's privacy. He decided he'd better explain his ill-advised statement. "I see his name is Robert. Maybe he goes by Bob."

"I'm with you there," Sheila said. "You don't want whoever whacked Not Bob to think he's succeeded this time? Why not?"

"I'm not sure." Tony had made his decision without thinking it through and didn't want to prove to everyone how rashly he'd behaved. Part of him thought they'd never catch the attacker if he felt like he'd succeeded. "Let's just hold off until we know more."

Hours later he decided it wouldn't have mattered. They scoured the woods, checked with witnesses, and finally accepted they had nothing to go on. The attacker had, or so they concluded, come upon Robert and hit him hard enough to crack his skull and then abandoned the man, unconscious by the side of the road. Nothing made sense.

"Sheriff?" Wade popped his head into Tony's office, not uncommon with his open-door policy. "Grace just called. She says she needs our professional assistance at the clinic."

"That's intriguing." Tony followed his fast-moving deputy down the hall and out to Wade's official vehicle. "We're usually calling for hers."

Wade nodded, flipped on the lights, and took off like his wheels were on fire. "She said something about a fight involving her patient and some relatives."

Tony could envision the Lundy clan creating problems. "But not who?"

"Nope." Wade made the last turn and parked, careful not to block either the ambulance or the helicopter landing site. "She said come fast."

The Law Enforcement Center and the clinic were almost neighbors. Tony had walked it frequently. "And, here we are." He had only one leg out of the car when Nurse Foxx, usually known as Foxxy, opened the clinic door and waved the two men inside. Tony was sure he heard her say "you'll love this" as she led them down the hallway.

In the largest room, there were a couple of curtained alcoves for the occasional overnight patients. The curtains to a couple of alcoves were open. This was not quite a hospital; the truly serious cases were transferred to Knoxville.

Orvan lay quietly in a bed, his head raised, watching the show on the other side of the room. His rheumy eyes sparkled and his mouth was slightly ajar. An IV into his scrawny arm delivered a clear liquid.

Tony and Wade didn't need a guide. The screeching sounds coming from the far alcove were impossible to miss. Above the din, a woman shouted, "Tell her you love me more." Followed by a different strident female voice, "No! It's me she loves best."

Sitting in a semicircle of plastic chairs were six Flowers women of various ages. Blossom, the youngest, sat in the chair facing the foot of the bed. Her orange hair glowed like a beacon. She and her sisters and cousins chatted among themselves while Blossom's father, Autumn, stood nearby wringing his hands, the only man in the scene. Almost hidden from view, the patient was Hydrangea Flowers Jackson, the oldest member of the Flowers clan. The two screamers were Hydrangea's only slightly younger sisters, Gladiola and Tulip. Tony

117

guessed the three women had to all be in their nineties. The sisters were taking turns moving Hydrangea's head to face themselves. The poor old woman had to be getting whiplash.

"Stop!" Tony didn't yell but used his command voice.

The women on chairs looked at him and fell silent. Frozen in place.

Hydrangea blinked a couple of times and closed her eyes. Dr. Grace Claybough checked the woman's pulse, then shook her head. "She's gone."

A howling of banshees could not have created a greater din than the six remaining Flowers women. They weren't crying, they were accusing all and sundry of having done in the old woman.

"Out." Grace pointed to the door. "Take your squabble outside. I have patients."

Realizing their role was shepherding the women to the parking lot, Tony and Wade went to work, encouraging them to keep moving forward. As they passed Orvan's cubicle, the old man looked disappointed. He had clearly been enjoying the melodrama.

Gladiola and Tulip, the two oldest women, the argumentative sisters, each had walkers. Neither was ready to yield an inch, although passing through the doorway in single file was their only option. Neither wanted to be first or last. Determined to fight it out for themselves, the pair were jammed into the open doorway, locking their supporting devices together. Whining and moaning, the ninety-year-olds banged into each other's walkers, slapped one another with purses, and pulled hair. One woman finally managed to squeeze into position and got ahead of her sister by dislodging the sibling's wig, tossing it onto the floor behind her, and sneaking past during the retrieval. The screeching did not stop until they were all outside.

Ears ringing, Tony and Wade did finally manage to herd the cluster of Flowers into the fresh air and stood guard, making sure none of them attempted to get back inside the clinic. They waited until every Flower disappeared.

CHAPTER TEN

Finally there was some good news. Mike and Ruby returned from Knoxville with a favorable report from the doctor. Dammit was so pathetically happy to see the couple, he lumbered from his nap on Tony's office rug, swinging his tail so hard he almost slapped himself in the face. Tony felt bad for the poor beast, separated from his family, and at the same time wanted to deny the dog's obvious claims of abuse and neglect during his stay in the Abernathy household.

The joy didn't last long.

"Sir, someone's been shot." Rex Satterfield's voice was calm as it came through the radio with the address. "The ambulance is on the way but, well you know, whoever was doing the shooting is still in the area."

Tony did know. Paramedics and ambulance crews didn't like being shot at. He didn't blame them. He'd been shot while he was still a Chicago cop and hadn't enjoyed any part of it. "What's the address?"

He and Mike were already headed to their vehicles even before they knew where they needed to go. They left Ruby and Dammit standing in the office talking to Ruth Ann.

Wade drove from another direction and beat them to the address, which turned out to be a lovely two-story home a few miles out of town. His voice came clearly through the radio letting everyone know there was no danger to anyone else.

Tony heard the wail of the ambulance through his radio as it approached the destination, a row of newer houses all built facing the same direction, giving them a lovely mountain view. Tony was a bit surprised to see that Sam Austin, a man Tony knew to be the homeowner of the house next door, had been handcuffed to a doorknob and was waving his free arm frantically, signaling his distress.

Ignoring everyone, Wade directed the paramedics to come to the house next to it, a single-story beauty. The home's exterior was marred by shattered glass where there should have been a sliding door.

"What happened?"

Tony and Mike joined Wade and listened to his description of events while watching, through the remnants of glass, the para-medics working on a middle-aged woman lying on a tile floor. She was bleeding copi-ously. "As far as I've been told," said Wade, "Mr. Austin shot Mrs. Marsh from his second-floor window. As you can see she was standing in her own kitchen."

"Who handcuffed the neighbor?"

"I did." Wade's eyes narrowed and a muscle in his jaw tightened. "I took away his rifle and I wanted to make sure he stayed put."

"How's Mrs. Marsh doing?" Tony kept his voice low.

"I don't know. The bullet hit about here." Wade tapped his upper arm. "But, her arms are a lot smaller than mine and there's a lot of blood. I'm guessing there's all kinds of possible damage."

"You wait here, Wade." Tony turned to-ward the other house. "Mike, let's go have a little chat with our shooter."

Mr. Austin seemed strangely calm when they reached him. Tony unlocked the hand-cuffs and led him out of view of the wounded woman. "Talk to me. What hap-pened?"

Mike took a few photographs of the only open window on the second floor.

"I want a lawyer." Austin said. His jaw

jutted forward. "I've got nothing else to say."

"Interesting." Tony put the handcuffs back on, this time placing Austin's hands behind his back, palms facing away from each other. "Let's get you to town and you can make your call."

"Is this necessary?" Austin waggled his fingers. "I'm not dangerous."

"Oh yes you are." Tony led him to the Blazer and opened the back door. "Anyone who will shoot their next-door neighbor, their unarmed neighbor, *is* very dangerous in my book." Tony placed a hand on Austin's head and pushed him down onto the seat. "Don't hurt yourself."

Mike said, "I'll stay and take more pictures and help Wade."

Tony thought it sounded like a great idea. He hated giving bad or frightening news to people. "See if there's a husband or family in the area. You know the drill."

It suddenly struck him they hadn't checked the shooter's home for other family or friends. "What about you, Austin, anyone else at your home?" Given the sulky behavior of the man, he was a bit surprised when he replied.

"No. Emily, my wife, is out of town."

For an instant, the idea of shooting his own neighbor lady while Theo was gone flashed through his head. Implausible. There was more to this story, he could feel it.

Theo was being entertained by Katti Marmot. The pregnant Russian bride was taking Theo's beginning quilting class. Her class project was, predictably, a small quilt for her unborn baby and, equally predictably, pink. Considering her refusal to learn the gender of the baby, Theo was a bit curious what her response might be if she produced a tiny little Claude, Jr. Theo pressed her lips together to stop herself from suggesting Katti sew a second quilt top, one using a novelty fabric of miniature trash trucks, just in case.

The other three members of the class appeared to be enjoying the convivial atmosphere as much as the actual sewing. Theo had seen them around town, at church, the store, or the doctor's office, but hadn't really gotten to know them until now.

"Make sure you all make plans to come to the quilt show. It starts on the Fourth and is taken down on Sunday." Theo gestured to their practice quilt blocks, in various stages of completion, hanging on the design walls. "If you examine the quilts in the show, I think you'll be surprised at how good these first quilts of yours are going to be."

"It was because of the show last year I decided to take this class." The speaker, one of the quietest students Theo had ever dealt with, was as subdued as her clothing. Beige with more beige. But her quilt and the fabrics she chose showed a different side of the woman. Her class project, a stunning combination of an oriental print of gold and teal and dark green, glowed in the classroom lights.

"Have I ever shown you the first quilt I made?" Theo grinned. "Every one of you has done a better job than I did." She pulled the ragged quilt out of its storage box and spread it out on a table. The pitiful quilt was poorly sewn, made of hideous maroon and blue fabrics, and the binding, which should have finished the edges, gapped away from the quilt's top. "See?"

"Well, the, um . . ." Each of the students in turn tried to find something nice to say about it. Finally one said, "That's a quilt!"

Their laughter attracted the attention of some of the shoppers. When they came into the classroom to visit, they all expressed their appreciation of their work. With the exception of Theo's first quilt. It didn't even receive any pity votes for being complete.

125

■ ■ ■ ■

Tony saw his mom's name come up on caller ID. He wasn't sure if he was glad the system was invented or not. This way, if he didn't answer her call, he felt guilty. Then he felt irritated she made him feel guilty. So, he answered it. "Hi, Mom."

"Tony, this is your mother speaking."

Tony rolled his eyes. There was no sense in his saying more, especially as he heard the distinctive ring of irritation in her voice. "What's going on, Mom?"

"You need to get out here. That bear of Roscoe's is sleeping in the back of one of our visitor's pickup. The man wanted to leave and now he can't because of the bear." She disconnected.

Hoping Roscoe was still working for his brother Gus, Tony punched another number.

"Yoo-hoo, Marc Antony, what's up?" Gus's merry voice boomed through the earpiece.

Tony was definitely not happy with caller ID today. "Is Roscoe with you?"

"Yep. And Baby too." Gus laughed. "We're trying to nail Quentin's porch back together and attach it to his old trailer. So far we're having a bit of trouble getting the odd bits all lined up."

Tony was momentarily distracted by the mental image Gus's words inspired. Quentin's porch was so ragged and old, Tony doubted there was enough rot-free wood to put a nail in. "Are you sure about Baby? Mom just called and is claiming Baby is sleeping in a visitor's pickup at the museum."

"No kidding." Gus paused. "Nope. I can see her from here. She's busy trying to get grubs out of an old chunk of wood. Picnic time for Baby."

"Let me talk to Roscoe." Tony wondered who else to call. Roscoe had a special relationship with Baby. Could that mean he would be able to deal with another bear? Tony guessed he'd have to contact the game warden.

"Sheriff?" Roscoe's voice was about an octave higher than his brother Gus's. "Did I hear right? Did you tell Gus you've found another bear?"

"Not exactly, my mom says there's one sleeping in a pickup at the museum. She thought it was Baby."

"I kin go out and look," Roscoe volunteered. "It's a bit of a drive you know."

"Meet me there." Tony thought they could

127

shoo the bear out of the truck and it would go home. Roscoe at least had some knowledge of bear behavior.

Tony arrived first. His mom was stalking up and down the gravel of the parking area flapping her arms at the bear. Ignoring her, the black bear, sleek and shiny, was clutching an upside-down, medium-size blue and white cooler with its big paws, and big claws. After dumping the cooler's contents into the bed of the pickup, it rummaged around in the untidy pile and came up holding an apple impaled on one long claw.

Roscoe arrived a few minutes later and stood next to Tony watching the older woman fussing at the bear. "Your mom ought not to be standing so close. She don't know that bear and worst still, that bear don't know your mom."

"Mom." Tony called out keeping his voice low. She couldn't hear him over her harangue. "Mom!" He yelled.

She turned and gave him the disgusted mom look. "What is it, Marc Antony?"

"That's not Baby."

Jane stared at him for a moment until his words finally made an impact. "Not Baby?" She seemed suddenly paralyzed. She didn't even blink. "Roscoe, is this Baby?"

"No ma'am," Roscoe sidled up to the

older woman and escorted her away. "I've never seen this bear. I'm going to open the tailgate and we'll see if we can handle this all gentle like."

Tony thought if it didn't work and they would have to call the game warden, it would be the second-best solution. The worst might be if someone had to shoot the bear to rescue Roscoe. The only reason Tony hesitated to call the game warden was the illegal nature of keeping a wild pet, and the fact that Tony had turned a blind eye to Roscoe's adoption of Baby. Tony now wished he routinely carried some kind of tranquilizer darts in the Blazer.

Roscoe walked to the rear of the bear-occupied truck and unlatched the tailgate. It fell open with a thud. Startled by the noise, the bear rose onto its rear haunches and made a low growling sound. Tony removed his pistol from the holster. Roscoe stood by the side of the pickup and clapped his hands together and said, "Get out bear!"

Possibly groggy from sleeping in the heat, the bear yawned in his face and looked around. Roscoe repeated the process, yelling this time. The bear lunged forward; the impact of its paws striking the metal floor of the pickup bed sent the apple flying forward and it landed on the ground. The bear followed the apple, looked up, saw a row of spectators, then turned and ran in the other direction, away from the people. Within seconds, it hurried past the last of the museum buildings and had vanished into the woods.

Everyone except Jane and the truck's owner applauded. The owner slammed the tailgate closed, got in, and drove away without a word to anyone, leaving most of his picnic items on the ground.

"Not Baby." Jane's face lost its last bit of color as she wobbled to a bench and more or less collapsed onto it. "I petted it. It licked my hand, just like Baby does."

Tony gave silent thanks to his mother's overworked guardian angel. What a job to be saddled with. A least, he thought, since he was already bald himself, she couldn't make his hair turn white. It was little comfort but it was some.

The Mystery Quilt
Second Body of Clues

Block One will need:
Fabric (A) 16 squares 2 7/8″
Fabric (A) 8 squares 3 1/4″
Fabric (C) 8 squares 2 7/8″
Fabric (D) 10 squares 2 7/8″
Fabric (D) 8 squares 3 1/4″

Preparation 1:
Place the 3 1/4″ squares of Fabrics (A) and (D)'s right sides together. Mark single diagonal line from corner to corner. Sew <u>scant</u> 1/4″ line of stitching on both sides of the line. Cut on line. Press to darker fabric. Trim to 2 7/8″ using a bias square ruler to maintain the center line and remove "ears."

Preparation 2:
Sewing with an accurate 1/4″ seam, make 2 Nine Patch blocks using the 2 7/8″ squares of Fabrics (C) and (D) with top and bottom rows — D/C/D and center row C/D/C.

Assemble, pressing to darker fabric.

Layout:
Place 8 squares 2 7/8″ of Fabric (A) in a stack, and place to the left of it, 8 half square triangle

blocks, arranging the triangles of Fabric (A) next to the Fabric (A) squares and along top edge. To the right of stack, place 8 half square triangle blocks with Fabric (A) next to Fabric (A) squares and along top edge. Before sewing make sure the layout shows a mirror image on sides with points (D) up on opposite ends. (Make 8)

Press to make seams interlock with Nine Patch blocks.

Sew one of the units of half square triangles and blocks of (A) on opposite ends of the Nine Patch blocks so points of (D) are facing away from Nine Patch center. (Make 2)

Add a square of (A) on each end of remaining pieced strips.

Finishing the block:
Place a row with squares of (A) on the ends, above and below the Nine Patch unit. Be sure points face away from Nine Patch center. Sew.

Make (2) blocks, trim to 12 1/2" and Label — Block One.

CHAPTER ELEVEN

Tony decided to pay a visit to the courtroom. A couple of brothers were on trial. More precisely, one was on trial for shooting at the other one. Neither of them seemed particularly bothered by the situation.

The judge was apparently the only person angered by the scenario. Archie Campbell, the county prosecutor, was presenting evidence, mostly the confession, that brother number one, Bradley, committed a felony when he went to his brother's house after they'd been arguing on the telephone, and fired several shots. Archie stated his case clearly and concisely just to have it on record.

Carl Lee Cashdollar, attorney and the mayor's nephew, was defending Bruce, brother number two. The defense involved brother number two — the one being shot at — accepting the plea agreement and explaining to the court how he'd provoked his brother and, therefore, "No harm, no foul." Bruce summed up the situation with, "After all, it's not like Bradley's a good enough shot to hit me where it counts."

The statement inflamed the judge. He appeared to be flapping his arms inside the robe, making him look like a man having a seizure. His lower jaw jutted forward and he pounded his gavel until silence returned, and he had the attention of everyone in the courtroom.

"There were innocent people in the area. Frankly, I wouldn't get out of bed to hear this case except for one reason. If the two of you want to shoot each other, go right ahead, but do *not* endanger the innocent people in this community, especially its children. I understand there were several children seen playing volleyball not too far away from your tantrum."

Both brothers nodded.

"I don't like it because I feel like my hands are tied, but I'm going to sentence you according to the plea agreement y'all worked out with the prosecutor." He pointed at Bradley, the shooter, with his gavel. "But if I ever see either one of you in my courtroom again, for any reason, I will throw the book at you. If you violate any of the conditions set out for this deferred sentence, I will throw the book at you." The judge's face was moving out of the red shades and into the purples. "If I see you at the grocery store and you're pushing the cart recklessly, I will throw the book at you and toss the key in the trash."

He stood abruptly. "Get out of my courtroom."

The judge watched the brothers run for the doors, their lawyers hot on their heels, before settling heavily into his seat. He signaled for Tony to approach.

The two men had a decent relationship. Occasionally Tony thought the judge was either too lenient or too harsh, but he usually found him to be fair.

"I don't suppose you'd let me shoot both of them myself?" said Judge Anderson. "You know, just to make the county a better place to live."

Tony shook his head. "I'd prefer you wait until I leave the room."

Judge Anderson released a heavy sigh. "What's up, Tony? You don't usually visit our courtroom, at least not during a trial, even if you are in charge of the court's security."

"Just thought I'd drop by and make sure everything is going the way it should be."

Tony, as the sheriff, had numerous responsibilities. He might be basically lazy, but he took all of his duties seriously. His favorite day was one in which he found his delegates doing fine without him.

"Sheriff?" Roscoe grinned, exposing his entire mouthful of crowded, crooked teeth. "Veronica has somethin' to tell you."

Tony thought, and not for the first time, how love had forged a powerful bond between the two most unlikely candidates ever. Never in his wildest dreams would he consider matching Veronica with Roscoe. Veronica held at least one Ph.D., and Roscoe held the record for the most years spent in Park County's middle school.

Tony couldn't even begin to imagine what their conversations must be like.

Veronica smiled and greeted Tony with a wave, never releasing Roscoe's hand. Today she was dressed in knee-length pants, sandals and a t-shirt proclaiming her love of books. The petite brunette did not appear, on the surface, to be a likely candidate for either Roscoe or medieval weaponry. Tony knew she was a fan of both.

"Tell him," said Roscoe in a stage whisper.

Tony felt his eyebrows rise.

Veronica obliged. "I've been seeing a

professor from a nearby university around the area. Often."

Tony hardly considered her statement alarming. After all, she fit the same criteria. Lots of people visited their county and many had weekend cabins in the area, but something definitely was bothering her. "Why is this professor a problem?"

"He's *skulking*," said Veronica. Roscoe must have looked confused by the term because she immediately added, "Sneaking around with binoculars."

"Bird watching?"

"Not unless they're invisible birds." Veronica shook her head.

Impressed by her adamant demeanor, Tony said, "Where have you been seeing him?"

"Usually, we've seen him in his car, up on the ridge near Kwik Kirk's."

Tony knew the place. The Ridge, as it had been called for at least two generations, was a dead-end road. The unpaved road saw more traffic in a week than the highway. Dating couples. Bird watchers. Occasionally artists with their easels and stools. Its semi-solitude was provided by fabulously overgrown vegetation, and the view of the mountains from there was breathtaking. He himself often enjoyed parking up there while eating a sandwich, letting the world pass him by for a brief time.

Roscoe chimed in, returning Tony's thoughts to the situation. "He wears this floppy hat, and he's got binoculars, and he's always looking into Candy Tibbles's back windows."

"A peeper?" Tony believed these two had seen what they claimed, but watching Candy Tibbles? Even a peeper ought to have higher standards and aspirations than that. In his opinion, she wasn't worth driving two feet to see. "How do you know this?"

"We've been looking at real estate." Veronica gently squeezed Roscoe's hand. "We have very specific needs. The most important ones are that it has to be out of town, with no neighbors to bother us, on a sizeable piece of land. We need space for Baby and the siege machines."

With those criteria, Tony guessed their real-estate search wasn't going to be an easy one. Park County was tiny, the smallest county in the state, and while there was land available, the county was dotted with settlements, flourishing or invasive vegetation, hills, ridges, and mountains. "Having any luck?"

"There are a couple of old farms with distinct possibilities." Veronica flashed him a grin. "But we have gotten lost from time to time. The roads are sort of randomly marked in places."

"They are indeed. When I became sheriff, I made a point of learning them all, every twist and curve, three-way intersections and five-way intersections, and I swear sometimes a new one pops up that I haven't seen before." Tony laughed, remembering his days of teenaged driving and getting lost every time he left the main roads. He felt lucky he wasn't still driving in the same circles. "What's that got to do with the peeper?"

"We passed Kirk's about forty times one day and kept seeing the same car, but it wasn't always parked in the same place. It's a white Cadillac SUV."

"And it's been there, or near there, every day," Roscoe said. "And the driver's had binoculars and a floppy hat each time."

"Is he alone?" Tony was curious enough to have a look.

"Don't know."

"Out of curiosity," Tony looked at Veronica. "What is he a professor of?"

"Botany," she said softly. "He was at my university, but I believe he might have been asked to leave. He may not be associated with any school now."

Tony assumed academia had gossip grapevines like every other business. "Why did he leave?"

"I did hear there was some 'impropriety,' but I have no idea if it was personal or professional. Our departments didn't exactly have much crossover."

After the flurry of gossip Blossom had spread about Tony and another woman, it died as quickly as it began, replaced by the surfing incident, and now the upcoming parade and the quilt show. Theo's classroom buzzed with women making award ribbons from scraps of fabric, poster board, hot glue, and marking pens with metallic ink. They chatted as they worked.

"Can you imagine thinking standing on a moving car would be fun?" Dottie, one of the regular older ladies, asked. "Honestly? I'm glad I didn't see it. Gives me the palpitations to just think about it."

"You always were a coward," Blind Betty disagreed. "When I was a girl, I'd have tried it."

"When you were a girl, cars didn't go faster than I can walk. And I use a cane." A voice from the corner reached them all. A white-haired woman hobbled toward the quilters. "I know we're the same age."

Pretty soon all of the ladies working were throwing mock insults at each other and laughing.

"What are you working on now?" one of the ladies asked another.

"A Civil War inspired quilt. Lots of small blocks."

India Parsons had only recently begun joining the quilters. "Did she say a silverware quilt?" India elbowed her neighbor and shouted the words.

"No," Dottie bellowed. The response was loud enough for people in the next county to hear. Several of the women jumped like they'd been slapped. "She said Civil War, not silverware."

"Maybe I should turn on my hearing aids." India fumbled in her purse and retrieved a small plastic case. "What about the Civil War? Isn't it over yet?"

"The Civil War quilt has scads of blocks, and they're each only six inches square and some have over fifty pieces." Dottie flapped the work in progress in front of the other women. "Can you imagine sewing all those teensy pieces together?"

"That's more ridiculous than using silverware." Betty shoved her needle in Dottie's face, needing thread, and almost blinded her friend.

"Did you see there's a new man coming to the center for lunch?" India whispered. The softly spoken words stopped all conversation. "He's pretty young, maybe only seventy."

"Does he have a wife?" All heads swiveled in India's direction. India stood up. It didn't actually make her head any higher than it had been. She was about as wide as she was tall, with silver hair cropped close to the scalp and rather elegant-looking glasses with mother-of-pearl frames. Silence reigned.

India shook her head. "No. He's a bachelor."

After a wave of interested oohs and ahs, Betty said, "Does he have his own teeth?"

"Yes."

Suddenly the workroom was filled with chatter. "Who is he? Where does he live? Who are his people?" India was surrounded by a cluster of excited interrogators.

Knowing the prospect of having a new male in the area, one possessing his teeth and his faculties, could entertain the women for the rest of the day, Theo made another pot of coffee for them and headed upstairs to get some of her own work done.

CHAPTER TWELVE

"Sheriff, we've got a suspicious death." Wade called on his cell phone, bypassing the radio.

Tony felt like he'd been punched in the gut. Not at all what he wanted to hear. "Who and where?"

"Candy Tibbles. I'm out at her place. In the back there's a sort of homemade greenhouse." Wade's voice faded and came back. "She's inside it. It looks like she's been dead a while."

"I've seen the greenhouse. Alvin showed it to me one time." Tony couldn't believe the boy's bad luck. "He's off at some botany camp. Is there anything obvious that might have killed her? You know, a bullet hole or an arrow?"

"No. But I'd say she didn't just drop dead."

Tony heard the sound of Wade being sick, and then he was back on the phone.

"She looks like she might have been pushed or hit with something, but I'm not going to do more than take pictures until you get here. Should I call Grace?"

"Yes. Tell your wife I'm on my way." Tony told Ruth Ann what little he knew and headed out. He wanted to see the scene, and then he'd determine if he needed to call in the TBI. The Tennessee Bureau of Investigation had wonderful forensic experts and would come help his tiny department if he thought it necessary. He didn't want to waste their time and effort on a whim.

Tony turned left at Kwik Kirk's convenience store on the highway about four miles from town. As usual, a few cars were parked there: people getting gas, buying snacks and bait. Across the road, there were four houses, widely spaced, on the little turnout, not quite a cul-de-sac. Alvin's home was the first on the left. Large old trees shaded the houses. Alvin's grandparents had lived there, and he assumed, their daughter, Alvin's mom, had inherited it.

Tony parked on the road, leaving the short driveway — two strips of dirt where the grass and weeds didn't even grow — for Grace to park her vehicle. As he walked up the driveway and then around the side of the house, he looked for anything that could be considered suspicious or out of place. There was nothing immediately noticeable. No sign with an arrow pointing to something, saying, "Look here."

Candy's brown sedan sat in the detached garage. It looked like it had when Alvin had returned it before going to camp. A cursory examination showed no blood, no sign of a struggle. Just a dirty car parked where it should be. Tony looked up at the garage's big overhead door. One of the springs to help raise it was broken. He made a note to remind himself to ask Alvin when it had stopped working.

Maple trees formed a backdrop for a hedge of japonica bushes with their fiendish thorns. He walked around them and entered Alvin's garden. The sound of buzzing insects seemed unusually loud. Above the fresh warm scent of trees and grass and freshly dug dirt was the rancid smell of rotting flesh. Candy Tibbles had been dead for a while.

Alvin's greenhouse was constructed of old storm doors, windows pulled from houses being remodeled, and all sorts of "rescued" materials. It sat next to Alvin's well-tended garden. In the garden, rows of brilliant green plants grew in raised beds made of sturdy, weathered-to-gray lumber. Clean straw filled the space between the beds. If there were weeds, they were young and small.

Tony glanced into the greenhouse. The makeshift tables were bare. No plants were inside the building; only the pitiful body of an unhappy woman, gazing sightlessly at the sky. It looked like someone had pulled a tarp off one half of the glass roof and left it in a heap on the ground. A second tarp covered part of the back of the roof, anchored with ropes and stakes, but it exposed more glass than it covered.

Wade waited nearby and upwind. "Grace said she will be here in a few minutes. She has a couple of patients who need her care."

"We can wait. Candy can't be saved." Tony stared into the greenhouse. "A few more minutes is not going to change anything."

"True. So true." Wade took a few more photographs. Placing his markers and making careful notes about each one. "You think she could have come out here alone? Maybe to water Alvin's garden."

"Nope." Tony couldn't imagine Candy being that helpful. "For one thing, there aren't any plants in there, and I heard Alvin talking to her about watering. The greenhouse was not mentioned."

"It's almost a hundred degrees out here. I can't begin to guess how hot it is inside there with all the glass and sunshine and nothing to circulate the air, you know, like an exhaust fan."

Tony felt a bead of sweat, not the first by any means but larger than the others, slip down the center of his back. "We need to know. Don't you have a thermometer in your case?"

Wade fished it out and handed it to Tony, continuing his photography.

Holding his breath, Tony pushed the thermometer through a space left between a former door with six small panes of glass at the top and an old aluminum storm door with no screen and watched the temperature rise. "Holy smoke, it's about a hundred and twenty degrees near the ground. It must be quite a bit hotter near the top. I wonder why there isn't a ventilation system in there. I'll measure the temperature again up higher after Grace arrives. I'd hate to disturb the ambiance." He stepped back and talked into his radio. Rex was on duty. Tony gave Rex a thumbnail sketch of their situation. "What's Sheila involved with?"

"She's got a school zone speeder." Rex's voice dropped into its disaster-calm cadence.

"Okay. Send her out here when she's done. Let's try to keep as much of this off the scanner as possible." Tony guessed a circus caravan of cars driven by the curious out on the highway would arrive in minutes. The citizens of Park County didn't seem to believe they wouldn't be able to see something fascinating if they drove past the scene of an accident or anything involving an official vehicle. "We'll need traffic control. You can send out Mike as well."

Wade's phone rang. After a brief conversation, he disconnected. "Grace is on her way."

Tony studied the body. Candy lay on her back, arms spread, almost like she'd been stargazing, except the position of her body would have been uncomfortable, if alive. One leg was twisted awkwardly underneath her. She wore pink shorts, a pink and yellow tank top more appropriate to an eight-year-old, and purple flip-flops with a flower on top. Actually, he could only see one shoe. He wondered if Candy had lost the mate, was lying on it, or if a killer had taken a souvenir. Until they knew the cause of death, speculation would be just that. Candy could have passed out. Had a heart attack. Eaten a poisonous plant. Been knocked out by the hammer and wrench attacker. Just because they couldn't see a wound from here didn't mean there wasn't one.

"First, let's check the house and make sure no one's in there. We kind of bypassed it," Tony said. "And now I think I'd like to hear how and why you found her body?"

"Kirk, over at the convenience store, complained about her radio playing day and night, loud, heavy metal stuff." Wade paused, as if just noticing the silence. Only a few birds chattering overhead and the sound of cars moving on the highway disturbed the peace.

Tony felt his eyebrows rise.

Wade stood still, looking at the ground, obviously deep in thought. Finally, he let out a deep sigh. "Wow, I forgot. When I got here I followed the screeching music and found an orange extension cord plugged into the exterior outlet on the side of the house." He gestured to the spot. "I pulled the plug and the music stopped. I followed the cord to the greenhouse because I wanted to tell Candy to hold it down. I never saw the radio."

Relieved that his deputy recalled the incident, Tony studied the outlet. "The radio might be inside the greenhouse. I didn't notice it. We can solve one mystery anyway." Tony and Wade followed the cord and quickly located the radio, on a stump, hidden by a shrub. "I'd like you to check for fingerprints on this too."

Wade nodded and wrote himself a note.

They walked to the front of the house and found the door was locked. Everything looked normal. Tony had hoped the killer, if Candy's death wasn't an accident, had left the weapon on the porch with a note of confession. A man could dream. The porch needed sweeping. Months, if not years, of mud tracked onto the porch had dried. There was a mixture of red clay and brown garden soil. Signs of frequent use, but no obviously new footprints stood out from the others. There could be some nevertheless. "Let's look in the windows."

So they went from window to window, looking inside. Nothing moved. No footprints were pressed into the ground under the windows. When they reached the back porch, they immediately saw the screen door was ajar and so was the interior door.

"What do you think?" Wade released his sidearm from its holster.

Tony did the same. "I don't think anyone's in there, but I'm not taking any chances either. Getting shot for being stupid is not a good plan."

As carefully as they could, trying not to smudge any possible fingerprints, they eased into Candy's kitchen. The smell of rotting meat hit them. A glance at the countertop showed them an open package of ground meat. And maggots. Another sign this was not a crime committed in the past few minutes.

"Gross," Wade whispered. "I hate maggots."

Tony nodded. "It looks like she was preparing to cook something and then died. Why did she go outside?" He was murmuring to himself as they studied their options. The pantry door hung open, exposing bags of potato chips, corn chips, all kinds of chips; if they could be sliced and fried, Candy had owned a bag of it. Chips seemed to be the only food stored in the pantry besides toaster pastries. Next to the pantry was a wide opening into the dining room. There was no door. It was go ahead or back out. They eased forward. No one. Clearing room after room, they checked them all. They climbed the stairs. The rooms were messy and dirty, but void of people.

On up to the attic. Unlike the chaos and clutter in the rest of the house, Tony guessed no one had been up here since Candy's parents died. There were a few items — a stack of things from Alvin's childhood, an old bassinet, a few boxes, a pitiful artificial Christmas tree, and a stereo system from another era. No people. No signs there had been anyone up here recently. The only footprints in the dust belonged to a mouse, and they were not fresh. Tony checked the temperature and said, "Let's go outside."

Wade did not argue.

Grace arrived minutes later, looking cool and well groomed. Her glossy brown hair with its gleaming red and gold highlights was pulled up into a knot, and her khaki slacks and white blouse were neatly ironed. Her crisp appearance lasted about thirteen seconds. Once she was inside the greenhouse, her clothes became sweat soaked, and her latex gloves filled with enough saltwater to make a barnacle happy.

Tony thought he should have used a stopwatch to see how fast she wilted, although he probably wouldn't have been able to push the buttons fast enough. He held the thermometer near the upper reaches of the greenhouse. One hundred and forty-eight. "Damn." He was soaked from the skin out himself.

Grace was a trooper though. While Wade's camera clicked incessantly, she measured the liver temperature and made a cursory examination of the body. "The back of her skull feels soft, like it's cracked."

"From the fall?"

"No way." Grace wiped the sweat pouring off her face with the side of her arm. "I can feel an indentation with my finger. It had to be something like a pipe or a tire iron. Wielded with a great deal of force." She leaned closer, shining her flashlight on the dirt under Candy's head. "It looks like blood might have seeped into the dirt. I'd say a lot of blood. You know how head wounds bleed. It's so much darker than the dirt farther away from her body. I don't think she died immediately."

Tony leaned over to look at what Grace was seeing. "I'll be interested to learn if she could have been saved with prompt medical attention."

Grace agreed. "Do you see anything she might have been hit with?"

The three of them studied the ground in the greenhouse, the garden area, and looked for something obvious they could see without trampling the evidence more than they already had. Nothing. Not even a trowel.

"Whoever hit her took the weapon, whatever it was, away." Wade stated the obvious and Tony and Grace nodded.

"Premeditated?" Tony wondered aloud.

153

"Or calm enough to think afterwards? I wonder where Alvin keeps his garden tools. Did anyone see a shed or a box?"

None one had.

The recent assaults on others bore a striking similarity to this scene. Tony grimaced at his mental pun. He looked at Wade. "This remind you of anything?"

"You mean our citizen wounded by an unknown attacker and then the hitchhiker knocked out on the highway and left there? Absolutely." Wade made a pounding gesture. "If Not Bob had been as small as Candy, he'd probably be dead too."

"I don't think we should assume Not Bob's attacker killed Candy. There're too many obvious differences."

"Besides her being a female, and therefore unlikely to be named Bob?" Grace threw in her comment.

"Yes." Tony flashed Grace a smile, even as he looked carefully about, searching for anything that might catch his eye. "Plus, it's probably five miles to Ruby's from here. What are the odds our tool guy would drastically change his hunting ground?"

"Probably not good. It could be a copycat though," Wade said. "Are we calling in the TBI?"

Tony considered the question. There

would be evidence on the body. Maybe the Tennessee Bureau of Investigation could find some footprints in the area, if he and Wade hadn't already destroyed them. He had a small department. He hated to call for help if he didn't really need it.

"No offense, Grace, but I think I'll have someone else do the autopsy." Tony called for the ambulance to come fetch Candy and deliver her to a pathologist in Knoxville.

Grace exhaled sharply. "I was about to insist the same thing. Just like with the surfer, you need someone trained to measure the skull depression and do a toxicology screen. I'm a physician, so I can declare someone deceased, but Doc Nash can't make me the coroner. Plus, even if I could, I'd hate to screw it up and let someone get away with murder."

"Wade?" Hearing the "M" word spoken out loud gave Tony a jolt.

"I agree," Wade said. "I can certainly do the camera work and fingerprints. I've had the training for those, but you might want someone else to do tire tracks and footprints."

"Okay, it's nice we're all in agreement. Let's get some help." Tony punched a single number into his cell phone. After a brief conversation, Tony disconnected. "The TBI

155

will be here in about three hours. Grace, you can leave now instead of waiting until Candy's been collected. The less we disturb the scene, the better our associates will like it."

"Well, I'm guess I'm off now." Scarlet-faced and perspiring, Grace managed a smile. "Y'all have fun. I'll think of you while I'm taking a nice cool shower and having a nice glass of sweet tea before returning to my patients."

Wade gave his wife an almost-amused smile. "You are a cruel, cruel woman."

She laughed and kissed his cheek. "The truth is closer to a quick shower and endless apologies to my patients for making them wait for an extended time."

Following Grace into the sweltering, but unpolluted, air, Tony and Wade paused, sucking deep breaths of fresh air into their lungs. Tony heard Wade continuing to give a running commentary into his radio. It sounded like he was trying to convince Rex to come out and smell it for himself. Tony handed his deputy the roll of crime scene tape, and they headed away from the house and back to work.

At first Tony thought the little building encased in a honeysuckle vine might be an old privy. It was so well covered, draped with the tenacious and heavily scented flowers, that he and Wade had walked past it without seeing there was a door. At least twice. The wood might be antique, but the padlock was modern. It dangled through the hasp. The key was in the lock. Tony eased the door open. It was cool inside and smelled like good clean dirt. A wheelbarrow leaned against one wall. Clean and neatly arranged garden tools, small and large, hung on hooks. Three of the larger hooks were empty. Tony really wanted to know what kinds of tools were supposed to be there.

And where they had gone.

Tony thought he could predict what the TBI unit would have to say when they arrived. He was right on every count.

"Hey, Wade," Vince, supervisor and lead investigator, called out as he climbed from the specially configured vehicle, a combination storage locker and laboratory. Two more men and a woman joined him. "Why do you stay in the crime capital of the state? Can't you get a job in a safer county?"

Wade just shook his head. "I'm never bored."

Tipping his chin down, Vince glanced over the top of his glasses in Tony's direction. "Job security, Tony. You're my job security.

As long as you keep your job, mine is safe." Even as he started pulling out bags and boxes for evidence collection, he kept up a running commentary on Tony's personal crime wave. "However, I would appreciate having some better working conditions though. What is it? Like a hundred degrees and ninety-nine percent humidity out here today?"

Tony grinned. "You're going to love the kitchen and the greenhouse. At least the attic, where I estimated the temperature at two hundred degrees, is clear. Only something small with wings could have moved around in there." As miserable as he was in his uniform and vest, he imagined the crime scene costume would be like being sealed in a portable steam room. "Come right this way."

All merriment stopped abruptly as the unit began working their way through the house and greenhouse and yard, collecting samples. Everyone was aware of the serious nature of their job. Doing their work properly could mean the difference between catching a killer and letting one run free.

Tony entertained himself by making notes of his own. What he saw, what he smelled. Who he saw drive by. Who parked at the store and watched from there. Who looked grim and who looked pleased. Although there had been no official news released, there were three houses with neighbors who undoubtedly reported to at least one other person, and so on. He'd be shocked if there were three adults in the county who had not already received word of Candy's death.

"Sheriff?" one of the TBI's younger investigators waved from the back of the house. "You asked specifically about garden tools?"

"Did you find some?" Tony walked closer but saw nothing.

"Stashed under here." The investigator lifted a chunk of prefab lattice away from one side of the raised porch.

Sure enough, an untidy pile of tools — a hoe, rake, and spade — all jumbled together, looked like they had been shoved under there to hide them. Tony had spent enough time with Alvin to know the boy was not responsible for this mess. "Alvin." He spoke the name aloud.

"You think someone named Alvin put these here?"

"No. I don't. I just remembered that I need to notify him. Our victim is his mother. You might want to examine those tools first." Tony frowned, even as he pulled out his cell phone. If anyone would know how to contact Alvin, it would be his own aunt.

Martha was Alvin's landlady and friend. Tony punched in the number. Thankfully, Martha answered right away. Tony started to explain when she interrupted.

"I was wondering when you'd call." Martha lowered her voice. "We heard about it hours ago."

"How?" But he knew. Within seconds of the call for the ambulance, not to mention Dr. Grace leaving her office, the rumors would have begun. "I need to tell Alvin about his mom. He sure doesn't need to hear it on the news. Did he leave you his contact information?"

"Yes, yes."

Tony heard the sounds of rummaging and finally, "Here's the number." Martha rattled off a series of numbers. "He told me he probably won't have his phone turned on. You can call the front desk. That's the second number I gave you."

"Thanks, Martha." Tony said. "I think I should drive up there and tell him in person. It's not the kind of thing a boy should learn on the phone, much less from a message left with a stranger."

"You call me when you get back, and let me know how he's doing and if he needs anything." Martha sniffled. "That poor boy."

Tony agreed and disconnected the call.

The ambulance arrived and parked on the crowded driveway. Tony told the ambulance crew that it could be hours before the body would be ready to transport. He signed his name on every form to insure the proper chain of custody.

And so, having signed over the body, and leaving Wade to help or answer questions for the TBI, Tony drove to plant camp.

CHAPTER THIRTEEN

The classroom at Theo's shop was abuzz with excitement. Candy Tibbles murdered! The announcement had come from a quilter who had heard about it when she stopped to get gas at Kwik Kirk's. Someone else said the woman was killed in her own bed, sending a chill of fear through the room. The woman possessed even less information than Theo herself, but if the facts were wrong, who knew? If Candy could be murdered, couldn't any of them be murdered too? No wonder Tony called her shop "gossip central."

There was also much speculation about the mysterious assailant who attacked the man now referred to in Silersville as Not Bob. The article in the *Silersville Gazette* had been short on facts and filled with the suggestion of violence and widespread crime. The true name of the victim had not been released.

The condition of the hitchhiker was discussed at length. The man continued to be in intensive care in a Knoxville hospital, and no one was releasing his name to the public. Theo knew Tony had contacted some family member, but for some reason, Tony was keeping the name to himself.

The quilters suggested, with not much confidence, that maybe the man had killed Candy, thinking she was Bob too. The whisper of a connection among the three events created speculation about a serial killer. Theo couldn't say the person wasn't a serial killer, except neither man had died. Both were gravely injured, but not dead. Candy's was the only death.

The similarities were not lost on her though. Both Candy and Not Bob were at their own homes when they were attacked. Park County wasn't exactly the kind of place where the residents usually had to lock their doors, much less fear their neighbors. Or it hadn't been until recently.

Theo had witnessed similar situations before — not the attacks, but her shop filled with the curious, hoping the sheriff's wife would have inside information. And be willing to share. Theo was very good at keeping secrets, but even she was in the dark. She didn't even have official word of Candy's death, and she certainly had no insight into the crime. Hoping it was all a big mistake, Theo pushed several women into the chairs around the frame and the charity quilt. "Put some stitches in it while you're sitting there. I know you'll feel better after doing a good deed. Just think of the joy this will bring someone."

Theo studied the quilt: a combination of maroons, blues, and greens mixed with cream pieced into interlocking stars. She thought it was one of the prettiest charity quilts they had worked on. The top had been "rescued" after a friend of a friend passed away and a family member didn't know what to do with all her unquilted tops. Over the years a large number of charity quilts had been finished in this room. Tiny little quilts for the Alzheimer's project, lap quilts for veterans, raffle quilts for every kind of charity, pillow cases for Benjamin Smiles. Quilts for first babies, last babies, animal shelters, and the homeless. If there was a cause, they made a quilt for it. If it didn't go to a designated person, it was raffled and the money donated.

As for the gossip, there was always some. It was rarely small-minded, petty speculation; Theo wouldn't stand for that. But news of illness or sorrows or joys traveled around the room. Theo knew when a grandchild arrived or a medical diagnosis was serious. People in cities might know a few of the same people, but in small towns, it was different. Lives intersected on all kinds of levels. The man living next door might be the mechanic. Children who had Mrs. Scott for third grade grew into parents of the children she was now teaching. All were children whose lives were better for hearing her tell mystical stories, always beginning with "Once upon a time," every day right after lunch. The sheriff's children played with the rich and the poor.

Plant camp was not what Tony had envisioned. In his mind "camp" was filled with games, laughter, pranks, maybe a tire swing you could jump from into the deepest part of the creek. Glancing around at the two-story building attached to a long greenhouse, Tony thought it was more like science class. All-day science class. The accommodating woman at the front desk led him through a labyrinth of hallways, past spotless rooms, some with visible plants and some with microscopes and people in lab coats. At last she stopped and tapped on a door.

A serious, professor-type woman wearing

laboratory glasses and a scarf tied over her hair opened it a crack. "What?"

"Sorry to interrupt, but there's a family emergency for one of your summer kids." Tony's escort delivered the words in a rush, almost like one long convoluted word.

The professor blinked, assimilated the information, then nodded her understanding. "Who?"

"Alvin Tibbles," Tony spoke up. "I'm the sheriff, and a friend of his."

Instead of ushering him in, she shut the door in their faces, startling Tony but not his escort. A moment later, Alvin squeezed through the doorway, carefully closing the door behind him. "Sheriff?"

"Tony," he automatically corrected him and tipped his head, indicating Alvin should follow him away from the perky secretary. "I'm afraid I have bad news." It didn't matter how many times he practiced the words; they never got easier to say. "We've found your mother in your greenhouse. She has passed away and there is an investigation under way."

Alvin listened intently, his expression almost that of someone who doesn't know the language and is trying to interpret it anyway. He shook his head. "No. I don't think it's her. She never goes in there. She always says it's creepy."

"I've known your mom for a long time." Tony led Alvin farther down the hall. "It is her. Whether she went into the greenhouse on her own, or someone else took her there is unclear." Tony watched as the boy blinked, suddenly looking less than his age. In spite of their problems, Candy was his mother and the last living relative Tony knew of. Set adrift by circumstance and a killer, Alvin deserved answers and justice.

"What do I do now?" Blinking hard, Alvin jammed his fists into his lab coat's pockets.

Tony didn't know the answer. Should he suggest the boy stay at camp, pretending his life hadn't changed, or take him to his own aunt's house where he'd have nothing to do? It could be a while before they had the results of the autopsy, much less any answers to their questions. "I don't know. I can take you back with me." He very carefully avoided the word "home." "Do you want to stay here during the investigation?" Tony deliberately didn't mention the autopsy. "It's up to you."

Alvin stared at the floor for a long time. "I'll stay here. I guess."

"That's fine." Tony wrote his private number on a card. "You can call me any time, even if you just want to talk, or if you change your mind. If you do, I'll come pick you up."

The fingers reaching for the card shook badly but finally managed to grasp it. "You find out who did it. Promise?" Alvin's eyes flooded with tears. "She's not bad, you know. I was not abused, and she was always fond of her family and good to animals, she's just not — " He paused, collecting himself. "It was always like she was under-baked or something. Not finished, you know? Like how sometimes bread don't rise."

Tony nodded. "I think that's the best description I ever heard of your mother."

Alvin wiped his flooded eyes, squared his shoulders, and returned to the classroom.

Dragging himself back to the Blazer, Tony hoped he could keep his promise. Who would bother killing Candy?

Tony called Theo and listened carefully to her report on shop gossip. He reached for the antacids in his glove compartment when she mentioned the fear level rising, and people connecting Candy with the other two recent attacks. Tony couldn't even promise her they were wrong.

"I'm going to Knoxville to have a little chat with Not Bob in his hospital room.

168

Maybe he can shed some light on his own attack." Tony disconnected and notified dispatch where he was headed.

Not Bob lay on a narrow bed, tubes running in and out and all around him while a bank of monitors flashed numbers. Tony studied their attack victim for a while before noticing the man was watching him.

Tony introduced himself then asked, "Do you feel up to a few questions?"

"Yes." Not Bob's voice was a soft whisper. "Some."

"Can you tell me what happened?"

After a moment, Not Bob said, "It was something like you'd see in the movies. One moment I'm squeezing the shampoo bottle." He paused and his eyes drifted shut. "Next thing, a raging freak screams at me and hits me with a hammer or a wrench, over and over. It seemed like he had one in each hand. I'm trying to dodge him, but I'm slipping, and blood's running down he drain and mixing with water, and he's like a mosquito buzzing around everywhere." He choked on his words.

Alarmed by the man's breathing, Tony interrupted. "I think you need to breathe. Relax. Take your time."

Not Bob nodded and wheezed hard, like he'd been running. "Next thing, I crawl for my cell phone. Left it on the sink. I tried punching in nine-one-one, wasn't sure I did."

"You made the call." Tony paused to let the man catch his breath again. "Do you remember my deputy arriving? A female."

"Was she the angel?" Not Bob grinned. "When she talked to me, I thought I was dead. She had pretty golden hair like a halo, but man, she was furious and kind of bitchy for an angel. She kept saying something over and over. It was like 'No. You do *not* get to die today.'" Not Bob's voice faded, and he drifted off to sleep.

Tony left Not Bob smiling at his memory. It wasn't until Tony was back in the Blazer that he realized he hadn't asked for a name of someone to notify. Luckily, Not Bob was well enough to do it himself. As Tony drove back to Silersville, his mind played with the pieces of their puzzles, hoping to line everything up.

Candy was hit in the head with something hard and slender enough to leave a dent in her skull. Only after the autopsy would anyone be able to say with any certainty if the blow was or wasn't caused by a hammer or a pipe wrench. The idea of some crazed person running around the county, invisible, hunting for the elusive Bob, gave Tony

170

the chills. Was it possible he had other weapons in his arsenal besides those two?

The acts might make perfect sense to the basher. Tony was torn. Without more information, he could create hysteria by claiming they had a serial attacker on their hands, or let his people suffer needlessly if they weren't warned.

He settled for having the department issue a warning to county residents to lock their doors and call if they witnessed anything suspicious. He only hoped they could service all the calls. If someone else was attacked, he'd have to borrow help.

Tony decided it was time to start the door-to-door investigation into Candy's death. More crimes were solved with footwork and interviews than in the laboratory. They'd talk to Candy's closest neighbors first.

The house directly across the road from Candy's, and therefore also across the highway from the convenience store, belonging to Kirk Kilpatrick. Diagonally from Candy's home was Opal Dunwoody's house. Opal was a nosy old lady well known by all of his department employees. She might hold the record for the number of complaints called in — everything from branches blown down to excessive noise to accidents on the highway. Occasionally she called to find out if her telephone was working.

When he returned from notifying Alvin of his mother's death, Tony turned into the cul-de-sac directly behind a car parking in the driveway of the house next door to Candy's. Tony watched the driver, a man in his late twenties or early thirties, hurry into the house and decided to start his interviewing there. Candy's next-door neighbors were people he did not know. He thought he would talk to them first, and with any luck, he would learn they witnessed the crime and he wouldn't need to talk to Opal Dunwoody, not because he didn't like her but because there was no such thing as a short visit with Opal.

Tony asked Sheila to stay with the TBI and asked Wade to join him for the interviews. Walking to the house next to Candy's together, Tony knocked on the home's front door and set off a frenzy of barking. Above the sound of it, he heard a woman's voice saying, "Hush, Reggie," just before she opened the door. In spite of the dark circles under her bloodshot eyes, she looked younger than he'd expected. Reggie looked about half poodle and half Corgi: long, low, and curly.

Tony introduced himself and Wade. "And you are?"

"Etta. Etta Vanderbilt, no relation to the more famous family. Won't you come inside?" She pushed the dog back from the doorway with her foot. "Go away, Reggie."

Surrendering, the dog trotted away. By the time Tony and Wade made it inside and closed the door, Reggie had returned with a well-dressed man carrying an infant.

Etta introduced them. Her husband, Paul, shifted the baby and offered his hand.

"We're investigating a disturbance," said Tony. He didn't want to give away any information; he just wanted to collect it. "Do you know your neighbors?"

"That woman!" Etta hissed the words. Anger chased some of the fatigue from her expression. "Did she call you to complain about the baby crying? She claims we're a disturbance. And all night long her radio is blasting — we had the windows closed and could still hear it!" Etta's voice rose with each word.

Her husband nodded but didn't speak; his lips stayed pressed tightly together.

Tony thought the man's expression said it all. These people thoroughly disliked Candy, maybe even hated her enough to go next door and bash her with a shovel, or whatever. "Did you notice anything different lately? More visitors? A new one? Arguments?"

"No." Etta, having given her opinion, was now considering his questions. "The visitors and arguing were normal for her. With the big trees separating the houses, it's hard to see, so it's mostly voices. And music."

"Anything else you can think of?" Wade glanced up from his notebook. "Unusual sounds? Screams? Notice anything or anyone unusual anytime in the last few days. In the entire area, not just at Candy's?"

"The baby rules my life." Etta shook her head. "I'm totally out of touch."

"Wait, there is something odd." Paul stepped forward. "It wasn't only yesterday though. It's been going on for days. I thought about reporting it, but it didn't seem, you know, criminal."

"What's that?" Tony straightened, paying closer attention.

"There was a car out on our little road, going back and forth and back and forth again. The driver, a man, kept checking a piece of paper," Paul paused. "It looked kind of like a yellow sticky note, and he had a map stretched across the steering wheel."

"That's right," said Etta. "Yesterday morning when I saw him, he was parked over at Kwik Kirk's, the store, and he had binoculars and this floppy hat with a long bill and the skirt-like thingy to cover his ears and neck. I have no idea what that's called." She sighed. "I might not have noticed, but he'd turned his car and backed into the parking space. Not many people at the store park like that. And not too many people drive around wearing what I'd call a hiking hat." She pressed her fingertips to her eyes. "Little Cooper has been awake more than he's been asleep. We're all barely holding together."

"We like Alvin." Paul swayed slightly and patted the sleeping baby, now curled up like a snail against his father's chest. "He's a good kid, and we talk sometimes out in the yard. I was glad when he was emancipated 'cause his mom's just not part of this galaxy."

"Does he come by the house very often?" Tony made a note about the driver wearing the hiking hat.

"Well, not to stay. He works in his garden or mows the lawn and leaves." David's eyes widened. "Come to think of it, I haven't seen him for a few days. Is everything all right?"

"He didn't tell you about plant camp?"

"That's now?" Etta laughed. "We really

are out of touch. I know he's been looking forward to camp. I thought I saw him talking to the trash guy not long ago. You know, Claude. He comes by fairly often."

"Let's go see what Opal Dunwoody has to add." Stepping outside again, Tony felt the contrast between the air-conditioned temperature and the midday sun. "I'm sure it will be fascinating."

"I'm sure it will be, too." Wade kept pace with Tony, even though he was still writing himself a note. "Seriously, the two sets of neighbors, Candy Tibbles and the Vanderbilts, were in touch with two different planets. It's kind of interesting."

"Interesting?" Tony considered the word and all its meanings. "Yes, I do believe you're right, but timing is important." Before they even reached the road, Tony saw Opal waving them over. The old lady sat in the shade of a grand old elm tree. Tony thought her lawn chair might have traveled over on the Mayflower and she might have been with it. Her face was nothing but wrinkles, discolored by years in the sun. She had no teeth, and her lips were sucked into the space where they should have been, making her look like a dried apple doll.

"How are you today, Miss Opal?" Wade

called out as they approached.

Behind the thick lenses of her glasses, she batted her snowy eyelashes. "You ready to get rid of that young wife of yours and try a real woman?"

"No, ma'am, not just yet." Wade laughed. "Ask me again next week."

Tony guessed the discussion was one his deputy and the old lady had on a frequent basis. "May we join you for a few minutes?"

Opal waved toward the ground at her feet. "I'd offer you a chair, but I'm a-sittin' on it." She cackled at her own joke.

"We can stand, thank you." Tony glanced over his shoulder to see what her view might yield. Then he walked to her chair and squatted so he would see the same view she did. With the heavy vegetation and this line of sight, she would not be able to see Candy's house unless she went down to the road. She would be able to see the mailbox and the patch of lawn near it. "Do you always leave your chair in the same place?"

She shook her head. Moving the chair would change everything about her view.

"Have you noticed anything unusual lately?"

"Well, those young'uns across the road have a baby." She grinned, exposing her gums. "He's pretty good looking."

"The baby?"

"No, the husband." Opal winked. "The baby's a charmer when he's happy. They let me cuddle him some."

"Anything else?"

"You mean the man with the map and the big spy glasses?" She leaned forward sharply, almost tumbling from the chair, mimicking someone holding binoculars. "Lawsy, but I never seen him afore, and he's driving back and forth like we're a Hollywood attraction." She waved a gnarled hand in the direction of the road. "You see any movie stars?"

"No, ma'am," Tony agreed. "You know Alvin and his mama, Candy?"

"That girl." Opal frowned. "She's been trouble since forever. Just can't help herself I guess, but I ain't sure how hard she tried. You'd think after all the trouble she was in she'd be more careful like."

"Trouble?"

"That baby boy who drowned. You know, the one who lived across the road way back when Candy was supposed to be taking care of him."

Tony didn't recognize the story. "When was this?"

"Oh, well, before she had her own young'un." Opal cackled. "We thought mebbe she'd give them hers when it was born. Be better for all concerned."

"So, at least sixteen years ago." Tony thought sixteen years would not be too long to feel the anguish of such a loss — and to carry a grudge. "Do you know where the family is now?"

"Nope. They moved away years ago, and there's been a couple of different families in the house since."

"How about their name?" Tony thought a name would help their immediate investigation.

Opal stared at the house, thinking. "It seems like the name was Pills, or Pingel, Partin, or something like that. I see them from time to time when I go to town, but I don't think they live hereabouts anymore."

Tony was sure his mom and aunt would be able to fill in the rest of the story. Those two women knew almost everyone in the county, between the two of them, and still had pretty good memory function.

"Wait now!" Opal's hands vibrated and she leaned forward. "Candy was outside and yelling at a girl the other day. Candy was some mad, flapping her arms around and screeching like a crazy woman."

"Did you recognize the girl?" Tony felt a

bit of hope. Maybe this was what they needed.

"No, she had her back to me and was over in the yard with Candy. I kin remember how that little ponytail bounced up and down when she stomped her foot."

"Anything else you remember about her?"

"She was a big girl. About the size of one of them Flowers girls and had, like, blue stuff on her arms."

"What color was her hair?"

"It was brown." Opal seemed pleased by her memory. "And she had on sunglasses."

Wonderful. A female with brown hair and sunglasses would stand out in Park County like salt in the sugar bowl, but there weren't too many with tattoos. "Any idea what they were arguing about?"

"No."

Tony stared down the road, trying to picture what the woman had seen. "That's fine. You've been quite a big help."

"You don't understand. No *is* what they were yelling. Both of them." Opal's faded, cataract-clouded eyes were sparkling with excitement behind the smudged lenses. "No more."

Believing they'd heard all she had to say, Tony and Wade turned to leave. Over on the highway a small group of vintage automobiles was moving past Kwik Kirk's headed toward town.

Tony couldn't suppress a groan. "I guess this means the day after tomorrow's the Fourth. Why not add escorting the parade to the search for our hammer-wielding attacker, and now a killer and all the bad behavior we'll have from people mixing beer and fireworks."

Wade whistled. "Those are some awesome cars."

CHAPTER FOURTEEN

Two of Candy's neighbors down, one to go. Tony saw no reason why they shouldn't go ahead and talk to the third one. Kirk Kilpatrick owned the convenience store. His wife, Elizabeth, was a teacher at the elementary school. Their children had probably been in school around the same time Candy was.

"Kirk's Kwik Korner" faced the half-block-long road and was usually referred to as "Kwik Kirk's" or just "Kirk's." The major attractions were gasoline, beer, and live bait. It wasn't a bad place to get a sandwich either. Kirk's had a small kitchen area to provide made-to-order cold sandwiches, hot dogs, and snack foods. Kirk worked long hours and sucked up gossip like a vacuum cleaner. Tony had been into the store many different times, and the owner was always there. If he lived farther away than directly across the road, he might never have seen his family.

"Hey, Tony, Wade," Kirk greeted them as they walked in. "What's happening over at the Tibbles's place? Everything all right?"

His avid expression showed Tony he was burning with curiosity. The yellow barrier tape was easy to spot from his post near the cash register. Tony thought about feigning ignorance just to make the man beg, but relented. "There's been a bit of an incident over there. Mind if we ask you a few questions?"

"Sure, what's up?"

Tony ignored Kirk's question and asked one of his own. "Have you noticed anything suspicious in the neighborhood recently?"

"Suspicious?" Kirk shifted behind the counter, a hint of excitement sparkling in his eyes. "Like?"

"Strangers? Odd noises?"

"I called to report the radio blaring all night long, and it wasn't until just a bit ago that someone did something about it." The man looked angry enough to incinerate bricks. "What took so long?"

"When did you make your complaint?" Tony pulled out his notebook.

"I called after I got to work. Guess it was maybe nine." Kirk calmed down a bit.

Wade asked, "And how long had it been noisy?"

Kirk shuffled his feet. "All night, I think. Well, it started much earlier. I'm not sure when, but I remember hearing the radio when I went home for dinner. It didn't seem too bad then. We have air-conditioning so all the windows were closed, and our TV room is in the back of the house."

"Did you call Candy and ask her to turn it down?" Wade asked.

Kirk's mouth dropped open in apparent amazement. He shook his head.

"Why not?" Tony could guess, but he wanted Kirk's answer. The longer Kirk thought they were here regarding his complaint about the noise, the clearer picture they might get of his relationship with his deceased neighbor.

"I've lived across the road from her for a long, long time, and I can promise that asking her to turn it down would only make her turn it up louder." Kirk's eyes rolled. "Once I suggested she might want to lower the volume on her television after ten o'clock because my wife and kids were having trouble sleeping. After that, for a month, she raised the volume at exactly ten o'clock. Turned it up as loud as it would go. I could hear the news here in the store with the doors closed."

"Okay, I get your point. So, anything else odd or annoying happening around here?"

"Some old guy has been driving up and down and spying on everyone." Kirk raised his hand to stop another comment. "I know, I know. Why didn't I call to report that? To be honest, I'm not sure. The guy came in a couple of times for coffee and to use the restroom. He seemed nice enough, maybe a little wonky, but who isn't?"

"What else can you tell us?" Tony tamped down his aggravation. "What kind of vehicle? Description of the man? Local or a stranger?"

"If he's local, he's new," Kirk said. "I can get a video of him for you." He pointed at a camera aimed at their faces. "You'll be able to see him and his car." He waved to his employee, who was busy putting drinks in the cooler while trying to eavesdrop. "Watch the register."

A few minutes passed before Kirk returned, carrying his prize video. "Here you go, Sheriff. Anything else I can do for you?"

"Just another question about neighbors." Tony checked his notes. "Do you remember the name of the family who lived in the house on the far side of the Tibbles's house when Candy was a girl?"

185

"The ones whose baby died?" All signs of joviality vanished. "I still can't believe they let Candy get away with it. It was murder, or at least criminal negligence."

"The name?"

"Pingel," Kirk said. "The couple moved away from here but her dad — I think it's her dad, but I don't know the last name — still lives out near old Nem's chicken farm. I've seen him around town a few times but we don't talk."

"Anything else catch your eye or ear?" Tony's mind was half on trying to place Mrs. Pingel's father. The woman's maiden name could help a lot.

"Nope. We're a pretty quiet area. The new couple is busy with the baby and Opal — " He laughed. "Opal hasn't changed since I was born."

Tony didn't give Kirk any information but made sure he took the video with him. Then he headed back to the Tibbles's house.

Theo stood by her office window. The second-floor view let her see much of this side of town and gave her a lovely view of the Smokies as well. Even though it was still days before the actual holiday, the traffic on Main Street was already clogged. The Fourth of July traffic meant good news for the businesses, including hers.

A small parade was planned for the morning of the Fourth, and it would include her children and Daisy. She was still working on the pea costumes for the babies, and the boys planned to decorate the double stroller to look like the pod. They were going to be farmers. The big golden retriever was going to be transformed into a cow. As far as she knew, no one had asked Daisy if she wanted to do it. Theo tried not to imagine what would happen if the hundred-pound dog decided to leave the parade route, and wondered if her status as the sheriff's wife would get her an extra blanket in the jail, or if she'd get the worst one ever when she got arrested for child endangerment because she'd agreed to let the kids do it.

There was no more space for anyone to park on the cul-de-sac. The sheriff's vehicles, as well as the TBI vehicles, clogged the driveway. The mail delivery truck was making the far turn when Claude in his garbage truck stopped, backed up, and parked along the shoulder of the highway. Claude had evidently realized, just in time, that if he made it into the cul-de-sac, he'd never be able to turn around. He lowered his window and talked to Wade.

"I'm supposed to water Alvin's garden."
Claude gestured to the barrier tape. "What's
going on?"

Instead of letting Wade answer, Tony
walked to the driver's side. "Did you come
out here yesterday?"

"No." Claude shook his head for emphasis. "Alvin said every other day. I thought I
could combine trash collection and watering this afternoon."

"Why are *you* doing his garden?" Tony
never ceased to be surprised by what people
did and who they did it with. What did their
trash hauler have in common with a fatherless boy? Or, was he fatherless?

"We're friends." Claude laughed. "Bet you
didn't expect that. Well, me neither. The kid
started coming out to the dump looking for
old boards and junk to build himself a
greenhouse and some raised garden beds.
We got to talking about this and that, and
the next thing I knew I was delivering the
rescued bits. I helped him build the greenhouse and plant beds."

"You helped build the greenhouse, not
just the raised beds?" Tony asked.

"Yep. It ain't pretty, and it needs some
major ventilation, but the tarps on top help
some. At least there's shade," Claude said.
"Still, I doubt he'll ever be able to keep

something alive in it past March. It gets powerful hot in there."

Tony couldn't disagree with his statement. Except the tarps were not both still on top. "Alvin's mom died."

Claude's head drooped. "That poor beggar." He squinted through the windshield. "That kid's had nothing but sorrow and bad luck. First losing his grandparents, and then having to try to live on his own and raise his mom. He inside, back from camp?"

"No." Tony cleared a sudden clog from his throat. "I gave him the news this morning. He's staying at camp until we have a better idea what happened. Neither of us saw any reason for him to come back yet."

"So I guess there's no date for the funeral?"

"No." Tony hesitated. "There needs to be a full investigation first."

Hearing "investigation," Claude turned his head to meet Tony's gaze. "What happened?"

Tony saw kindness, curiosity, and honesty mixed with compassion. It was the compassion that made him ask. "What do you know about the Tibbleses?"

"I can tell you there's several of us who pay Candy each month. Cash on the first. We drop the money into the mailbox. It's a great one for secret drops, with the lock and all."

"How many? How much?" Blackmail? Tony stifled a groan. He wasn't sure he understood Claude's comments about the mailbox. He'd have to examine it later.

"I don't know how many, for sure. I'd say at least three, maybe four, maybe even more than that." Claude shook his head. "I swear I don't know who else is paying. I never really thought Alvin might be mine, but he could be. Anyhow, I had the money and couldn't bear thinking of him being hungry or cold. So I paid. Three hundred dollars a month."

"Does Katti know?" Once again, just when Tony thought he knew what his electors were up to, he was wrong.

"That I pay blackmail? Yes. Does she know Candy?" Claude thought about it. "I don't think so." He absently scratched his hairy belly where the shirt didn't quite meet his jeans. "Katti understands that I was a randy teenage boy and Candy was giving it away."

CHAPTER FIFTEEN

"Blackmail is a dirty word." Tony frowned. "Why do you think she was blackmailing someone besides you?"

"The mailbox is only part of the reason." Claude Marmot scratched his hairy belly again. "It's like a secret drop-off."

"Really?"

"Come, I'll show you." Claude didn't wait, but turned and walked briskly in the other direction.

Tony and Wade followed Claude from the highway, down to the gravel road, avoiding getting close to the house as they walked past. Four homes shared the stretch of unpaved road, two on either side. The Tibbles home and the one facing it were the closest to the highway. Each house sat on an approximately two-acre wooded lot.

As soon as Tony saw the mailbox on its post, he understood what Claude meant. There was a slot for mail to go in, but then it dropped into a lower box, one needing a key to allow someone to retrieve it. Unlike all the other rural mailboxes in the area, Candy Tibbles, as lax a person regarding security and personal safety as he'd ever met, had a locking mailbox. And not just a locking mailbox; a large one.

It wasn't shaped like the average rounded-top mailbox with a hinged door. This was a white box about a foot wide and high, and maybe a foot and a half deep sitting on a sturdy pedestal. The small red flag looked undersized.

Claude laughed, Tony assumed at his expression.

"See what I mean?" said Claude.

"Any other reason you suspect others are being blackmailed?" Tony opened the door covering the mail-slot opening, but saw nothing sticking out of it.

"I saw her pull three envelopes out one day when I was picking up the garbage. It looked like there was nothing written on any of them, and the mail lady — you know, the one who wants to be called a 'postal carrier' — was just turning off the highway on her way to make her deliveries." Claude scratched again. "Unless it was mail from the day before."

"Want a job in my department?" Tony offered. He didn't know why or who was involved, but he was firmly convinced Claude was onto something. He was also convinced Claude wasn't telling him the whole story. Tony pulled on the neck of the protective vest he wore under his shirt. A wave of hot, moist air rose from his chest, hitting his face. He sighed.

Claude roared, laughing, sending his belly bouncing up and down like a fleece-covered basketball under his too-short t-shirt. "No way. Look at you, Sheriff, it's got to be a hundred degrees and your shirttail's tucked in. You've got sweat stains on everything from your hat to your shoes, and if you say a cuss word, every old lady in this town is all over your case and writing letters of complaint." Claude looked right at a passing driver and spat on the street, then waved and smiled at the clearly irritated driver. "Bet *you* can't even spit without your voters calling you out about it."

Tony couldn't dispute anything Claude had said. It was all true. If he hit his thumb with a hammer and displayed some of his swearing prowess, someone would write a letter to the editor. And, since the editor hated his guts, she'd print it. "You're a free spirit Claude. No wonder Katti thinks you're a keeper."

Claude chuckled all the way to his truck. It was blocking the mail delivery van, and the chubby mail carrier didn't look very happy. Claude swore a blue streak, just to show he could, until he saw Katti drive up in her bright pink Cadillac. Suddenly, his vocabulary took a change for the cleaner.

Tony laughed. Claude might be a free spirit, but Katti owned him. This time, though, Katti actually ignored her blasphemous spouse and climbed awkwardly from the convertible before heading toward Tony. Under her maternity top, a festival of pinks, her belly was growing, but she still had some months before her baby was due. Tony bet her belly would pass her husband's in size before then. He was also fairly certain she'd frown every time Claude used a word she deemed inappropriate. On some level, Katti had an advantage. She could swear in her native Russian, and as long as she smiled, they'd never know.

"Can I help you, Katti?" Tony met her halfway. He could see residents watching from windows and porches. Investigation: a performance art. If he'd been in a better mood, he might wave and take a bow.

"You, I help, you." Katti's command of English slipped when she was excited. "I know who is in big fight with poor lady."

194

"What big fight?" Tony led Katti back to her car.

Katti waved her arms. "Is in parking lot at food store."

Tony hadn't heard about this. "When?"

Katti looked confused for a moment. "Is second. My Claude is working on truck so I go for apples and bread. I come out, and lady is very angry with man who does not pay. She say 'Money due on first,' and you no pay."

"Do you know the man?" Tony considered two blackmail stories to be the equivalent of a flashing sign saying "investigate here."

"Yes, yes," Katti pointed toward the convenience store. "Is owner."

"Thank you, Katti." Tony shepherded her back to her car. "You ought to get out of this sun." She obligingly climbed into the convertible, and with a wave to Claude, headed back toward town.

Claude whispered, "Can I water the garden?"

Tony looked at Claude, surprised he was still there. Tony shook his head. "I can't have you walking around the property until the tape is taken down."

"I understand." Claude stared toward the back of the house. "It's awful hot. How about you throwing some water on the boy's garden? Can you do that? There's a hose and sprinkler already in place, all you'd have to do is turn 'em on."

Tony thought the least they could do for Alvin was save the boy's precious plants. "How long should I let the water run?"

Claude wiped a line of sweat from his cheek. "Feels like at least a half hour, maybe forty-five. If it goes a bit longer, it'll be all right."

"We can handle it." Tony made a few notes.

As Claude drove off, Tony looked at his deputy. "Any guesses who else has been paying sixteen years of blackmail? Our list seems to be getting longer."

"And maybe someone finally decided it was time to stop?" Wade shook his head. "I can't say I'm surprised, but I don't have any names to suggest."

"I'm going to start watering," said Tony. "Then we are going back to Kirk's. You might want to watch and see if he tries to run."

Kirk stood facing Tony, his expression unreadable. He had elected to have his second interview outside, away from his employee's radar. Standing in the shade cast by the building, Tony's new vantage let him see not only the right side and most of the front of the Tibbles's home but about the same amount of Kirk's home.

"There's been some talk about you and your relationship with Candy Tibbles and something pretty nasty. Blackmail." Tony barely got the words out before Kirk planted his fists on his hips and leaned closer.

"Shut up." Spittle flew from his mouth, along with the words.

Tony wrote Kirk's statement in his notebook. "Anything you'd like to add?" Kirk looked like he'd like to add a fist to it. Just before he swung, reality intervened and he dropped his hands.

"Sorry, Sheriff."

Tony waited.

"I paid that woman for years. I heard she was dead, so I thought, why pay?"

As lies went, it was a poorly thought-out one. "I have a witness who saw your argument with Candy one day after your payment was apparently due." Tony shifted positions slightly, moving the notebook up higher. "Any comment?"

Kirk blew out a breath and looked away. "You ever do anything stupid, Sheriff?"

Tony just raised his eyebrows.

Kirk turned back. "I was lucky I could build my store here, right across the road

197

from our house. I could walk to work. I could see the kids over lunch. It was perfect." He sighed. "I've known the Tibbleses forever, I guess. I lost all track of the years. Candy seemed way mature for her age. My wife was out of town. Candy was working here and . . . well, you know. It was just the one time."

Tony thought he should write "stupid" next to Kirk's name. "And then the blackmail began?"

Kirk said, "The next thing I knew, Candy was claiming she was pregnant, and she'd keep quiet about my involvement if I'd give her money every month. So every month I had an envelope with cash in it that she'd pick up at the store. After her folks died" — Kirk paused and looked up — "I really don't think her folks knew anything about the blackmail, and I really don't think I was the father. Well, anyway, she had a new mailbox put up and I dropped the money in it every month."

"Until this month," Wade said. "Why not pay this month?"

"We went off on a family vacation and didn't get home until the second. We no more than pulled into town when I had to stop for a few things over at the grocery store. Next thing I know, here comes Candy, traipsing across the parking lot while waving that stupid pink notebook at me and shouting, 'Where's the money?' " Kirk stared across the road at his house. "I told her to go home, and I'd be over about lunchtime and give her the cash. I told her I'd put it right in her grubby hand."

"But you didn't." Tony guessed. "What happened?"

Kirk swallowed convulsively, like he was fighting his lunch back down. "It was quite a bit later than I promised when I finally went over there, maybe about three. She was dead, in the greenhouse, but I swear I had nothing to do with her death."

"You didn't call anyone?" Tony's first thought was to lock Kirk up and throw away the key. That kind of behavior was so stupid, it had to be illegal. "Not report her death? Really? Who does something like that?"

Kirk hesitated for a moment. "I'm telling you, Sheriff, she was dead, and nothing was going to change that, so I left. I turned on her radio, even louder than she usually played it, and thought I'd let someone else complain about the noise and then Candy would be found." Kirk's voice rose. "Leave me out of it."

"Did you take anything?" Tony thought about the missing flip-flop.

"God, no."

Tony thought Kirk's revulsion was honest.

"Please don't tell my wife. She doesn't need to know, does she?"

Tony almost felt sorry for the man. One stupid moment sixteen years ago, coming back to haunt him. Almost. "I have to talk to her. As far as telling her about your adventure with Candy, I don't intend to, but I'll not lie for you." He walked away from Kirk, headed for Kirk's house.

Almost as if she was waiting and watching for him, Kirk's wife, Elizabeth, came outside to meet Tony on the sidewalk in front of her house. "Let me guess, my husband's done something amazingly stupid."

Tony nodded. "Do you know what it is?"

"Not really." Kirk's wife was a pleasant-looking woman, whose years of teaching elementary school seemed to have given her a perpetually childlike expression. "If this is about Candy, well, Kirk's been paying her blackmail for years."

"You knew?"

She nodded. "He thinks I don't know, but really, how dumb does he think I am? He trots across the road to her mailbox on the first of each month with an envelope. Candy yells over to remind him a payment is due. If the whole thing didn't make me mad enough to spit, it could almost be amusing."

Tony thought *amused* was not the expression he saw. The set of her jaw spoke volumes of hurt and old anger. "Why not tell him to stop?"

"If the boy is Kirk's, he deserves the money. But it hurts our children and their futures. Education costs. The price of everything is going up." A tear slid down her cheek. "Kirk is stupid, but not a killer."

Until Tony had more details, facts, and a solid time of death, he was fishing without bait. He said goodbye and wandered back toward Candy's house, wondering if Kirk's wife could have been involved in the killing herself.

CHAPTER SIXTEEN

Theo slipped through the crowd in her shop. The national magazine publicity, coupled with holiday traffic, was creating a banner day. She made her way over to Gretchen. Her only full-time employee was smiling, but she looked worn out. Strands of blond hair stuck out of her normally neatly braided coronet.

"I'll cut fabric for a while. You go take a breather." Theo reached for the rotary cutter. "Thank you for bringing your daughter to work. She's great with the girls."

Gretchen's relief was palpable. "It works out for all of us. She earns some money, I know where she is, she's having fun, and Ziggy doesn't keep calling to ask me if I know where our children are."

Theo laughed, but only because Gretchen's husband, Ziggy, maintained an incredibly calm, organized persona while working as the county disaster coordinator, as well as running a fast-food restaurant and refereeing sports. He couldn't quite maintain the same façade off duty when his wife and children were involved. Storms and fire and hail damage, he could handle; his child five minutes late from school was an emergency.

The shop door opened, distracting Theo's thoughts. The ringing of the tiny bell was almost lost in the clamor of excited voices. She watched several of her elderly regulars coming in for their free coffee and charity quilt time. They displayed more spirit and energy than usual. Leading the charge was Theo's favorite, Caro.

"Can you believe it?" said the woman walking with Caro, Blind Betty. "I'm surprised no one has killed her before this."

"Hush, Betty," Caro steered the woman through the maze of shoppers and bolts of fabric. "We'll talk about it later."

"I'll bet they've come back for their revenge." Betty would not be silenced, but Caro managed to drag her into the workroom and over to the latest charity quilt where it sat on a large square frame. Betty couldn't see, but she could still hand-quilt by touch. She needed a needle-threading assistant. "I'd have killed her myself if she murdered one of my children."

Caro arranged a couple of chairs and said to Betty, "Sit."

Theo glanced at her shoppers. It was easy to pick out the tourists. They stood open-mouthed, clearly curious and hoping to hear more. The locals, at least the elderly, were making their way into the workroom as well. As they chatted, they showed less curiosity and more excitement than the younger women. There was a fair amount of "got what's coming to her" from the old timers, as well as the question, "Who are they?" from the newbies.

Betty, finally settled into a chair, quieted somewhat. "It was the family who lived next door to the Tibbleses. You remember who I mean, don't you Caro?"

Caro headed for the coffeepot. "It's been years, Betty. They moved away years ago. Can you really think they would go away, wait this long, and then come back to kill Candy? It doesn't make sense."

"Would you forget someone who killed your baby?"

Betty's words sent a chill through Theo. She had to force herself not to run upstairs and check on the twins. Theo tried to remember who Betty was talking about. Theo would have been in her twenties at the time and unlikely to have been involved with either the mother or the babysitter, but such a tragic story would have impacted the whole community. She must have still been in grad school. Taking advantage of a lull at the cutting table, Theo eased into the classroom and greeted the older women.

Betty wiggled into position and, using her fingers, explored the unquilted portion within her reach. Moments later, she accepted a threaded needle from Caro and began quilting. "You tell that oversized husband of yours I've solved the case for him."

"Tell me about it, Betty. I don't recall the incident." Theo remained standing so she could keep an eye on the front of the shop. Once she saw Gretchen return to the cash register, Theo relaxed her vigil. "When was this?"

"Well, I remember it like it was yesterday," Betty began. "It was summer. Hot, like now. The story was that Candy was babysitting the next door neighbors' little one and left him alone in a wading pool. He drowned."

Theo shivered.

Betty wasn't through. "As if that wasn't bad enough, Candy didn't seem to care. She didn't act like she was sorry or anything, and just because she was young, I guess, no one charged her with anything."

"Who's the family?"

"Pingel, I believe. They haven't lived in Silersville for years, but I still see them from time to time." Betty laughed. "Okay, I'll admit I haven't exactly *seen* them, but you know what I mean." Betty stabbed the quilt a few times with her needle, just for emphasis. "At the very least, I think Candy should have given them her baby, Alvin, in exchange. It's not like she bothered to take care of her own. He might have had a better life."

Theo patted Betty's shoulder, trying to calm the older woman. The way she was waving her hands, she could poke someone in the eye with her needle. "What about the baby's extended family?"

"Oh, her dad still lives in the area. Turned himself into a hermit." Betty slurped some coffee and turned to Caro. "I need another thread."

Theo hurried up to her office. Her main intent was to call Tony, away from prying ears, but the mother in her needed to see her children.

The story Theo relayed would have made Tony's hair stand up if he wasn't bald. Hearing almost exactly the same story from two sources on one day was remarkable. It surprised him there had been so little said about the baby's death over the years. Stories like that had a tendency to be replayed forever, and every time one of the parties involved was mentioned.

As for him, at the time of the incident, he would have been either about to finish his tour in the Navy or already enrolled at Northwestern. Silersville had been left behind, physically and mentally. He had moved on.

Tony knew someone who could, and would, fill him in. His mom. Signaling for Wade to join him, they headed to the museum site. On the drive out, he asked Wade, who had grown up in the county, what he knew about the story.

"I sort of remember Candy," Wade said. "She left school when I was in tenth grade, I think, and there was a fair amount of curiosity about the father of her baby. None of the guys I hung out with would have anything to do with her. And vice versa. She was interested in older guys."

"And the suspicious death of an infant?" Tony hadn't found any file about it. "Were there rumors?"

Wade shook his head. "If there were, they didn't travel to the school. You could ask Sheriff Winston."

"True." Tony had occasional visits with the former sheriff. The man had run the office his way, not necessarily the way Tony thought it should have been run. Tony wouldn't be shocked if Harvey had made his own decision about what happened and closed the case without much investigation.

Arriving at the museum, Tony felt an itch start between his shoulder blades, and he tried to scratch it away against the seat. It was a very nice folk museum, but he thought maybe he was developing an allergy to it. Just thinking about going there again made him feel itchy all over. Maybe it was the memory of his mom petting a wild bear that made him itch.

Tony and Wade finally tracked Jane down in the museum café. She was standing near the windows overlooking the new garden, planted the old-fashioned way, with home-made tools and using seeds from heirloom vegetables. Tony was no expert, but he'd swear the corn had grown a foot in the past two days. He wondered if Alvin had ever visited his mom's garden. He'd bet the two of them would have a lot to talk about.

Sally Calhoun, hired to be the cook in the new facility, greeted them with a shy smile. "Can I get you something?"

Before Tony or Wade could greet either

woman, his mom turned and snarled at Tony, saying, "Now what?"

It shocked Tony. He knew his mom could get a little testy from time to time when one of her plans didn't work the way she expected, but this was uncommonly rude behavior for a normally sweet woman. "Mom? Is there a problem?"

Shaking her head, Jane frowned and sipped her iced tea. "I'm sorry. It's just so hot today."

Tony suspected there was more to her mood than heat, but he smiled at Sally. "That iced tea looks like a good idea."

Wade agreed. "And could I have one of those carrot cupcakes as well?"

Sally smiled and disappeared into the kitchen.

Jane, her face filled with angst and despair, whispered, "Sally has a boyfriend."

"I'd think you'd be happy." Tony hoped Sally's boyfriend was a better man than her late husband. Possum Calhoun had made pond scum look and smell attractive. "You don't like him, I gather."

"He's a perfectly fine man." Jane managed to look shocked that her youngest child could have suggested otherwise. "He's nothing like Possum, if that's what you're thinking."

"Then what's the problem?" Tony glanced over his mother's shoulder and watched the arrival of Wade's carrot cupcake. He smiled and said to Sally, "That looks delicious. Maybe I should have one of those too."

Sally nodded and headed back to the kitchen.

Returning to the subject gnawing on her nerves, Jane said, "I'm afraid she'll marry him."

Feeling as though he'd come in halfway through the story, Tony just stared at her. He flipped through his mental dictionary for the right word to describe his mother's attitude. Searching for the perfect word amused him when he didn't have time to actually do any writing on his novel of the Old West. *Peevish* was the word coming to his mind. He smiled, knowing he had a winner. Peevish, for certain. His mom was peevish. He felt joy at finding the answer.

Jane frowned at his merry expression and drummed her fingers on the table. "The man lives in Tullahoma and comes through here maybe once a week. It's been going on for a long time."

The switch in his brain finally clicked on. "And you're afraid she'll get married and move away and you'll lose your cook."

Jane nodded.

"So, it's really all about you." Knowing there was nothing serious going on and that he was not the cause of his mom's bad attitude, Tony savored the little, nut-packed, incredibly rich cupcake covered with cream cheese frosting. "Oh, my," he moaned, fearing he was going to be addicted to another dessert. Between Blossom's pies and Sally's cupcakes, he suspected he'd have to run three hours a day just to keep from outgrowing his uniforms.

Sally laughed at his reaction, then turned to Jane. "I'll be leaving now. You promised I could have the holiday off."

Jane's smile did not reach her eyes. "Yes, I did. Have fun, and we'll see you on the fifth."

"Yes, Miss Jane." Sally was untying her apron as she scampered back toward the kitchen.

Turning back to face her youngest child, she said, "Why are you here?" Jane laced her fingers and rested her hands on the table. Her lips pressed tightly together, as if she was forcing herself to be polite.

Wade kept his head down and his eyes on his plate.

Tony decided his mother had *not* liked his comment suggesting a bit of self-centered behavior on her part. Fine. He kept eating.

For a moment, the delicious cake had about driven his purpose from his brain. "Tell us about the Pingel baby incident from maybe sixteen, seventeen years ago."

"I'm ashamed to say I haven't thought of the family in years." Jane's expression changed to sorrow and her eyes flooded with tears. "Pingel. Yes, the last name was Pingel."

"What happened?"

"No one really ever knew. The Pingels swore Candy Tibbles let the baby drown and Candy said the baby was fine when she left and the mom and dad or grandfather must have done something. As far as any one ever said, there wasn't any proof either way."

Tony felt sick. "What did you believe?"

"Actually, I believed Candy." Jane finally quit squirming on her chair and drank some of her tea. "Her parents supervised her babysitting from a short distance and . . ." She hesitated.

"And?"

"There was always something wrong with the baby. It was born with multiple problems." Jane paused. "There was some talk at the time suggesting the parents could have saved it but chose not to and then claimed it was Candy's fault so they wouldn't get into trouble."

Tony suddenly lost his appetite.

CHAPTER SEVENTEEN

Tony dropped Wade at the Law Enforcement Center and started thinking. Where should he go to get the best gossipy information? Theo might have a guess about who else might have fathered Candy's child, but he immediately discarded the notion. When Candy gave birth, Theo would have been in college. His aunt, the high school teacher, on the other hand, might know something useful. He drove from the museum to her house. She wasn't there.

Exasperated, he called her on his cell phone, only to learn she was headed to the museum. His back started itching the moment he turned the Blazer and headed out there again.

"I need to know what you remember about Candy Tibbles. As a student," Tony asked his aunt after going through all the ritual greetings.

"You always assume I hear every piece of

gossip in town and remember it," Martha snarled at him, shocking him with her bad attitude. Not like his aunt's normal behavior.

Tony discarded the idea she might be trying to appear uninterested in gossip. He knew she was thrilled to be asked for information about a student. He guessed her attitude was connected to her unexpectedly having to fill in for Sally. Maybe Jane had not warned her of the change in duties. Martha was a good cook, although not in the same league with Sally and Blossom, and she wasn't keeping up with the order coming from a late lunch for a bus tour group. He stepped into the kitchen, wrapped an apron over his uniform, scrubbed his hands, and stepped up to the grill.

Clearly relieved, Martha handed him a metal spatula and explained their system. "Good to see you. Let's see if your time cooking in the Navy taught you anything." She gave him a happy smile.

Tony was curious himself. He remembered how to make cinnamon rolls in huge quantities, but he'd never mastered making only a few dozen. He was pretty sure he could cook one burger or BLT at a time. With Martha's advice and his own experience, they made it through the rush.

She brought him a tall iced tea and gestured to a pair of chairs overlooking the new lawn. "Candy was not one of my students. Thankfully. I can still remember another teacher talking about how much trouble she was having with the girl. Candy could read, only she wouldn't. She spent as much time applying makeup in class as she could get away with. Homework assignments were not turned it. The teacher had a conference with her parents. Yes, they understood, promised to encourage her, offered incentives. Nothing worked. One day Candy came to class, stood next to her desk, plopped the textbook down on it, and washed her hands of the whole thing." Martha sighed. "Candy never went back to school."

"And she could just quit?"

"She was sixteen and pregnant. There was no way to force her to come to class. I don't know for sure, but I doubt anyone tried very hard." Martha sighed. "I'm not saying it's right, but there is a reason for the old saying 'you can lead a horse to water.' "

"No one could make her learn."

Martha sipped her tea. "I remember she was often seen hanging out with older boys, maybe some men. Locals and visitors. She looked much older than sixteen."

"Great." Tony was not pleased. "That will

make my investigation much easier."

"Don't be sarcastic, Tony." His aunt thumped his badge. "You didn't get this out of a cereal box. Go back to work."

The TBI crew looked so miserable, Tony felt a bit guilty he had called them for help. He guessed they'd guzzled sixty gallons of water and were wishing for more.

The TBI lead investigator, Vince, wiped his face on his handkerchief. "We were able to get your victim processed and sent her off to the medical examiner in Knoxville. As much as I understand the importance of documenting the details, including taking photographs of the victim's final position, I feel guilty, you know, almost ignoring the deceased while we work around them."

"That why you're always chatting with them?" One of the team ribbed Vince. "You should hear him work, Sheriff. 'So what did you think when someone came at you with a blunt instrument? Did you try to run? Did you attack? Here, let's put bags over your hands to protect the evidence.' "

Vince laughed. "Yeah, like you weren't going on about what kind of person would pull back the tarps so she'd bake."

Under the ribbing was concern. No one wanted to miss the tiny fragment of evidence that might lead them to find and convict the guilty party. If talking to a fragrant corpse was what it took, that's what they did. Tony thought they were geniuses. He looked at the floor in the greenhouse. Packed dirt and a fresh hole.

"Did you happen to find her other flip-flop?"

"Nope." Vince glanced around the yard again. "Just the one. I thought it would be under her body, but it wasn't. We kept lifting branches on the shrubs and looked underneath, as well as shining a flashlight into the shrubbery. Nothing." He sighed. "She could have kicked it a long way. My four-year-old can launch a flip-flop into the neighbor's yard without even trying."

"A critter could have hauled it away too. Anyone see signs of animal tracks or bites?"

"Nope. Insects, yes."

"It could be a trophy for a freak." The words created a moment of silence.

"We dug up a lot of dirt and packed it in a bucket. It looked like she might have bled out from the head wound. Don't know if the lab can tell or not." Vince shrugged. "My money is on her being cooked."

"Okay, are we through out here and ready to work in the house?"

No one showed any enthusiasm for working in a hot house with rotting kitchen smells, but no one balked.

"I promised to water." Tony pulled the sprinkler close to the garden beds. "Any signs any of the garden plants were disturbed?"

"If they were, I'd say the regular gardener put everything back in its place."

Tony wanted to know why the garden tools had been stashed in the wrong place. Why hadn't the killer put them back into the unlocked shed? Unless he hadn't gotten them out and didn't know where they belonged.

Theo wiped the kitchen counter after dinner. The boys had vanished and the babies were in view, playing with a colorful toy hanging close enough for them to bat it with their tiny hands or feet. Daisy was guarding them but staying out of their reach. Tony was almost through loading dishes into the dishwasher. "Did Candy have any friends? Like girlfriends she might talk to or go to the movies with?" Theo felt a combination of sympathy and irritation for Alvin's mother. Candy might have brought most of her problems on herself but no one deserved to be murdered.

"Not as far as I can tell." Dishes done,

Tony draped a cold wet cloth over his bald head and wandered about the kitchen heedless of the water dripping onto the floor. "She just seems to have been empty. That's not the right word, but I don't know what else to call it. If she had friends, hobbies, favorite foods, we have no idea who or what they might be." He paused. "She did have an awesome collection of chips. Corn chips, potato chips, you know, like she bought a bag every time she went to the store and forgot and bought them again."

"I know how that works." Theo felt a laugh wedge in her chest. "That's why we have three bottles of ketchup in the pantry."

"I did wonder about that." Tony flashed his pirate grin at her. "Anyway, I'm not sure I've ever been in a house, especially one inhabited by the same person for over thirty years, containing nothing personal. Photographs. Hobby stuff. There's still some of her folks' stuff, I'm guessing right where they left it, and Alvin's room has some of his old clothes and old toys, but nothing we think belonged to Candy."

Theo glanced around the combination kitchen and living space. She was everywhere. A quilt, a book, a potted plant. Her favorite mug. Tony was there too. His chair, magazines, and papers. The boys had toys and games scattered around them. Even the twins had their own favorite items. "That's creepy. Who doesn't have favorite things?"

"I know. We even went under the house. We found some old canning jars and half a bicycle but nothing that spoke of her." Tony removed the cloth from his head and wiped his face with it before taking it out to the laundry room and dropping it into the washing machine.

Theo followed. "Did you find jewelry or trinkets?"

"Nope," Tony said. "We looked. Our best guess is someone smashed her head with a garden tool and left her unconscious, bleeding and dying. Other than a missing flip-flop, nothing appears to be taken. Her purse was in the house, complete with her wallet containing a fair wad of cash, an unopened pack of gum, a tube of lipstick, and car keys. Nothing special in the car but dirt. It needed vacuuming."

Theo tried to imagine Candy's world and failed. "She didn't even have a cell phone?"

"Thank you, sweetheart." Tony kissed her. "I can't believe we all missed the obvious. What should have been there and wasn't. I'm sure she did. I'll find out."

Chapter Eighteen

Before nine in the morning of the third, Tony thought Ruth Ann had earned a raise. It had taken some real detective work by Ruth Ann to find the file connected to the Pingel infant who died presumably under Candy's supervision. Former Sheriff Harvey Winston had put it in the box containing his personal papers.

Harvey, when he was asked, fished it out of the box and brought it to Tony. Most of the contents were letters accusing Candy of "murdering that precious baby." Each letter had been filed with accompanying notes from Candy's parents, refuting the accusation and accusing the infant's parents of wrongdoing and trying to blame a fifteen-year-old babysitter for their own misdeeds.

The bottom line remained the same. No blame was ever established, officially or otherwise. There was simply no evidence on either side, but the overwhelming impression Tony got was that the youngster's parents might have set Candy up to take the blame. The baby was born with multiple "issues." If he had survived, he would always require a great deal of special care. The baby's physician described a multitude of possible reasons the baby died. None linked the death to Candy. Or to the family.

With some reluctance, Tony and Wade drove out to discuss the past with the baby's maternal grandfather, Charles Yates.

"Can't you let it rest?" Yates said. "They've moved on, have two *healthy* children. They have made themselves a nice, normal, happy family."

Tony shook his head. "We're not here about the baby. Not specifically." He did not like Yates and believed he might have had more to do with the family's loss than Candy had. "What do you mean by letting it rest?"

The man narrowed his eyes and spoke with a sour twist to his mouth. "Just because it wasn't her fault don't mean they shouldn't blame her."

"Really? You think the innocent should be punished and the guilty go free? That doesn't sound much like justice to me." Something in the man's expression triggered a suspicion in Tony's mind. "How well did you know Candy?" Had the father been involved with the babysitter?

Yates made no response to Tony's question.

Tony did not like having his question ignored. "What about your wife? Can we talk to her?"

Anger crossed Yates's face again, deepening his appearance of disdain. "She don't live here. Hasn't since the kids moved away." With that, he stepped back inside and slammed the door in Tony and Wade's faces.

Tony stared at the closed door for a full minute, then turned to Wade. "Well, I think I'll put a little S for suspect note next to his name." He headed back to Wade's vehicle. "I'd like to talk to his ex-wife. What do you think?"

"I think I'd leave him too, if I was dumb enough to marry him." Wade fell in step next to Tony. "I also think I'd like to know a lot more about his finances. But if he's been paying blackmail all this time, why suddenly kill her?"

"I'd be willing to bet he's not one of Candy's supporters. I'd guess he'd brag about having a young girlfriend. Unless . . ." Tony climbed into the passenger seat. "Maybe he's been paying to keep her quiet for another reason."

Wade sighed loudly. "That brings us back around to motive. Why wait so many years, and kill the woman now?"

"Speaking of suddenly killing a woman, why don't we go pay a visit to Mrs. Marsh and see if she thinks her next-door neighbor, Mr. Austin, shot her by accident or if it was the culmination to an escalating problem?"

"Lots of accidents happen in the kitchen." Wade turned the key. "I'd like to think she'd be the first to cry foul if she thought he did it on purpose."

Tony was silent for a moment. "I quit thinking people would do anything sensible years ago. There is absolutely nothing rational about humans. We get straighter answers from caterpillars." Tony glanced at his watch. "I'm supposed to go hang some quilts."

Leaving the quilters' husbands, including Tony, hanging the largest quilts for the show in the museum barn, Theo hurried to the shop for the forgotten name cards and award ribbons. As she was leaving, she ran into, and almost knocked down, a woman standing on the stairs just outside her office door, the one with the huge "Private" sign on it.

"Mrs. Abernathy?"

Theo nodded. The woman looked vaguely familiar. She was probably forty, but she dressed as if she were seventy in an old-fashioned print dress and heavy makeup. The overly dark dyed hair was glued into a smooth cut at chin level and made her head look just like a bowling ball.

"I'm Bonnie Hicks from Children's Services." She was not smiling.

Theo's first thought and her immediate comment were both wildly inappropriate. "Thank you, but I have all I need." When she saw the woman's whole face suddenly flush scarlet, Theo found herself wondering if someone thought she was being a bad mother and had reported her. Humor might not be the best approach. "May I help you?"

The woman sniffed. "This is private."

Theo glanced around but didn't see anyone within hearing. "What is it?"

"You employ Alvin Tibbles." Mrs. Hicks made a firm statement, not a question.

"Yes. He does yard work for us."

"Would you recommend him?"

"Yes."

"Fine, thank you." Mrs. Hicks turned and walked down the stairs and out of the shop.

Theo simply watched her until the door closed. "That is the single strangest conversation I've ever had." She was so distracted by the event, she went back into her office and sat down.

"Mrs. Fairfield wants to talk to you, Sheriff." Rex's voice sounded a bit muffled. Tony suspected he was chewing on his hand to keep from laughing. "She's here, in person."

Since he'd been dodging Mrs. Fairfield's calls, not her complaints — those had been carefully investigated — for a week, he assumed his time was up. "Send her back."

He postponed his visit to Mrs. Marsh, telling Wade to be ready to leave the moment his visitor departed. He removed a stack of papers from the center of his desk and placed them on the floor. Tony also popped three antacid tablets into his mouth although he doubted they'd be enough to prevent his heartburn from flaring up. It promised to be a long, difficult day. He'd finally signed all the forms and papers involving Candy Tibbles. Tony really wanted to go home.

Ruth Ann ushered the woman in and left, leaving the office door open. She was obviously not going to miss a word. The increased workload and upcoming holiday would require his staff to work extra hours. No one was going home at their normal time.

"Let's not beat around the bush, shall we, Sheriff?"

Mrs. Fairfield had a stage-ready voice, capable of reaching the back of an auditorium, and she spoke with an unidentifiable accent. He guessed, without any facts to back up the idea, that she'd created her own personal accent. Maybe it was supposed to sound British, but it failed. Instead, it made her sound like a cartoon character.

Mrs. Fairfield launched into her complaint. "I have been waiting to talk to you for hours. We must work together to solve this mystery."

Thinking the woman had been watching too much television for her own good, Tony tried the polite approach. "It's been a busy day. Please remind me, Mrs. Fairfield, what mystery?"

Her mighty bosom heaved and her eyes filled with tears. She dabbed at them with a lace-edged handkerchief more suitable for a wedding than a visit to law enforcement. "Why, the disappearance of Mr. O'Hara, of course. We had an appointment, and he failed to arrive. I'm positive something dastardly has occurred."

Tony sighed. If he had a rating system for complaints, he'd give the woman points for persistence and vocabulary. Dastardly wasn't a word he'd heard before in an investigation. Mrs. Fairfield had purchased a home in Silersville and moved in only about a month earlier. In that time period, she'd begun working on breaking the record for the most calls by an individual to the sheriff's department in a three-week period. If it wasn't witches in the park, it was the amount of noise created by the garbage truck or a Peeping Tom. She had reported lost glasses, lost keys, phone messages from people making vile threats.

It seemed only prophetic that she had purchased the house once occupied by Nellie Pearl Prigmore, a woman whose mental decline had created frequent calls and a strong bond with the sheriff's department. "I don't recognize the name O'Hara. Is he a resident of Park County?"

"Oh, no, I'm sure he's not. He must be from a very special place." She flapped her handkerchief. "Not that Park County isn't lovely, after all. Isn't that why I'm here?"

Tony had no answer to her question. He was pretty curious about how she'd ended up in his jurisdiction. If it weren't patently ridiculous, he'd accuse his old partner in Chicago of setting up an elaborate prank. It might not hurt to find out what Max had been doing lately.

"Are you listening to me?" Mrs. Fairfield slapped the cleared-out section of his desk with the handkerchief. "I demand you find Mr. O'Hara and bring him to me. At once."

"Have you a recent photograph of the gentleman in question?" Oh, goodness, he thought, now he was starting to slide into her trap.

"Of course." She reached into her voluminous handbag and pulled out a large framed photograph of a distinguished-looking gentleman.

Not a man he could remember seeing. Tony might not know everyone by name, but he was pretty good with faces. "And do you have his address or telephone number?"

"Certainly not." Mrs. Fairfield sniffed and lifted her chin in a haughty manner. "Ladies do not possess such information."

"Really?" Tony was losing his patience. Whoever had hired this woman to antagonize him had gotten their money's worth. "How did you meet him?"

"We haven't actually met." Mrs. Fairfield dabbed a tear from the corner of her eye. "My late husband and he were friends, and I'm sure we'll get along splendidly, once I find him."

"Ah." Tony sensed the light bulb over his head start to glow. "When did Mr. Fairfield pass away?"

She took a deep breath and then eased it out in a prolonged sigh. "Sixteen years ago."

"No kidding?" Tony was sure he heard Ruth Ann giggle beyond his office door. He was delighted to provide entertainment for his secretary. Maybe she'd take a pay cut because she only worked for the fun of it. Or maybe he could teach a hog to waltz. "And did you have an address for Mr. O'Hara at that time? Perhaps he was at the funeral."

"Oh, there was no funeral." Mrs. Fairfield flapped her hanky. "Mr. Fairfield's in the parlor."

"His ashes," Tony said. He thought she looked confused by his statement. "You had him cremated and have the ashes in the parlor, don't you?"

"What are you accusing me of?" Mrs. Fairfield lunged to her feet. "Mr. Fairfield is as handsome as ever. I keep him under glass." She gave Tony one last glare before heading toward the door. "I didn't want him to need dusting."

Tony was still considering the possibility that Mrs. Fairfield was using her deceased spouse as a decoration when Wade pulled into the driveway where one neighbor had

231

shot another the previous day.

"It was an accident." Mr. Austin met them outside on his driveway. He was still adamant, although after his trip to the jail, in handcuffs, his attitude was tinged with apology and embarrassment.

Tony wasn't satisfied. "I don't believe you." His own embarrassment was being erased by irritation. He was embarrassed because he hadn't taken the time to do as full an investigation of the shooting as he should have. He was irritated because he was sure the man had lied to him. "Shall we try this again?"

"I thought the gun wasn't loaded." Austin's voice grew louder with each word.

"Even unloaded, why aim a gun into your neighbor's kitchen?"

Sam Austin shook his head.

The arrival of Mrs. Emily Austin attracted the attention of everyone, especially the dogs, who ran toward the car, barking and enthusiastically wagging their tails. When she climbed from the car, she smiled at Wade and Tony and walked toward them, even as she greeted the dogs. "I've been visiting our neighbor, Mrs. Marsh, in the hospital. She has the most amazing story to tell." She turned to her husband. "I had no idea you were so chivalrous."

"Hush, Emily, not now." Sam Austin tried to push his wife to stand behind him. "I'll explain later."

Mrs. Austin shoved him right back. "You might as well tell them the truth." She smiled up at Tony. "I shot our neighbor, but Sam here was my intended target."

"Why?"

Her cheerful expression could not hide her pain and underlying fear. Tony thought he could guess the reason for it, and he disapproved.

"Sam was cheating on me." A wash of tears filled her eyes. "I'm not expected to live much more than two months, and Mr. Chivalrous here can't behave until then."

Tony had been so fascinated by her facial construction, he almost missed her meaning. The nose was perfect. Too perfect. And the space between her eyebrows was flat and too wide. "Cancer?"

"No." She didn't explain. "FYI, I watched him in the neighbor's kitchen, their lips locked, hands where they should not have been, so I pulled the rifle from under the bed, aimed, and fired. Just as I pulled the trigger, he moved, and I couldn't stop the bullet. The scum."

"Why confess? If he's guilty of cheating, why not let him be accused?" Tony thought the story sounded implausible. Irrational. And stupid.

"I considered it. That's why I didn't immediately run downstairs and explain." She shrugged. "This way, I'll be dead soon and he'll have to live with the guilt — he didn't pull the trigger but *he* is responsible for her injuries, and *she* will never be the woman she was before either. I mean, scars are exotic but there is a limit to their appeal."

Tears streaming down his weathered face, Sam stammered a heartfelt apology. To his wife.

Tony wasn't sure what to do. The two combatants were busy kissing and apologizing to each other. The jail was full to capacity. He said, "Promise you'll behave and I'll let you stay here until we can get this situation resolved. Do not leave the county."

And, they did. Promise. Tony headed for town, hoping he'd done the right thing.

CHAPTER NINETEEN

The morning of the Fourth of July started with the heavy boom of a cannon. The sound echoed through the hills and signaled the beginning of Park County's celebration of America's Independence Day. Unfortunately, Tony and his staff believed it would also signal the start of an outpouring of midsummer madness. Or, more accurately Tony thought, an increase in the madness already brewing.

The parade down Main Street involved not only the visiting classic cars and his children, Chris and Jamie, pushing the twins and leading the dog, but the Silersville High School band also marched. Flatbed trailers were converted into floats by every civic organization in the county and various youth groups. Uncle Sam, a regular participant, marched the parade route along with any number of festively dressed or decorated horses, dogs, and even a pig. There were all sizes and all shapes of people and animals.

Santhe Flowers displayed her colorful tattoos as she walked along Main Street, playing patriotic tunes on her flute while two of her plus-size sisters did an impromptu dance involving yards of red, white, and blue tulle.

Tony and Wade worked the parade route, mostly to keep the citizens from diving under an anxious horse while going after a piece of candy tossed from a float. While the black powder group was shooting blanks, the smoke and explosions were enough to startle the animals. The little girl riding the pig fell off, and the parade was halted for a few minutes while she was dusted off, calmed down, and put back on the pig to the sound of cheering.

One of the antique cars from the touring group overheated and had to be pushed out of the way of a goat pulling a cart filled with red, white, and blue balloons.

Bringing up the end of the parade was Claude Marmot, pushing a rolling trash can and carrying a shovel. He was dressed in blue and white striped pants and a red shirt and had a huge pink cowboy hat perched on his head. The crowd responded with a cheer and applause each time he scooped something off the street.

The winner of the children's category was his own family. The peas slept in the pod, and the boys maintained control of Daisy, dressed in her doggie superhero cape and mask. The bagpipe group from North Carolina won the musical category, and grand prize for the best float went to a highly decorated flatbed trailer belonging to the senior citizens' group.

After the parade, Tony was on his way back to the office when Clyde Finster waylaid him.

"Say, Sheriff?"

"Everything okay now?" Tony had personally delivered the unpleasant trophy fish. "You have your prize catch hanging on the wall?"

"Not exactly." Finster stared at his feet. "The wife don't like having it in the house. Says it's her or the fish."

"How about hanging it in your garage?" This was not Tony's problem. He didn't understand his compulsion to try to make things work out for the fisherman. The man just seemed so crushed.

"Truth, Sheriff?" Finster glanced back over his shoulder as if getting ready to share an important secret. "It's not quite as pretty as I remembered it."

Tony kept his opinion to himself. "Well,

it's up to you, I guess." As he watched Finster weave his way through the crowd, Tony considered calling Claude Marmot, trash collector and recycling and repurposing guru, to warn him to watch out for the prize catch.

Tony eventually got to his office. It was too soon to have any official report on Candy Tibbles's cause of death. Holiday or not, he spent an hour digging through the papers he'd ignored the day before. He planned to go home for a while and have a cookout with his family. After a short celebration, he'd be back in the trenches, on duty all night.

"I had an encounter with a social worker yesterday." Theo carried a tray of condiments and dishes out the back door and down to the yard. With Tony's schedule, this was the first chance she'd had to talk to him. "She wanted me to verify that Alvin works for us and wanted to know if we were satisfied with his work."

"Odd woman? Bubble hair?" Tony lowered his voice. "Looks like she's wearing a helmet?"

"Yes," Theo whispered. "I'm not sure what she uses on it, but it's got real holding power."

"That's Bonnie Hicks." Thinking how much he preferred his wife's wild curls, Tony followed Theo, his arms loaded down with buns, hamburger patties, and hotdogs. As if building a garage and the addition to the upstairs was not enough for Gus, he'd added a paved patio and constructed a picnic table big enough to seat ten. Tony thought the very least they could do was host this small celebration.

The Fourth of July and the completed addition gave their afternoon a gala feel. Tony felt like an old grump at the party, knowing he'd be leaving soon. He was the only one there who had to return to work. Theo's shop was closed, and even the museum wasn't allowing visitors.

Gus sat at the table with his wife, Catherine. Each of them was holding one of Tony's baby girls, still dressed like peas, and they were both laughing at some story Chris and Jamie were telling. Soaking wet from playing in the sprinkler, the boys' story involved lots of waving arms, scattering droplets of water, and sound effects from the brothers, united for the moment in their storytelling.

"What did you tell Bonnie?" Tony pulled his mind back to Theo's story about the social worker.

"That he does work for us and the work is

239

good, and then she just turned around and left. It was bizarre." Theo snagged a couple of potato chips from a bowl.

"That *is* odd. She's usually pretty easy to deal with." As the county's sheriff, Tony had fairly frequent dealings with Bonnie. Aside from her imposing hair, she was a reasonably normal, helpful woman. She truly wanted to help children and families, and he was sure she dealt with even more paperwork and more frustrations with difficult people on a daily basis than he did.

"I thought I might have offended her with a comment I made." Theo explained her wise crack about the children.

"No, that can't be it. I've said awful things, and she laughs or takes them in stride." Tony pushed the subject from his mind and grinned at his wealthy sister-in-law. "We want to thank you, sincerely, for the amazing addition to our home, Catherine. Would you like to choose one of our children in payment?"

Catherine's smile was luminous. She shook her head.

Gus gave his wife a kiss on the cheek and laughed. "Don't need one of yours. We're getting one that actually needs a family. Your kids don't qualify."

"Really? You're finally getting a baby!

More. Tell us more." Theo hurried to put her tray on the table and give the happy couple hugs. "What fun!"

"We've been on several lists to adopt for quite a while now." Catherine continued patting the baby niece she held. "Now there's a baby for us."

"That's wonderful! No, it's better than that." Tony felt like his grin might split his face apart. He knew his brother and sister-in-law would make great parents. "When?"

"Any time." Gus lifted the cell phone in his shirt pocket halfway out.

If Tony had needed proof, seeing Gus with a cell phone at a picnic was it. His brother usually called them instruments of the devil and only used his at work.

"Boy or girl?" Theo whispered to Catherine. "Or surprise?"

Catherine laughed. "Are you already planning the quilt?"

"Maybe." Theo lifted a shoulder and lowered it in a slight shrug. "Someone says *baby* and I think *quilt*. It's like hamburger and bun."

"Well, you'll just have to wait along with the rest of us." Catherine glanced over at her husband and gave him a loving smile. "Gus has painted the nursery the same yellow as your girls' room. We're not doing anything more until we are actually holding the baby."

"You'll want the cradle," Tony said. "I'll bring it to your house when you give me the word." His father had made that cradle, and he and all his siblings had all used it themselves and for every baby each had of their own. Gus was the oldest of the siblings, and would be the last to need the cradle, probably until the next generation. Which reminded him . . . "Have you told Mom and Martha?" The idea of scooping his mother and aunt with the joyous news had some appeal, but not seriously.

"We stopped by the museum on the way into town and told them." Catherine's face glowed. "We're not telling anyone else. Before."

"That reminds me." Gus glanced around. "Aren't the dynamic duo coming here for lunch? They never miss a family picnic."

Tony felt a jolt of concern. Gus was right. The sisters should be here, squabbling over whose potato salad tasted better.

As if conjured by black magic, the older women arrived, carrying covered bowls and already trying to organize everyone, feed everyone, and enjoy themselves.

Theo leaned against Tony, enjoying the

evening and watching fireworks lighting the night sky. He was still wearing his uniform, and she guessed he'd be called out again soon. Not a holiday for him, he'd been gone more than he'd been with the family. It wasn't just the sheriff's department. The volunteer firemen had to hate this holiday — day and night. The trucks had passed by the Abernathy house at least three times, going out on calls probably connected to careless fireworks fiends. There were other roads out of town, and Theo assumed they'd traveled those roads as well.

Chris and Jamie were running in the park with their friends, armed with glow sticks. Wide awake, sitting in their double stroller, the twins stared at the sky, fascinated by the flashes of light.

Tony's cell phone rang at the same moment a huge burst of light exploded overhead, starting red and shifting to gold. He answered, listened for a moment, and kissed Theo's cheek as he turned and walked away.

CHAPTER TWENTY

"Sheriff?" Mayor Calvin Cashdollar stood in Tony's office doorway. "May I talk to you?"

Tony didn't love paperwork, and after working most of the night, he felt mentally and physically sluggish. He willingly set a stack of papers aside. "Come in."

Looking even more awkward and stork-like than usual, Calvin tiptoed in, closing the door behind him. He stopped in front of Tony's desk and cleared his throat over and over, punctuated by numerous "ahem" sounds.

"Have a seat?" Tony wasn't the mayor's biggest fan but the man had not done anything to seriously harm their working relationship. At least not permanently.

"I prefer to stand." Calvin stood at attention, but he was shaking, making the overlong thatch of blond hair flap against his eyebrows.

At least he'd stopped the "ahem" chorus. "Speak," Tony said.

The command snapped Calvin into speech. "I, um, well, that is, um . . ." Calvin paused, pulled his handkerchief from his pocket, and blew his nose. He exhaled. "I thought I'd better tell you, there's a chance I might show up on some list of Candy's as Alvin's father, but I swear I did not kill his mother and I am not the father." The message delivered, he stood, still shaking, huffing and puffing like he'd just run a marathon.

It took Tony's brain a second to translate the hastily delivered message. "You and Candy Tibbles?"

"No. I swear I never touched the girl. A long time ago, when I saw her hanging out in bars, drinking and smoking, I always told her to go home." He sighed. "What a wasted life. Candy couldn't have been much past seventeen, but she looked almost forty in the dim lights. Her skin was coarse, and her hair hadn't been combed. She said she'd tell my wife we were having an affair if I didn't pay her each month."

"Doreen knows you pay?"

"I told her." Calvin wiped his face with one shovel-sized hand. "It was after we'd had a fight and she moved to her family home. I was a lot younger then and went drinking at The Spa. It was long enough ago that there was a huge red spot still brightly painted on the building. Otherwise, it wasn't much nicer then than it is now."

"So you and Candy?" Tony really didn't want to know this. "You never had an affair?"

"No. We did not." Calvin's voice was emphatic. He gazed past Tony as if he was looking into the past. "Her father, we called him Tib, was my best friend, and her accusation was false, but it would have hurt my reputation as much as if it were true. Candy contacted me when she found out she was pregnant. I paid three hundred dollars every month. Even if I told the truth and claimed her story to be the lie it was, there would be lingering doubts in some minds, especially when there was a baby. There were a couple of times when I had to be out of town on the first, and Doreen drove out and made the payment. I can't say it improved our marriage."

"I imagine it didn't." Tony wondered how Theo would handle making such payments in his absence. He assumed it would not be a pleasant feature in their marriage. Theo was tiny and gentle, but she had her limits, and Tony was thankful this sort of thing hadn't happened to them. "You didn't demand a paternity test?"

"Oh, I thought about it." Calvin sighed and sat — collapsed really — onto the visitor's chair. "Doreen knew Candy's story was a lie and we discussed it, but it seemed easier to both of us to just pay the money than go through the testing, knowing no one would believe the results anyway. So I took the easy way out."

Tony had to ask. "Did you know you were not the only one paying?"

"Yes. Or at least I assumed so. I hope the father was actually one of those she black-mailed. One night I drove out to drop the cash in the mailbox and saw another car pulling away from it." Calvin shook his head. "Before you ask, no, I didn't see the driver's face."

"Did you tell Tib about the blackmail?"

"I did. It broke my heart to tell my best friend what his only child was doing. And what she claimed." Calvin threaded his long fingers into a knot. "I still miss him."

"So over the years, you probably got to know Tib's grandson pretty well." Tony was glad Alvin had such good grandparents.

Calvin smiled for the first time since he'd sat down. "I'd be proud to claim Alvin. He's a good boy. I used to see him a lot more than I do now, you know, because his grand-dad and I would take him fishing with us sometimes or to a ball game."

"When was the last time you saw his mother?"

Calvin thought about it. "Maybe a month ago. I'll admit I tried not to see her. Paying blackmail when you're innocent doesn't create much warmth. And the last time I saw her — " He stopped speaking abruptly and stared at the ceiling.

Tony had never seen the mayor look so pensive.

"She looked so bad. She looked older than her mother did when she died." Calvin shook his head very slightly. "Half of Candy's teeth were gone, she was dirty, her hair needed washing and cutting. It would have made her dad cry if he saw her look like an old hag."

Tony asked Alvin about his mother's cell phone and the mailbox key over the telephone. "I don't know what we'd learn, or even if we'd learn anything at all, if we find them."

"Mom wore her key on a chain around her neck. She always said I had to guard my mailbox key. That it was precious. It's in the ashtray of my truck."

Tony had not seen a chain or key on Candy's body. "I presume the truck is parked in front of my aunt's house?"

"Yessir. It's okay to drive around town, but I wouldn't trust driving it for more than five miles at a time." Alvin sounded amused. "But I only paid fifty dollars for it."

"Sounds like a bargain." Tony had been reluctant to call Alvin, but he needed the information he might provide. "May I go get the key?"

"Yes. The truck's not locked." Alvin's voice lowered. "I trust you. I don't know what happened to Mom's phones. She has two. I have one. All of our cell phones are the kind where you buy time in advance."

"Did she usually carry both of them with her?" Tony found their disappearance more suspicious every minute.

"Oh, yeah." A touch of humor infused Alvin's voice. "She didn't go anywhere, not even to the bathroom, without them."

"Can you describe them?"

"Actually, they looked a lot alike. They were pretty small and flipped closed. One was black and one was black and white." Alvin fell silent. "She kept them in her jeans pockets. The black and white one she used to contact her drug dealer. She'd call and then drive off and be back in minutes."

Tony did not like the sound of this. Some-one had taken the cell phones. "Do you know the numbers? I might be able to trace them, or at least learn something."

Alvin rattled off one number. "That's the one I always called. I don't know the drug phone's number."

Tony wasn't surprised. He had found nothing easy about Candy's murder. "Are you enjoying camp, or would you like to return home? I can have someone pick you up."

"Do you know any more about what happened to my mom?" Alvin dodged Tony's question.

"No." Tony wished they would receive the results of the autopsy, or that a clue would turn up to point them in the right direction. Sometimes patience was hard won. "We're looking into several leads though."

"Then I'll stay here." Alvin's voice was steady, but he sounded tired. "I feel guilty for having such a good time and learning so much, while . . . well, you know."

"Believe me when I tell you this," Tony said and paused, searching for the right words. "There is nothing you could have done to prevent your mother's death. I do not think sitting around watching and wait-ing for our investigation to move forward will make you feel better, and from what I've learned, your mother had her problems but she wanted you to be happy. She was proud of you."

As much as he didn't want to, Tony realized he needed to go out to The Spa and have a chat with the owner, Fast Osborne. The Spa was the short name of a tavern on the highway. It was actually named The Spot, and time had not managed to totally destroy the old sign with the name in faded letters. Even more faded was the paint on the exterior of the long building. Once painted white, now the cinder blocks were mostly their original gray. There had been a painted accent, a huge red spot covering part of the front wall, including the door. Years of neglect had worn away almost all the red paint and now just the faintest mark remained where it had been. Tony didn't think the interior had been cleaned during the same period of time.

Fast Osborne was the owner and main bartender. He greeted Tony and Wade when they stepped inside by smashing a bug on the dark wooden bar with the bottom of a shot glass. He proceeded to wipe its guts on a dirty towel and put the glass back on the shelf. "Howdy, Sheriff."

"Afternoon, Fast." Tony glanced around the room. There was no one inside. He could see plastic tables and chairs outside. A couple of men sat out there drinking beer in the sunlight. It had to be miserably hot, but the air was clean. "Did anyone tell you we found the man we were looking for? The one involved in the pickup and tree incident."

"That so?" Fast showed zero interest. "You come all the way out here to tell me?"

"No," Tony said. "I came out here to ask you about Candy Tibbles."

"Ain't seen her for a few days." Fast squinted through the hazy air. "She's generally one of my best customers, although I got to say, she looks much better in the dark." He sighed. "She's kinda let herself go, if you know what I'm sayin'."

"Does she drink much?" Tony thought they'd start out with a general discussion and work up to the real business.

"Sorta depends on who's payin'." Fast seemed to be choosing his words with care. Tony guessed he thought they were investigating a drinking and driving situation and wanted to avoid getting into trouble. "She does drink a fair amount when she has a date, usually likes those sweet drinks like rum and cola. Put an umbrella and a cherry

252

in it, and she'd probably drink antifreeze."

Tony had no personal experience with this side of Candy's character, but imagined it was true. "She's been getting drugs from someone. You have any idea who?"

"Nossir. I know there's some talk about 'em. I've overheard a bit, but I sell booze, not drugs." Fast launched into a dissertation about how drugs were cutting into his income. "You know, she is one of my best customers, but man — she *is* startin' to make the place look bad."

Wade cut Fast's lecture short. "How about who she dates? A few months ago, we know she was hanging out with a married man."

Fast appeared to be considering his answer. "Sad to say." His voice lowered. "I think most of her men friends are married. She's been absent. You think she's off shacked up with one of them?"

If Fast hadn't heard about her death, Tony didn't think he needed to break the news. "Any one in particular come to mind?"

"Well, she and Stuart, that is Mr. Stuart, was pretty thick for a while. I'm not sure if they is still though. I guess his wife pitched some kinda fit when she found out. He had a shiner, an' couldn't open one eye for a couple of weeks. I don't know what the missus clobbered him with but, I would *not* want to get on that woman's bad side."

"Anyone else?"

"Not that comes to mind." Fast had the reputation of guarding his customers' secrets, often lying about whether a particular person was in his establishment when someone was asking.

As for Mr. Stuart, Tony knew him. The man had a strong wife and a weak spine. The combination made Tony think he would be interesting to talk to. Even better without his spouse.

Satisfied they had learned all they could expect to, Tony and Wade raced for the fresh air and sunshine.

"What do you think?" Tony said.

"I'd say we might want to have a chat with the happy Stuart couple. Either one of them could have had a motive to clobber Candy."

If either Mr. "Cheater" Stuart or his wife, the Enforcer, killed Candy, they were not only covering for the other one, but doing it in style.

Tony had carefully separated the pair so he and Wade could keep them from copying off the other's paper. "Ladies first."

Mrs. Stuart was in her mid-forties, attractive, well groomed. The only thing preventing her from being lovely was a mouth with an unfortunate shape. Even when she smiled, her lips turned downward, giving her an unpleasant expression. "What's this about?"

"Candy Tibbles."

If possible, the downturned mouth became even less attractive. "Yes?" She looked neither curious nor interested. "What about her?"

"Do you know her?" Tony was careful not to suggest there was anything amiss with Candy. The up side to having no daily paper was not everyone had heard the news.

"We've met." Frost edged her words. "Why?"

"Can you tell us when you last saw her?" Wade made sure she could see him writing down her words.

"Maybe a month ago, or it could have been six weeks." Mrs. Stuart continued, "We — that is, my husband and I — saw her at the Riverview. We were having dinner, and she was out in the parking lot, screaming at our mayor." Her smile was bitter. "It looked like he was positively rude to her. It makes me believe I'll vote for him the next time he's up for reelection."

When it was his turn to be interviewed, Mr. Stuart told them essentially the same story. He did have to tell them about his fleeting relationship with Candy, but it was nothing they hadn't heard before. No one mentioned the rumored black eye.

"Hot enough for you?" Ruby welcomed Tony and Wade to her café. The large white apron wrapped around her didn't disguise her pregnancy, but it made her look larger than she really was. The men settled into shaded chairs on the back deck, and she gave each of them a tall glass of ice water.

"I'm starting with a gallon of iced tea, please." Tony waved away her offer of a menu. "Then a double apple pie with ice cream." He lowered his voice. "Is Blossom still mad at me?"

Wade started choking on his water. "You two have a spat?"

"Not exactly." Tony gave him a glare. "I don't want her suffering from a misunderstanding and sharing it with all her friends and family. Since the Flowers are legion, they're an important group in an election year."

Ruby patted Wade between the shoulder blades even as she answered Tony's question. "I explained you were not making a social call. At first I didn't think she believed me, but she's solidly behind you again. If necessary, the Flowers will swing the vote in your favor."

"Thank you." Tony's thanks were sincere. "I meant to ask, have you ever had trouble with Candy Tibbles? Your name, along with everyone else's in the county, has crossed my desk."

"Really, was she complaining about me?" Ruby's eyes flashed. "I threw her out and told her to stay away."

"When was this?" Tony retrieved his notebook.

Ruby's mouth dropped open. "Is there something I should know?"

Tony merely waited.

"It was maybe a month ago. She was harassing a customer, asking for money. The next thing I knew, she punched him in the face and starting swearing a blue streak." Ruby was breathing hard. "I threw her out and told her never to come back into my café. I might have thrown your name into the threat along with Mike's." She fidgeted a bit with her apron strings. "Sorry."

"Did it sound like a panhandling situation, or maybe something else?"

Ruby considered his question for several minutes. "It was definitely something else. Like she'd been expecting money and hadn't gotten it."

"I don't suppose you remember who the

customer was?"

Ruby shook her head. "I'll call if it comes to me."

After she left them, Tony and Wade sat not talking, just eating pie and guzzling more water and iced tea. Sitting at the next table was a young man in low-hanging jeans, half of his underwear showing, and myriad tattoos exposed by his muscle shirt. He had a ring in his nose and a chain connecting it to the ring in his ear. It was his educated, articulate telephone voice that captured Tony's attention as he chatted on his cell phone with what might have been a client — something to do with computers.

"Can't tell anything by the wrapper, can you?" Wade slid his sunglasses down from their perch on the top of his head to cover his eyes.

"Nope," Tony agreed. "I'd have expected the conversation to be more, or rather less, well spoken." Tony watched a few people walking up the zigzag path away from the highway and over the hill to downtown Silersville.

Wade said, "I ran into Matt Barney this morning." Tension tightened the skin over his cheekbones. "The man would set law enforcement back about a hundred years if he's elected."

Tony couldn't disagree. Barney might even take it further back than that. He wasn't completely convinced the man could read. It irritated him to think how much valuable time he'd had to spend defending his own actions in the past four years. "He actually called our county Murder Central."

"What will you do if you lose the election?" Wade shifted in his chair.

Tony sighed, suddenly tempted to withdraw from the election and let Barney have the job. Tony could be a stay-at-home dad and spend the entire day with his baby girls and enjoy the quality time and intelligent conversation. Only the spector of chaos and more crime to follow his departure made him hesitate. "If I lose the election or quit, will you stay on the job, Wade?"

Intelligent dark blue eyes turned to meet his gaze. Wade's shock was obvious. "Are you kidding?" His head was moving from side to side. "I'd end up in our jail. The temptation to shoot him would be too much for me to handle. You could fit his whole brain into one of those little pimento jars and have room to spare."

Unable to suppress a smile, Tony said, "I probably shouldn't use your description in my campaign, no matter how true it is."

He changed the subject. "Sounds to me

like Candy's been a busy blackmailer."

"Yes, it does." Wade leaned back in his seat. "I know there has been a fair amount of rumor and speculation surrounding her lifestyle, but there is a definite pattern here."

"Suddenly people have stopped paying her." Tony drained his glass of tea. "Why not? Why would you suddenly stop paying blackmail you've been paying for sixteen years?"

"If you broke down and confessed, got it off your conscience." Wade shoveled pie into his mouth. "You wouldn't need to keep her quiet anymore."

Tony nodded. "Or your marriage disintegrated and there was no further need to try to cover up the affair." He tried to remember if any of the names they'd heard belonged to someone recently divorced.

Wade said, "What if the blackmailed person simply moved away?"

"Or you're too broke to pay." Tony crunched a few pieces of ice. "Maybe he recently lost his job and Candy wouldn't cut him any slack, even after sixteen years of payment."

"Maybe the father's decided he'd been supporting the boy, not the mom, and Alvin has moved out, so the payments stopped." Wade lifted an eyebrow. "Any chance Alvin's started receiving money that used to go to his mom?"

Tony moaned with frustration and loathing. "Can we even guess how many people have been sending or delivering cash? And for how long?" The vision he had in his mind developed nightmare implications.

"And why?" Wade looked confused. "Surely there aren't that many men who could have fathered the boy. In a town this size?"

"A few older men, some younger men, boys her age." Tony gripped the edge of the table. "I don't want to consider all the possible choices. I'm feeling lucky I can scratch myself off the list."

"Me too." Wade laughed, but it was humorless. "That's two, as long as neither of us is lying."

Tony said, "She was definitely getting money for Alvin. And I suspect we can add in a category for 'cheating spouses.'"

"Drug dealers." Wade suggested. "That one's a two-way street though."

From the highway came a series of honking horns, and they turned to see a caravan of antique cars winding down the hillside, near Not Bob's home. The last Tony heard, the man had been moved from intensive care but was still not nearly well enough to go home.

"I talked to Alvin this morning." Tony rubbed his temples with his thumbs, hoping to relieve some of the tension growing there. "He told me where to find the second mailbox key. Let's go to the house and see what we can learn. Knowing Candy's energy level and low-level imagination, I'll bet she has a simple system for keeping track."

"Names, phone numbers, if everyone was expected to pay the same amount on the same day." Tony stood, put his money on the table, and trudged around the side of the café. "I hope we're jumping to the wrong conclusion."

CHAPTER TWENTY-ONE

Tony had seen a few mailboxes similar to Candy's on other rural routes. There were several different brands and styles but with each kind, the mail was slipped through a slot, then it dropped into another portion of the box requiring a key to open it. It prevented someone from stealing the mail, or having it blow out if the door opened, and it allowed the mail to accumulate without anyone being aware that no one was collecting it. Alvin's key unlocked the mail storage compartment below the outgoing mail shelf and incoming mail slot. The small door covering those did not require a key.

"Alvin told me that his mom said he always had to guard his mailbox key, protect it with his life. For a woman who seemed to care nothing about anyone or anything, I find that interesting, don't you?"

Wade agreed, studying the outside of the box, as he pulled gloves on. "Let's see what she has."

With a turn of the key, the front panel opened, exposing a moderate accumulation of mail. Tony imagined the upper layer of mail would be the most recent deliveries. There were a few advertising flyers and a coupon book. No magazines, but why get magazines if you have no interests? There were also two sealed envelopes with "Candy" printed on the front. No stamps.

Tony wondered how they had been delivered. Obviously not through the U.S. Mail without a stamp, unless the postal carrier was one of the blackmailed persons and dropped them in with the rest of the delivery, which was possible. Anyone could drop an envelope in the box. But how likely was it that none of the three sets of neighbors would not have seen it done over a period of sixteen years? Not very. Even if the delivery happened at three in the morning, someone would very possibly be up ill, or with a child, or on a bathroom trip, or hushing a barking dog. Get up in the night, look out the window, and see a strange vehicle next to the box. Seen a second time, it would form a pattern, not an oddity.

With gloved hands, Tony held the box they'd brought along for the job, while Wade carefully removed the contents, his own hands in gloves. "This mail on top is loose and looks like it fell in naturally. The bottom stuff is neatly stacked, like she's been storing it in here."

Tony pulled a bag from his pocket. "Put the stack in here."

"Out of curiosity, do you see a flip-flop?" Wade asked. He illuminated the inside of the box with his flashlight while Tony looked over his shoulder.

"No." Tony looked in the top, toward the back of the outgoing mail shelf. It looked like something might be blocking the light. "Wait. This mailbox is huge. I think I can see it, jammed all the way against the back. There's a kind of silhouette. Let's see if the key will open the box's back door."

Sure enough, when they opened the large back panel, a purple flip-flop, complete with attached flower, was lodged into the space. "Let's get this bagged and tagged and see what, if any, fingerprints or skin or whatever we can find to nail the SOB."

A cursory examination of the neatly stacked envelopes made Tony think of a filing system. Envelopes presumably filled with cash were labeled with handwritten or typed names on each envelope. Fun names like "Blue Cow" and "Yellow Buzzard" couldn't disguise the smell of extortion.

Sorted by name, the system looked more organized than they would have expected from Candy. This was her passion.

Although they discussed it briefly, Tony and Wade couldn't shove everything back inside the mailbox and lock it again and pretend they'd never seen it.

"You're going to have to fingerprint the envelopes before we open them. Front and back."

Wade nodded. "It will take me a while to dust, photograph, lift the prints, and label each of them."

"It takes as long as it takes." Tony knew the job would be tedious but the county had paid for Wade to take the course of specialized training so he would be able to do it, and do it correctly. "If you don't have enough of some supplies, I'll bet we can borrow from our friends."

At least they were saved from having to dig through all of Candy's belongings looking for her records. She had left a cheap spiral notebook under the stack of envelopes inside the mailbox, along with a pen with a bright green feather on its cap.

They made a quick check through the house to make sure it was undisturbed, and Tony placed fresh seals on the door when they left. "I'll bet you're as anxious as I am to spend the day in there." Hot and rancid were the words he'd use to describe it.

Wade wiped a line of perspiration from his cheek. "I'm thinking we're lucky the TBI got rid of the rotten meat for us."

"That's right." Tony felt a rush of relief. The house still reeked, but at least the worst offender had been removed from the kitchen. The air did smell better. "Okay, tell me, Wade," Tony popped a handful of antacids into his mouth and chewed slowly, meditatively. He felt a bit like a cow chewing its cud.. "If the killer took the key from Candy's neck, why not use it? Collect some free money and destroy some of the evidence?"

"Maybe she wasn't wearing it. Or," Wade mulled the problem for a moment. "Maybe whoever killed her knew nothing about her blackmailing business."

"Oh, good. Now we can add everyone else in the county to our list of suspects."

Tony needed to talk to the neighbors again. But how could he bring up the people making deliveries to Candy's mailbox without suggesting the idea? "I'm going to check Alvin's garden before we go next door. Might as well be watering while we work."

Tony stood on one of the tidy paths through Alvin's garden and slowly turned, looking up and down, searching. He wasn't sure what he was looking for — inspiration maybe — before they turned the water on and talked to the neighbors. He focused on the house next door. The house where the Pingel baby had reportedly died.

It reminded Tony of how little he had liked the baby's grandfather. If hunches were admissible in court, he'd have arrested the man on two charges, murder and false testimony. Tony had no evidence, no facts, but deep in his gut, he knew the lies told about Candy had scarred her and made people either shy away from her or condemn her.

The house wasn't close, not really, and it was separated from the Tibbles property by some mature trees. What caught his eye was movement behind a second-floor window. "If I can see you, you can see me." He spoke out loud.

"What's that, Sheriff?" Wade's head popped through an opening in the vegetation.

"I was just thinking. We might want to

have another chat with the family next door."

"You think they lied?"

"I think they have a ringside seat to the most popular of all spectator sports," Tony said.

Wade grinned. "Watching the neighbors?"

"Exactly." Tony continued his survey. "Let's go over now. I can see someone's at home." As he walked past, he turned on the faucet, sending a spray of hot water into the air. The plants, drooping in the afternoon heat, would be happier soon. "Don't let me forget to turn this off when we leave."

"Should I go with you or go work on my fingerprints?"

"Come with me. This shouldn't take long."

"I know what it's like," Tony used his most soothing and sympathetic voice. "You're up all hours. Day and night get confused. The baby is only calm if you keep moving, so you stand in front of a window and sway back and forth." Tony watched Etta Vanderbilt's expression.

The young mother looked surprised. Tears rose in her eyes. "Yes, that's it exactly. I guess I thought ours was the only baby keeping a parent on the move."

"Not even close." Tony gave her a re-assuring smile. "Just tell us. What did you see as you wandered from window to window? Don't try to sort it out or make sense of it."

Etta sighed and met his gaze. "One night is like all the others. I don't know what day of the week it is, or was."

"That's fine." Tony waited.

"We didn't lie." The tears — Tony guessed most likely from fatigue rather than sorrow — slid silently down her face. "We did *not* like Candy. She played loud music, some-times all night long. There were men com-ing and going. The cul-de-sac should be quiet, but cars came past at all hours, pull-ing into her driveway, stopping by her mail-box."

"She was interesting to watch." Wade sug-gested.

"Better than the soaps." With a gasp, Et-ta's tears turned to laughter. "Paul, my husband, and I are quiet people. We work, have a meal, play with the baby, watch a little television, off to bed. We grew up in homes like ours, and I guess we thought that was the way everyone lived. Being next door to Candy was amazing because of the contrasts between our worlds."

Tony nodded, listening carefully for what

270

she did not say as much as for what she did say.

"One night, the baby and I were doing exactly what you described. I was walking around in the dark, trying to get her to fall asleep. I saw headlights up on the old road on the ridge that runs behind our house and Candy's. The vehicle was stopped. That's normal." She suddenly laughed, humor dissolving some of her fatigue. "I see a lot of cars up there on the ridge from early morning to late night, but they usually have the headlights turned off."

Tony smiled. He thought he might have parked up there a couple of times himself, when he was in high school. "Which direction were these lights facing?"

"That was the weird part. The driver must have parked at a right angle, you know, facing Candy's backyard directly, so the lights shone right at her house." She paused. "And then I thought I saw a shadow moving down the hill, like someone was using the headlights to see where they were going."

"You didn't call to report it?" Tony knew the answer before she opened her mouth.

"Sheriff, if I called your office to file a report every time some person was parking on the ridge or visiting Candy in the middle of the night, you'd need a much bigger department."

"You're right, of course." Tony found himself reminded, though, of the recent seemingly random attacks on the citizens of the county. Was someone ignoring what they saw because they didn't want to bother him or his staff? He hoped not.

As soon as Tony and Wade returned to the Law Enforcement Center, Wade carried the mail to his fingerprinting cubicle and began the process of checking the exterior of each envelope. Front and back.

Tony called out, "Ruth Ann, I need you to make notes as we go along."

Arriving in the room, she whistled at the stack of envelopes. "Candy was a real cottage industry."

Tony placed Candy's notebook on the top of the stack. "First thing. Let's see if anyone besides Candy has been reading this."

Wade removed his fiberglass latent-print brush from its protective tube and poured a small amount of black print powder onto a clean sheet of paper. He picked a little powder up with a brush and swept it across the front of the notebook, side to side and top to bottom. A couple of smudges appeared. He photographed them. Then he made a note on the lifter he was preparing.

"Because it's paper, I have to use special lifters."

Ruth Ann looked over his shoulder, studying the small hinged item designed to lift and protect a fingerprint permanently between thin plastic pages. The hinge on the lifter was like a paper tape, where the date and case number could be written on it. "Look at all the different sizes you have."

Tony heard the sound of the cash register ringing in his head. "Use what you feel you have to, but . . ." His words ground to a halt.

Wade grinned. "Money still not growing on trees in Park County, is it? We could use the TBI resources."

"That's true, but I'm not prepared to wait in line for this information. Carry on."

Quickly but carefully, Wade finished processing the front of the notebook, the back, the inside covers, and the most recent page used. Then he lined up his lifters, and using a magnifier, studied each in turn. "I'm only looking for something not consistent with the others." Wade looked up. "Whether it's Candy's or not, I'm not prepared to say, but whoever handled this was the only person leaving fingerprints on it."

"Okay, that's a start." Tony pointed to the stack of envelopes.

Wade finished both sides of the first envelope, made his notes, and passed it to Tony.

Tony took the envelope in his gloved hands and slit the top open. Pushing the slit wider with tweezers he saw cash. Not unexpected. "Do you want to fingerprint the money too?"

Wade hesitated. "We're possibly going to get lots of matches to the mail carrier on the ones with stamps. But, so many people touch money and . . ."

"Just do the envelopes, front and back," Tony said. "We'll just hope it's not the wrong decision."

"You know, if the mailman killed her, his fingerprints will be on the envelope." Wade's perfect teeth flashed in his handsome face. "I'm just saying."

"I think I saw that movie too." Ruth Ann shifted on her chair.

Wade pointed to the stack of envelopes. "Ah, but most of these were hand delivered. No stamps."

"Open a few, and let's see if something inspires us." Tony absently wondered if Candy had moved on to committing a federal crime. If she had, he could hand the case and all the evidence over to someone else. A man could dream.

"These have different amounts of cash. Fifty, a hundred, two hundred, and three hundred." Wade carefully dusted each envelope, and Tony divided them into categories according to the amount of money inside.

"Red Dog, Blue Cow," Tony studied the envelopes. "It's like some weird spy game."

"Some envelopes don't have names on them." Wade continued his work.

Ruth Ann said, "Do one of those next. I'm dying to know what's inside. Not even a really stupid person would pay blackmail and not make sure they got credit for it, would they?"

Tony felt his eyebrows lift. "Never overestimate the lack of brains or sense in this world. After recently having someone die 'surfing' on a pickup, I'm thinking the sky's the limit on idiocy."

Wade handed Tony another envelope to open. Nothing was written on the outside of it.

"This one has the donor's code name paper clipped to the cash." Tony handed it back. "You'll want to do the note."

One envelope held the expected cash and a note. This one was pretty straightforward and echoed Tony's opinion. "I'm paying you, but I'm not playing your dumb spy game." It was signed, "Claude Marmot."

Claude Marmot was the closest thing to an expert on Candy's blackmail that they knew about. Tony and Wade decided to talk to him away from the crime scene and prying neighbors. Out at the dump, Claude was busy welding a roundish car shell onto motorcycle bits.

Tony saw no way it would work, but Claude had transformed an old Crown Victoria into a serviceable pickup; why not attach a cover to a two wheeler?

"Sheriff? Wade? I'll be with you in a minute. Why don't you two take a load off?" Claude smiled and waved them to the former rear seat of some vehicle now arranged in the shade near his project. He waited until they were settled before continuing his welding.

Tony watched Marmot-the-Varmint work. His hands were small for the size of his arms and obviously possessed great tensile strength. He squeezed the parts together with one hand while manipulating a drill with the other. Before releasing it, he slipped a bolt through the holes and finished with a flourish. Then he stepped back with a wide grin lighting his face. "Awesome."

Tony cleared his throat. "We'd like your help."

"No kidding." Claude wiped his hand on his jeans. "It's about Candy, I'll bet."

"It is." Tony glanced at the ground and up again, considering his next question. "When you dropped off your payment for Candy, did you always place it in the box?"

"Yep."

"Did you ever see anyone else placing money in the box?" Tony leaned back on the seat. "Or did you have any knowledge of others who were making payments?"

Claude looked uncomfortable. "I might have some ideas but nothing you'd call proof."

"People you saw there?"

"No. I never saw nobody." Claude crossed his arms over his chest. "I wasn't the only man in Candy's life back then. I'll reckon she never lacked for dates, even with married men."

"She was just a girl." Wade frowned. "Sixteen."

"That's so. She didn't act like a girl. Don't forget, I was a lot younger in them days too." Claude frowned and rubbed the stubble on his face. "I'm not sure I was shaving yet and I'm not sayin' it was right. I'm just sayin' that's the way I recall it."

Chapter Twenty-Two

"I've got a complaint from a Mr. O'Hara about the aroma of the pig farm next to them." Rex's voice carried through the telephone, speaking loud enough so everyone in the office could hear him.

Tony thought Rex sounded like he was ready to laugh out loud. "And what do *you* know about this situation that is so amusing?"

"The pig farm in question has been in its current location for at least twenty-five years. The new property developers planted a living fence of poplar trees to disguise the situation." Rex continued, "I live a couple of miles away and am usually upwind of the pigs unless the weather is changing. Believe me, a few trees do not create a good disguise."

Ruth Ann giggled. "Why would anyone think a few trees are going to eliminate the aroma of pig poop during the heat of the season?"

Tony would have been amused himself if he thought that the argument between the pig farmer and the property owners would be settled in a peaceable manner. "Is this a new situation?"

"No, sir, but from what I gather, it is of grave concern to a new resident out there. He's threatening to shoot all of Mr. Henry Rankin's porkers." Rex's voice returned to its normal professional tone. "I tried to diffuse the situation on the phone, but I think someone with a badge ought to pay them a visit. I'd hate to have this escalate."

Tony knew Wade was still tied up with the fingerprint project. "Tell Mike to go now. I'll be out later."

Besides being a smart, capable deputy, Mike and his bloodhound, Dammit, comprised the county canine unit. But more importantly in this situation, Mike also had a black belt in aikido. Tony thought it might be nice to have Mike's special skills at hand when he interviewed the irate resident and Mr. Rankin, the pig farmer. Other than diffusing the argument, there really wasn't much he could do. The pigs were there first, and they were a fair distance from town. Unless the homeowner was prepared to buy the pig farm, so to speak, he was stuck.

The name O'Hara was jiggling something in his brain but he couldn't place it. Too much excitement of late and too little sleep. He thought he should identify it before heading to the farm.

Mrs. Fairfield.

"Sheriff?" The muffled voice on the other end of the call was one Tony had become all too familiar with in the past few days. The pathologist assigned to do the autopsy of Candy Tibbles had the unfortunate name, Dr. Death. Actually, his last name was Deaton, but no one used it, including the doctor. He was as wide as he was tall and had a flair for telling jokes. "I've got a cause of death for your Ms. Tibbles."

"What killed her?" Tony guessed blood loss but was not qualified to make the call.

"Sunlight." Death waited, presumably for a reaction. He didn't wait long.

"Excuse me?" Tony said. "Sunlight?" For a moment he wondered if the doctor was telling a joke, but as macabre as the man could be, he was all about having justice for the dead. "How is that possible?"

"Ms. Tibbles suffered a terrible blow to the back of her head. Cracked the skull, and you know how head wounds like to bleed. A bit melodramatic, if you ask me. Well, anyway, she was undoubtedly knocked out cold, and the dirt boys will have their own job figuring out the blood loss."

Tony started to wonder if the man was being paid by the word instead of the body.

"I've examined Ms. Tibbles, and I've studied the photographs of your scene," Dr. Death said. "I'm going to say she would probably have survived if she had been hauled out of the greenhouse and into the fresh air. She would have needed a hospital to get that head fixed up, but your woman was baked to a crisp. Freshly sunburned where she lay. I can show you. It's not a lot of sunburn because she died fairly quickly, but it's there."

"When you say she might have lived if she was pulled outside," Tony said, "are we talking seconds, minutes, or hours?"

"Well, the sooner the better. I'd say minutes." Deaton must have shuffled some papers into the receiver and it created a terrible racket, then stopped. "When whoever pulled the tarp back and exposed her to the midday sun, they killed her as sure as if they'd shot her in the head. The angle of the sun and the missing tarp put her face in the direct path of the light. Hence the sunburn. Living bodies are not happy in ovens."

"So the manner of death is homicide?" Tony asked.

"Yes," Dr. Death said. "Excellent question, Sheriff. I believe you're getting the hang of this business. By the way, good luck with the upcoming election. I've met your opposition, Mr. Barney, and I can't say I think he'd be an asset to any department. I'll bet he can't even cut his own meat much less run an investigation into missing chicken drumstick at Sunday dinner."

"Thank you, Dr. D."

CHAPTER TWENTY-THREE

Tony hated to question the boy. Alvin had been back from plant camp for only a few minutes. He had called Tony's office for a ride home when Candy Tibbles's remains had been returned for burial. After a short visit with the undertaker, Calvin Cashdollar, Alvin was delivered for a visit with Tony.

"Blackmail?" Alvin Tibbles looked bewildered. "Why would people pay her?"

"For the usual reasons." Tony didn't think the boy was really taking in the whole situation. He looked ten years older than he had when Tony visited him at plant camp. "People will pay to keep people from finding out something potentially illegal or embarrassing."

"I'd have paid too, some days, if she'd have promised to tell people she lied about being my mom and said she had kidnapped me from a normal family. I knew she couldn't really help herself, but some things she did were more awful than others." A flash of humor lit the boy's wan expression. "Did you know she told me your aunt owed her big bucks and wouldn't pay? I didn't understand what she meant at the time or why your aunt would owe her anything."

"Any idea what for?" Tony could imagine his aunt getting into an argument with Candy, especially if there was a student of hers involved. He could not quite wrap his mind around his aunt having any secret worthy of cash payments. Not even the fifty-dollar variety.

"I asked Mom." Alvin shook his head. "She said I should stay out of it, and I told her to leave your aunt alone."

Not for the first time, Tony found himself feeling sorry about the burden the boy carried. Children should not have to take care of their parents, at least not until they were adults, certainly not when they were still in school. "Your mom has a notebook where she apparently checked off monthly payments. Some appeared to be only once-a-year items, but there are only code names. Did she have a great memory?"

"Not even close." Alvin started laughing. "She loved the whole idea of spies and having secret codes. We played secret agent games all the time when I was little. Before

my grandparents died, she was irrespon-
sible, but she could be kinda fun." His laugh
trickled away, turning into obvious grief.

"So the names she assigned each person
probably mean something? Were they based
on initials? You know, maybe switching
Triceratops Aardvark for Tony Abernathy
kind of thing?"

"Not necessarily." Alvin gulped back
threatening tears.

Tony hated having to ask the boy these
questions. "We can do this later."

"No." Alvin remained in his chair. "Did
you find the code book?"

"There's a code book?" Tony felt like slap-
ping himself. No wonder it had seemed so
easy. Easy even for Candy on one of her
bad days. "What does it look like?"

"It's this little pink book, with a white kitten on the cover." Alvin's hands shook as he
indicated something about the size of a deck
of cards. "When we played spy, she kept it
in her pocket so she could reach it and
interpret her code. I had to help her set it
up, but she coded everything for years. I'm
sure she couldn't come up with another one
on her own. She wanted to be a spy."

"Do you know where she kept it after you
stopped playing the game?"

Alvin nodded. "She keeps it under her

pillow."

"Either Candy has changed her hiding place, or someone else beat us to it." Wade frowned. He'd checked every bed in the house, had been through the covers inch by inch, inside the pillow cases and under the bed where he'd had to fight through monster dust bunnies. Nothing.

"I'm calling Vince. Maybe the TBI boys have it." Tony wasn't on hold for very long when the answer came. No. None of them had found the code book. It would have been bagged, tagged, and on the list they'd given him.

"Did you read the list?" Vince's words burned through the telephone.

Tony had. He had also heard the undertone of righteous indignation in Vince's voice.

Tony apologized profusely for his ever even considering such an improbable scenario and heard himself promising to never imply such a thing again. "I was desperate and not thinking clearly."

Only his offer to buy the whole team dessert the next time they had to explore a crime scene in Park County soothed them. The responding comment about the probability of their being needed again fairly soon in the crime center of Tennessee, he let pass without comment. He deserved the backlash.

"You know, for such a messy house, there's nothing in the trash cans." Wade returned from his search of the upstairs. "Either she never even threw away the cardboard center from a roll of toilet paper, or someone collected all the garbage about the time she died."

"Claude." Tony liked the trash hauler, but he didn't like the way his name keep coming up in their investigation. He also thought Wade might be adding one and one and coming up with three but he was grasping at straws himself. "He could have taken the code book and the trash out to the dump."

Wade shook his head. "He signed his name, so we know he made the most recent month's payment."

"True. I'm not saying Claude knew about the code book. The killer could have slipped it into the trash to protect his — or her — identity, knowing Claude would probably pick it up before anyone knew she was dead. Once it arrived at the dump, it would be next to impossible to find."

"You think the killer came into the house after bashing her in the head and threw it away?" Wade looked out the window and down the driveway where the trash would have been placed. "There's a lot of people who could see someone, not Candy, putting something in her garbage in broad daylight."

"If I thought there was any chance the notebook would connect me to a murder," Tony mumbled as he chewed absently on an antacid, "I'd take it with me, rip the pages out, and run them through a paper shredder."

Wade said, "I might just rip out the page that listed my code name and leave the book in place. But if I was really smart, I'd leave it alone and be interviewed with all the other names in the book. It's the blackmail payer who is not in the book I'd like to talk with."

Tony sighed. "We have so many theories, they have their own zip code."

"If you've got your heart set on digging through the stuff I collected" — Claude stared out at the pits and piles in the dump — "I do have a master plan."

"So you can suggest a general area where we should search." Tony squinted against the blinding light reflecting from a piece of mirror. The hot garbage gave off a powerful aroma. He did *not* want to do this.

"Yep." Claude walked toward a medium-high pile. "This is the most likely area. You'll know if you start finding Kwik Kirk's on napkins and bags, it's probably near Candy's stuff. She doesn't generally have much more than a black plastic bag or two. Not like the couple with the baby. They make up for Candy with all those diapers."

"Do you have a shovel we can borrow?" Tony walked along the edge of the pile, hoping to see a bag from Kwik Kirk's on top.

"Yessir." Claude ambled off and returned with two shovels, two pairs of work gloves, and a gallon jar of water and two chipped cups. "Have at it."

It didn't take Tony long to decide he didn't enjoy digging in garbage. The stench was amazing. He'd never imagined this aroma, plus the sound of flies. He'd have opened his mouth to complain but was afraid the bugs would fly in. Nasty. A glance at Mike, who was filling in for the fingerprint-occupied Wade, showed another unhappy man. Dammit lounged in the shade of a massive magnolia tree by the house. The bloodhound looked quite comfortable.

About the time Tony was ready to call a halt to their search, Mike found a couple of black bags surround by Kwik Kirk's trash.

Opening them crushed their excitement. Lots of empty chip bags, plastic pop bottles that should have been recycled, and an exceptionally revolting collection of chicken bones.

No book.

CHAPTER TWENTY-FOUR

"I've located the Pingel family. The parents of the baby who died and accused Candy of negligence." Ruth Ann handed Tony a piece of paper with an address and telephone number written in her beautiful calligraphic penmanship. "And I looked into their employment situation, as well."

Tony wasn't sure if he wanted to cheer for Ruth Ann or hide from her. "What did you learn?"

"They're living in the tri-cities area. He's driving big rigs, and she has a home-based business, selling cosmetics." Ruth Ann hesitated. "They are behind in their mortgage and credit card payments."

Tony applauded her work. "Okay, so Wade, you can continue your fingerprint work, and I'm going to ask the sheriff up there to have a little chat with the couple."

Wade nodded and trotted off to his cubicle again.

It didn't take long for Tony to get his counterpart, a Sheriff Brown, on the telephone. He explained the situation and almost before he finished his tale, the sheriff was promising to find out all he could about the family and their lives in the past few days. Tony's contribution was to supply, thanks to Ruth Ann, their employment information and address.

While he waited, on hold, Tony plowed through several reports and files. Paperwork was the bane of his existence. He was deep into the arrest records for the Fourth of July, awestruck by the number of calls taken by 911. The dispatch team deserved medals. If he was doing the math correctly, one firecracker exploding had created thirty phone calls.

"It didn't take me long to get your answers," Sheriff Brown's voice boomed through the line. "Always happy to help. Maybe someday your department will help us."

Tony promised they would. "I don't suppose you know where the husband was at the approximate time Candy was left to die?" Tony couldn't help but believe the motive for the heinous way Candy was murdered had to be revenge. But revenge for what? Why else would someone treat her that way? As soon as he had the idea, he pushed it aside. Never make assumptions. He wasn't some naïve boy anymore. He knew people were capable of committing any number of horrors. They only had to make sense to the perpetrators.

"Oh, yes, and I think you'll find it very interesting indeed." The sound of pages of a report being shuffled came through the receiver. "The husband was making deliveries in the Knoxville area. According to what I've learned about the man's timetable and route, he could have passed right by your office on the day your lady died. I'll fax you this schedule." Sheriff Brown cleared his throat. "But also — "

"*But* is not my favorite word." Tony waited for the other shoe to drop. He didn't wait long.

"But . . ." Ignoring Tony's statement, the sheriff plunged into his story. "I talked to the babysitter. Evidently the mom left her kids with a sitter that evening and got home quite late the following afternoon. She apparently did not give anyone a makeup demonstration or whatever you'd call it. And furthermore — "

Shoes numbered three and four crashed around them. Tony said, "Let me guess. She asked the sitter not to mention it?"

"And paid with cash. And gave her a healthy tip," Sheriff Brown added. "Why not just take out an ad in the newspaper and say she was going to be bad?"

"Thank you." Tony tipped his head slightly to one side, holding the receiver with his shoulder while he made himself a note. "Now I have to find out if she was bad at Candy's house," Tony mused. "Or did she merely have a date with a man, not her husband, while her own was in our area, possibly doing a bad deed?"

"Let me know what you learn, Tony. I love it when we can find a bit of justice in this world."

Abandoning his office for the conference area, Tony drew a giant timeline on the white board and invited his entire staff to check it when they passed by to verify the details. "Let's start with the last time someone saw Candy alive. Someone we trust."

"Alvin saw her last."

Tony nodded and marked it on the board. "We have not only Alvin's word for it, but corroboration by several different people that he went to plant camp and stayed there."

"Wade found her body, and at that time,

Candy was definitely deceased and had been for a while."

"Okay, so between those two times, let's fill in some other bits."

"Theo, honey?" Tony gingerly opened his wife's office/studio door about six inches and peered inside. He sniffed, struck by the scent of the air up here. Theo's office aroma was comprised of lavender starch, coffee, and fabric sizing, and was vastly different from his world of sweat, gunpowder, disinfectant, and unwashed humans.

Through the opening, he could tell Theo hadn't heard him open the door. She was concentrating on her task, standing on a step stool, facing her design space — a full wall covered with cream-colored flannel. She was busy arranging quilt blocks on it. The flannel magically held the fabric pieces in place without the use of pins, making them easy for her to rearrange.

He rapped on the door.

She glanced over a shoulder at him, her expression curious, but not really with *him*. "Tony?"

"Yep, it's me." He waited another moment for her to process his presence. He hated to interrupt her when she was designing and usually tried not to. He watched her expression turn from puzzlement to concern. "I need your help," he said, as he walked across the room. Her step stool held her high enough off the floor for their eyes to be almost at the same level.

Theo's hazel eyes blinked behind the lenses of her glasses. She exhaled, releasing a deep sigh. "What do you want me to find out?"

Tony didn't bother to try to deny his intent. "I need to know more about the Pingel baby, the parents, and their relationship with Candy." Tony toyed with one of the blocks on the wall until Theo slapped his hand. "I doubt we'll ever know the whole story, but I'd guess some of your ladies, the older ones, know more than I can ever learn from the remaining parties involved. Nothing creates more silence than a badge some days."

Theo nodded. "If you promise to leave before I forget what I was thinking about, I'll promise to try."

Without another word, Tony kissed her cheek and left, taking extra care to close the door quietly behind himself.

Theo had to admit she was intrigued by Tony's request. What had happened to the Pingel baby that day? Was Candy the fall guy or the villain? Or neither? The bits of the story she had heard did not connect together like two halves of a cookie. She abandoned her design project almost immediately after Tony left the room, picked her own babies out of their crib, and headed to the classroom. At this time of day, there would almost certainly be a gathering of women who had lived in Silersville at the time of the event and didn't mind being bribed with a baby to hold.

"Who wants to snuggle with Kara or Lizzie?" Theo hoped she didn't look like a spy on a mission.

"Me." Dottie stuck her needle into the quilt and wiggled on her chair, making her lap larger.

"No, no." Blind Betty waved her hands. "Pick me. Dottie held one yesterday."

"It's a bribe." Caro whispered loudly enough for people on the outside sidewalk to hear. "She wants gossip."

Theo couldn't refute her comment. "Okay, let's see who has the information I need."

The face of every quilter in the room turned toward her. "What?"

"Were any of you living here at the time Candy Tibbles was accused of killing her neighbors' baby? The Pingels?"

Three hands raised.

"I don't usually auction off my children, but did any of you think Candy was guilty?"

All three heads moved from side to side.

"Why not?"

Caro began, even as she reached for a baby to cuddle. Lizzie. "I didn't spend much time with Candy, but several of my friends hired her to babysit their children. They all said she was nice to the kids. A bit unimaginative, maybe, but she read them stories, changed them when they were dirty, and followed whatever rules the parents gave her. To the letter. If they said apple juice at noon, she served apple juice to the kids at noon, and even stopped their playing a game to do it."

"It's true." Blind Betty held her arms out and Theo gently placed Kara in them. "Thank you, Theo." Tears welled in Betty's cloudy eyes as she sniffed the baby's neck. "Doesn't she smell sweet, though." Her fingers traced over the baby's face and moved up and smoothed Kara's wild hair. "Candy stayed with my nephew's children quite a bit. The story from them was the same. She kept a close eye on the children but didn't try to entertain them." Betty adjusted the baby's position. "They were shocked when the family accused Candy of negligence. They claimed there was no way

Candy would have had the baby in the wading pool unless the parents specifically told her to put the baby in the water and what time to do it. No way."

Theo settled at the frame, picked a spot where someone had abandoned a threaded needle, and began quilting. "Did anyone come to her defense? Or did it get that far?"

"The way I remember it" — Dottie, having no baby to hold, returned to her own stitching — "the family swore it was Candy's fault, but then they said they were sure it was an accident and got all sappy and maudlin about not punishing another child for their grievous loss." She started quilting again, but her hand trembled and she stopped. "Sheriff Winston looked like he was about to have a stroke, he was so mad. His face was scarlet, and he swore he was going to get to the bottom of it, but of course, they couldn't find the bottom. No evidence one way or another. No witnesses except Candy and the parents."

"What smells like fish but looks like cat? And it's not a catfish." Tony had listened to Theo's report and shared it with his staff. Everyone wanted to know the rumors, the half-spoken truths, the lies, the fragments pieced together to show them the truth.

"Answer. It's a very guilty cat."

Mike lifted his pencil into the air. "Why did the Pingel family move away so quickly after the death?"

"There is no statute of limitations on murder," Wade suggested. "Would moving away stop the investigation?"

"Out of sight, out of mind?" said Sheila. "I remember hearing the gossip around town. I'd say the split was pretty close to fifty-fifty between those believing the parents and the ones believing Candy."

"Just because you don't like someone, does not mean they're bad," Tony muttered.

"But they might be." Sheila waved her pen. "If it looks like a duck, and quacks like a duck, it still might not be a duck."

Distracted by her statement, Tony sat. "What is it, if it's not a duck?"

"I have no idea. Maybe I was crossing a mockingbird with a duck in my mind." Sheila marked through the note she'd just written.

Tony massaged the back of his neck. It felt like the muscles grew tighter, more tense every day. "Sheila, you've been looking into this for a while. What do you think is the probable truth, even knowing we'll never be able to prove it?"

Sheila sighed. "I think Candy and the

baby were playing in the yard when the parents returned home and she left. Maybe the little boy cried when she started walking back to her house, and he tried to follow and fell into the water. Either a parent, or both parents, were not paying attention to him, and he drowned." Sheila voice hardened. "I really think they saw an opportunity to avoid dealing with his special needs."

"Not acceptable." Tony snapped his pencil in half.

Mystery Quilt
Third Body of Clues

Block Two:
Sew a 2" wide strip of fabric (A) on both sides of each of the 3 1/2" wide strips of fabric (B). Press to (B). Cut into 10 segments 3 1/2" wide. Label as Center. Set aside.

Sew a 2" wide strip of fabric (B) on both sides of each 3 1/2" wide strip of fabric (A). Press to (B). Cut into 20 segments 2" wide. Sew one on two opposing sides of the 10 Center segments.

Cut one of the 6 1/2" wide strips of fabric (C) into 20 segments 2" wide. Sew one of these (C) on two opposing sides of the new Center segments. Press to (C).

Sew 2" strips of fabric (B) on opposing sides of 6 1/2" strip of fabric (C). Press to (C). Sub-cut into 20 segments 2" wide. Take care not to have the joining of the (B) strips in a cut segment. Sew one segment on each side of the center, completing the square with (C) on all outside edges.

Cut 2 of the 9 1/2" strips of (A) into 20 segments 2" wide. Sew a 2" by 9 1/2" strip of (A) on two opposing sides of the new Centers. Press to (A). Sew a 2″ wide strip of fabric (B) on opposing sides of the remaining 9 1/2″ wide strips of fabric (A). Press to (A). Subcut into 20 segments 2″ wide. Sew one of each side of the Center, completing the square with (A) on outside edges.

Trim each of the ten blocks to 12 1/2″. Label Block Two.

Chapter Twenty-Five

Thanks to the wonderful people who invented computers and telephones, Tony's office obtained in mere seconds the makes and models of the vehicles driven by trucker Max Pingel, his wife, and those of his mother-in-law, Mrs. Yates. A few more seconds produced license plate numbers and official photographs of the threesome.

Tony gave the information to his small staff. "If all, or any, of them are in Park County, I want to talk with them. In the meantime, I'm going out to Rankin's pig farm."

As Tony headed out to the pig farm that was irritating the new resident, he found himself thinking that being an all-purpose sheriff had its perks and drawbacks. This trip fell in to the drawback category. Nothing quite like visiting a pig farm on a hot day to add a little something extra to an already unpleasant day.

At least the pigs were happy. Their owner was not. The people living downwind were not. But a pink and black spotted hog wallowed in some mud, chasing away the flies and was presumably cooler than the ambient temperature. The hog chortled and squealed a bit, and Tony found himself envying the porker. Sure, he was destined to be ham, bacon, and assorted chops, but he was unaware of his fate. And in the meantime he had plenty of food, fresh air, and zero responsibility to anyone.

The farmer, a genial bachelor named Rankin, met Tony at the road. "I suppose the suburbanites are unhappy."

Tony didn't try to deny it. He sat in his vehicle, the window rolled down. It was all about show business. The cranky neighbors could see he'd taken their complaint to heart and come out for a visit. Nothing would change. The farm had been here for ages. "How old's your place?"

Rankin squinted at the house, a two-story white frame building with green shutters. It had fairly fresh paint. "Oh, I'd guess the house to be a hundred to a hundred and fifty years old. Can't remember offhand whether it was great-granddad or great-great-granddad who built it."

"Did he raise porkers too?" Tony watched

a couple of big green flies head into the Blazer. He managed to wave one back outside. The other one buzzed loudly against the inside of the windshield.

"Oh, yes, it runs in our veins, pig juice."

Rankin smiled as he watched Tony's battle with the insects, but when a breeze blew in their direction, his nose wrinkled a bit, making Tony think the farmer might not be completely unsympathetic to the aroma complaints. "You do know why I'm here?"

The farmer nodded. "There's nothin' I can do about the smell. I clean up the best I can."

"I never thought there was." Tony sighed. "You'd think people moving in next to a pig farm ought to know the score. If you move next to a railroad line, do you complain about the trains?"

"Well, nice to see you sheriff." Rankin waved and headed back toward the house. "You tell 'em I'm doing my best, won't you?"

Tony agreed, shooed another fly out the window, and raised the window before it could dive back inside. Then he drove back to the office.

Parked in the street in front of the Law Enforcement Center was a semi truck. The name of the owner was painted on the door.

Pingel. Tony hurried inside to have a chat with the man.

Moments later, Tony was pouring coffee for their visitor, treating him like an honored guest.

Mr. Pingel added three teaspoons of sugar to his coffee, then stirred it. He didn't pick up the cup. "I suppose this invitation has something to do with Candy Tibbles. I heard she has passed away."

Tony nodded his agreement about the invitation but privately thought Candy's manner of death a bit more grievous and unnatural than "passing away." He hoped he looked relaxed as he leaned back in his chair. Wade slipped into the room and sat in the chair not occupied by Pingel. "Candy babysat your son?"

Pingel stirred the coffee some more. Then he blew across the surface of it, as if trying to cool it down. "Yes."

"If you wouldn't mind, tell me in your own words about your relationship with the girl." Tony tossed the statement as casually as he could.

"We didn't have a relationship." Pingel looked up.

Tony noticed a flash of anger on Pingel's face. "All right. Let's start easy. How long did you and your family live next door to the Tibbleses?"

Pingel sipped his coffee. "I'd say about five years."

"Did Candy babysit for you often?"

"Yes, almost every day. She and the little guy got along just fine." Pingel paused. "She didn't do anything wrong. The boy's days were numbered from the beginning." Pushing his handkerchief under his glasses, he wiped away a tear. "Born with too many problems to count."

"I've heard some stories that contradict your account." Tony pretended to study a file. "What about those?"

"I'm ashamed to say that right after the boy died, my wife lied, and I let her." Pingel blew his nose. "It seemed to make my wife feel better to have someone to blame for the boy's death. If she didn't use poor Candy, she was bound to turn on me or herself. I was afraid she'd do something rash."

"But you didn't try to correct the story." Tony clenched the pen, breaking another one. He was going to have to find stronger pens or find another outlet for his anger.

Pingel waved his hands, forgetting he held the coffee cup, and black coffee flew through the air. "Yes, yes, we did. Right after the funeral we apologized to Candy. Gave her some cash to add to her college fund."

"College?" Tony hadn't heard anything about plans for higher education.

"Well, she was planning to become a hairdresser. We said we'd give her a good recommendation as a babysitter, if she needed one." Pingel's words tumbled over each other. "But the gossip had started and couldn't be stopped. It got worse and worse, and my father-in-law added false details and spread the story, and we finally moved away just to shut him up." Pingel fell silent. "We thought it would be better for us and Candy if we moved away."

"Where is your wife now?"

"I'd guess she's gambling." Pingel frowned. "I called earlier, and the babysitter said she'd taken off for the weekend. She does it about four times a year. I can give you a phone number for her."

Tony called Mrs. Pingel and learned her location. Thanks to a cooperative deputy in the North Carolina casino town, Tony verified in only a few minutes that Mrs. Pingel had been at the poker tables during the time of the murder.

After Pingel left his office, Tony felt a deep sense of relief. He believed Pingel's story, especially after he asked Sheila to check it with Mr. Yates. The bitter man admitted the truth, and Tony felt they could cross the Pingel family from the suspect list.

"Let's see what other dots we can connect." He stood in front of his white board, talking with Sheila. "Opal Dunwoody claimed she saw a woman walking toward Candy's house." Tony checked his notebook. "Then they argued."

Sheila didn't look convinced the story meant anything. "Opal would not have been able to see if the woman went into the house through the front door or walked around the side toward the garden and greenhouse area."

Tony agreed. "Or neither. It's possible she talked to Candy out front and then left. Opal was pretty vague about the time."

"And unless her glasses were clean, which I seriously doubt has been the case for years, she could have been watching through a smudge as thick as a curtain."

"They certainly were not clean when I talked with her." Tony suspected cataracts caused Opal all kinds of visual confusion that, mixed with some greasy dirt on her glasses' lenses, would render her almost blind.

"And as for the day" — Sheila fanned herself with her hand — "she's a nice old lady, but she spends lots of time in her front yard watching the neighbors and the traffic over at the convenience store. Even as mentally sharp as she is, Monday and Wednesday would be easy to mix up."

"True." Tony gestured with the marking pen. "I don't think we can ignore or confirm the events seen from her angle."

Sheila studied the board. "Who took the code book? And how did they even know it existed?"

Tony's shoulders twitched. "I'm guessing our victim, the something-less-than-brilliant blackmailer, probably let the information loose herself. Can't you just hear Candy going on about her code book? She could have waved the notebook in their faces, telling each one how she'd know if someone didn't pay on time."

"Silence at any cost." Sheila nodded. "It's the blackmailer's job security. Can you imagine having something you needed to keep hidden so desperately that you handed over your family's grocery money to Candy Tibbles every month?"

"Thankfully, no." Tony considered that particular situation well out of his area of personal expertise. But all people, including himself, were fallible. "We all like to think we're too smart, too lucky, or in control of our destiny, but it might not be true."

Sheila nodded her agreement. "Especially when someone is fighting an unseen enemy. The story doesn't even have to be the truth. Think of the mayor's situation, paying blackmail even though he didn't need to. The same thing could happen to you. I could claim I saw *you* steal something at the grocery store. Even if it was untrue, the accusation would tarnish your reputation. Maybe you're afraid you won't be reelected. You don't want your family to suffer from embarrassment or your joblessness, and so I suggest you give me your lunch money every week and say I'll keep my silence." Sheila frowned. "Maybe Candy was smarter than we give her credit for."

"Or maybe not. Maybe one day you want a raise. Greed raises the cost of silence. The payment increases." Tony lifted an eyebrow. "What if I can't pay? Trying to save the family budget, Theo begins packing me a lunch instead of having me buy my own."

"I'm screaming at you, telling you to give me the money," Sheila jumped in. "I don't care where you get the cash."

"So I whack you in the head to shut you up," Tony said. "It works. You fall down and all I care about is you aren't yammering at me anymore."

"So," Sheila said, smiling. "What did you hit me with?"

"I wish I knew." Tony shook his head. "It was hard, cylindrical, and smaller in diameter than any of the tools we found under the house."

"Who was our guy with the map?" Tony himself had almost forgotten the odd report. "On a cul-de-sac with only four houses, it sounded like he couldn't find the right address."

"Maybe he didn't have any trouble finding the right house but was just covering his actions. Spying on your neighbors is a sport played everywhere. Spying on strangers is encouraged as a crime deterrent." Wade had joined the impromptu meeting.

"So he could have as easily been watching Mrs. Vanderbilt as Candy." Tony thought the young mother was much easier on the eyes, but probably not fascinating to watch for long periods of time, and Candy might have been.

"What about the surveillance video from the convenience store? Maybe it caught the license plate." Sheila flipped through her notebook. There is almost always traffic at Kwik Kirk's.

313

"Maybe he went into the store for a snack."

Tony sprang to his feet. "The video. I forgot all about it. Kirk gave it to me days ago and then I went back to Candy's place."

"Hopefully you put it some place safe." Sheila gave him a smile. "And still have it."

He had. The moment he remembered it, he knew he'd shoved it in the briefcase he kept in the Blazer and almost never used.

It didn't take long to find the information they were looking for. Only one man wore the hat described by Roscoe and Veronica. A few minutes later, the mysterious man with the binoculars was finally positively identified as Ulf Erikson, a botanist from North Carolina.

It wasn't much after that when Sheila found him sitting in the car on a back road and called in her sighting. She said he appeared to be studying the back of the Tibbles's property. As expected, he had a pair of powerful binoculars, a camera equipped with an extra-long lens, and a notebook on the seat next to him.

Tony said, "I'd like to have him in my office."

"I'd be more than happy to arrange it." True to her word, only a few minutes passed before Sheila ushered Erikson into Tony's office. "I checked him for weapons, and he didn't do anything stupid when I suggested he come with me." Aggravation laced her words. "He did whine the whole way here. Not a pleasant sound at all." She took a step toward Tony's open door.

Tony raised a finger, signaling for her to wait.

"I didn't do anything wrong," Erikson said. "I heard the boy had discovered a beetle-resistant strain of beans. I just wanted to talk to him about it."

"Interesting, but the last I heard, no one uses binoculars for conversational purposes." Tony found the man annoying and a liar, but he couldn't imagine Erikson was likely to bash Candy in the head and leave her to die in an overheated greenhouse. Why would he bother to pull the tarps away and leave her in the full heat of the sun? Unless . . . "Did you sneak into the garden and get caught?"

"Caught? Sheriff, you make it sound like I was doing something illegal." The weasel's eyes moved constantly, hiding something.

In spite of his bluster, he wasn't convincing. Movement of his Adam's apple showed he was swallowing convulsively. Tony relaxed in his chair, toying with his pen. "I'm convinced the law is still on the side of the

315

homeowner. Trespassing is frowned upon."

"I knocked." Erikson fidgeted a bit. "When no one came to the door, I walked around back to see if someone was in the garden."

"And?" Tony leaned forward abruptly.

Erikson flinched at the sudden movement. "I didn't see anyone."

"So you left?"

"Well, not right away. I did take a few photographs." He seemed to be strangling on his words. "I needed to be able to compare the plants with their later appearance." His words ground to a halt.

"But these are not your plants. Are they?" Tony pointed his pen at the man.

The botanist meshed his fingers tightly together and leaned forward. An expression of great intensity pulled his lips tight against his teeth. After a few moments, he shook his head.

"So you *were* trespassing?"

Erikson nodded.

"Did you go into the greenhouse?" Tony guessed some of the man's reluctance to tell the truth came from what he witnessed in there.

Erikson's head swung back and forth like the clapper in a bell. "I heard the insects and looked in." He suddenly gasped as if

he'd been holding his breath. "It was hor-
rible. They were feasting, but I couldn't help
her. I mean, she was obviously dead, and I
didn't want to be involved."

"Why not make an anonymous phone
call?" Tony could not understand the way
the man thought. "If you weren't doing
anything wrong, how could you just leave
any person, a human being, in the dirt, in
that situation? Have you no feelings, not a
whit of conscience?"

Silence. One shoulder twitched.

It was all the answer Tony received. He
glanced past the man to Sheila. "Get copies
of his ID and cut him loose. I want to be
able to locate him if we decide we need him
after all."

"I think he's a liar and a potential thief,"
Tony snapped, adding more documents to
the ever-increasing file on Candy's murder.
"What do you think I can charge him with?"

"Do you think he ever encountered
Candy?" Wade leaned against the door
frame.

"Yes. I do." Tony didn't know why he was
so certain the man had not told them
everything he knew. "I think he'd been stak-
ing out the greenhouse for several days
before she died, and he's still doing it."

"Why?"

"I don't know. It doesn't make sense to me, but maybe rivalries in botany operate under special rules. I assume they are much the same as in other industries, though. Whoever crosses the finish line first will win."

"Let's say he's telling the truth." Wade stared off into the distance. "He went out there, and Candy told him what? That Alvin wouldn't be home for a while, or that he didn't live there any more, or that for fifty dollars she'd give him a couple of plants, thinking Alvin wouldn't miss them?"

Tony sensed Wade was on to something. "But he comes back with the money and doesn't find her. He's angry. She's promised him one thing and doesn't deliver. He stomps out to the garden, and she taunts him and starts to walk away. He picks up a hoe or something and swings it like a baseball bat and hits the back of her head."

"She falls into the greenhouse. Or maybe that's where he struck her. He can see she's still breathing and panics. He begins ripping the tarps off the glass ceiling and stops when he sees he's making the situation worse. The temperature is increasing, and he hears someone coming."

Tony rubbed his bald scalp. "And?"

318

"Panicking, he slinks away and tosses the hoe under the porch. But that's all wrong, because the weapon wasn't the hoe, and nothing under the porch was the right size. He has to pretend he's still looking to talk to her and Alvin." Wade appeared less certain.

Tony took up the thread Wade had started. "He slips away so he can come back, pretending to just be arriving. Maybe the weapon was under there with the other tools, and he took it later. Maybe he even intended to call for help, saying he arrived and found her. That he was just doing a good deed."

"Okay, so why's he still spying on the house from a distance? He's established his reason for being there and his reason for leaving. Why stay?" Wade shook his head. "I don't get it."

"He wants the plants." Tony glanced at the white board. "People are coming and going from the convenience store until after dark and on to midnight. If he trots up there with a flashlight, one of the neighbors will see."

"True," Tony agreed. "So what's he going to do? He plays innocent, and when he sees that it's safe, he can walk down from the road without anyone seeing him. Then maybe he slips and slides a bit on the ridge, but digging deep enough to grab the plants is quick work. Walk back the way he came until he's out of sight of the neighbors, slip over to the highway, and walk the rest of the way to his car."

"That works," Wade said. "Mostly."

Tony thought the scenario had possibilities, but it didn't make him want to jump up and yell, "That's it."

"I'm not sure if this is good news or bad news, Tony." The voice on the phone belonged to Vince of the TBI. "We've gotten the preliminary information back and so far, nothing links your wrench wielder and your female victim."

Tony wasn't sure if the news pleased him or not. "What *have* you learned?"

"There were any number of substances on your wrench, mostly around the adjusting screw, and they transferred to the injury sites. Oil, grease, soil, paint, and that's just for starters. And, of course, some of the victim's blood transferred onto the tools." Vince growled like a bear. "We did find blood from the guy Sheila calls Not Bob on the shirt belonging to the hitchhiker someone clobbered later on. Definitely transfer."

Tony considered the possible implications.

320

"And the Tibbles woman's injury?"

"Clean." The sound of computer keys provided background sound for a moment. "She had soil in her hair, not imbedded in the wound. What you might expect if you fell onto a pile of dirt. There's no connection between the tools, but it could be as simple as the attacker using whatever is available."

"Back to square one." Tony mumbled.

"Not necessarily. At least, if you find a dirty wrench and your attacker hasn't developed a miracle cleaner, we should be able to match the substances. Right down to matching the blood. It would be a slam dunk, evidence-wise."

"And the other weapon?" Tony thought he knew the answer.

"Probably not, but we could try." Vince used his professional voice. "It does not appear, at this time, to possess any unique qualities. However, just because it didn't transfer much onto your victim, that doesn't mean she didn't transfer conclusive evidence onto it."

"In other words, we need to find the right weapon."

Theo stood in the kitchen, staring at their backyard. The boys and Daisy were tearing through the grass but avoiding the new garden patch. That might have had something to do with the new wire mesh fence surrounding it. She felt concern and affection for their teenaged gardener. "Do you think Alvin is going to be okay? I heard he decided to come back from camp today, and I told Martha she should bring him along for dinner. I guess he didn't feel up to dealing with all of us."

"He's a strong young man. Thankfully. Between Martha, Mom, and Sheila's mother, he'll crave the day he can get away from all the surrogate mothers in his world. I just hope they don't drive him crazy."

"Aren't you including me in your wish list?" Theo teased. "You, of all people, should know I have a gift for nagging."

Tony kept his mouth carefully closed.

CHAPTER TWENTY-SIX

Theo kept smiling. There was nothing else she could do. Winifred Thornby from the newspaper was taking pictures and asking questions at the same time. A few of the questions had nothing to do with her shop and it being featured in a national quilting magazine, and everything to do with her husband's investigation.

Sometimes Theo felt like the referee. Tony and Winifred did not have a good relationship.

Thinking what an understatement this was made Theo's smile widen. Tony and Winifred didn't just have a strained relationship — they destested each other. Luckily, Winifred took a photograph that satisfied her before Theo dissolved into hysterics.

Winifred put her camera in the bag and stared at Theo. "That worthless husband of yours had better catch the attacker with the wrench, and what else, a hammer? If he'd spend more time doing police work and less time eating pie, our county would be a safer place to live. Two victims, no, three with Candy, and maybe more to come. How can you tolerate it, living with someone that lazy?"

So much for the good mood. Theo couldn't address Tony's investigation. "You might want to talk to some of the quilters working on the charity quilts." Theo tried to move Winifred closer to the frame surrounded by women working on the current quilt. "It would make an interesting story."

Tenacious and single-minded, Winifred didn't budge. "I'll assume your refusal to discuss the matter as agreement with my assessment."

"No." Theo shook her head for emphasis and felt her curls bounce. "I do not agree with you. He's working hard, but I do not have specific information to give you."

Winifred's eyebrows flew up in an overly dramatic fashion. "Are you implying he is withholding information?"

Theo couldn't respond. Or, at least, she managed not to.

"Haven't you heard of freedom of the press?" Winifred moved closer, stalking her.

Theo pretended to hear a baby cry and trotted up the stairs. She locked her office door behind her.

"Where did Candy get her drugs?" Tony stood in front of the day shift. Roll call was over, and they were going over a list of situations needing attention in the county.

"We've got several possible dealers on our radar." Wade stood. "I suggest we talk to Quentin Mize. He's clean now, but he and Candy hung out together when he was deeply into drugs."

Sheila agreed. "I imagine he still knows how to find them if he wants them."

"Oh, good, Quentin as a confidential informant." Tony thought it would be like asking a feral dog to guide them to a meat market. The last thing he wanted was for Quentin to fall back into drugs.

"If not to tend Alvin's garden, why would Candy have been in the garden or greenhouse area? The way everyone has described her to me, I doubt she developed a sudden determination to raise prize-winning roses." Tony studied their chart. "What's there for her in the daylight?"

"Sir." Sheila leaned forward. "Do we know it was daylight when she went out there? Maybe she went out in the dark."

Tony lifted the extensive report from the pathologist. "According to the experts, she

325

became overheated while she was unconscious. They seem to consider it unlikely she would have regained enough consciousness to at least squirm around in the cooler night air. All indications suggest she lay motionless where she landed. No heel marks in the dirt."

"So she and her companion did not pull back the tarps to watch the moon rise?"

"Well, maybe." Tony considered it. "I guess they could have pulled the tarps away and spent time in the greenhouse. Maybe she came back later, when it was hot, and they got into an argument. She died where she landed." He discarded the jumbled idea. "I'm just connecting people and places. Her being hit in the dark doesn't work."

"What about J.B.? He knows everything that happens in Park County after dark," Sheila suggested. "Did he see anything unusual the night before? You know, like a car where it shouldn't be or a person sneaking through a yard?"

"Nothing in his report. I'll talk to him. There's always a possibility that there's a regular visitor to the house after midnight who wouldn't be classified as unusual." Tony said, "Sheila, I want you to check with your contacts in the schools. Who's dealing what?"

"I know a couple of kids who might be able to supply a few names, if I can promise to keep them anonymous." Sheila jotted herself a note, then met his eyes. Waiting.

"Forgive a past deed, but not a future one." Tony hated drugs. "I don't want you handing out any get-out-of-jail-free cards."

It didn't take Tony long to locate Quentin. A quick call to his brother Gus produced the address where he had sent Quentin and Roscoe to build a mower shed. It was a simple enough job that even the two friends could complete it without much supervision from Gus.

Tall, thin, and a bit twitchy, Quentin ambled toward Tony's vehicle with a wide grin on his face. "Howdy, Sheriff."

"You're just who I was looking for," Tony said. "Have you got a few minutes to talk?"

Quentin glanced at Roscoe.

The smaller of the two men was the brains of the operation. "Sure." Roscoe flipped his hammer into the air and nimbly caught it. "Take your time. I'll call Veronica."

"He's crazy about the professor." Quentin lowered his voice as though he were telling a secret he was supposed to keep. "Once they find a place to live, I'm thinkin' they'll get hitched."

"More surprising things have happened." Tony herded Quentin away from his friend. "I need your help."

Quentin's jaw dropped. "No kidding? That's great."

"I know you've been doing well, working hard, staying away from drugs." Tony watched Quentin's head bob with every word. "I'm proud of you."

The gangly man blushed. "Thank you."

"What I need to ask is if you know who might have been dealing drugs to Candy Tibbles?"

Eyes wide, Quentin's head moved from side to side. "No. I've got no idea. It's been a while since I bought any, you know. Sorry."

Tony was surprised at how relieved he was to hear Quentin's words. "I'm not. I'm glad you've gotten this far away from all those poisons."

Quentin glanced in Roscoe's direction. "Couldn't do it without friends."

When Tony and Wade went looking for the night patrol, they discovered that as was his custom, Deputy J.B. Lewis had left the building as soon as he turned in his reports. The deputy loved the night shift, wrote decent notes, and didn't gossip about anything or anyone he witnessed.

Tony and Wade caught up with him in the grocery store parking lot. Tony said, "I read your reports. Is there anything you saw you thought was maybe wrong but nothing you'd put on paper?"

"Clandestine or suspicious activity?" The creases around J.B.'s eyes deepened as he grinned. "Sure, Sheriff. I'm pretty up to date on who is cheating and with whom. Who are you interested in?"

"Candy Tibbles," Tony said. "Maybe in the past few weeks."

"Pitiful woman." J.B. shook his head in obvious sorrow. "Such a lost soul. I've seen her with so many men." He paused, studied the sky. "Well, there is a guy, Sinclair, who drives a mid-aged dark blue Toyota. I've seen it parked pretty often in Candy's driveway late at night." J.B. shook his head again. "They might have been friends or he might have been selling her something. I don't know. I've seen the same car over at Kwik Kirk's. It's right across the highway, so why not walk over from Candy's house?"

"Anything else? Not necessarily related to Candy."

J.B. rubbed his forehead. "I've seen several guys coming out of The Spa with women who were not their wives, and women with men who were not their husbands. Bad behavior on both sides. You want the names?"

"Yes. Make me a list. Sounds like it will be a long one." Tony didn't really want to know as much about the county residents as he sometimes learned. There were times his knowledge made it difficult to deal with them on unofficial business. Chatting over coffee at church with a cheating husband or wife stretched his meager diplomatic abilities.

"Sheriff, I have a report of a fight." Flavio paused for a moment, then continued. "Mayor Cashdollar requests — his words not mine — you come to the funeral home. As soon as possible. Or faster."

"The fight's at the funeral home?" Tony hoped he'd misunderstood.

Flavio's voice was muffled, sounding like he was stifling a laugh. "Yes, sir. I gather it has something to do with the viewing for Hydrangea Jackson."

"I'm on my way." Tony walked toward the Blazer. "Notify Wade to meet me there. He'll never forgive me if he doesn't get to come along."

"I wouldn't mind seeing it myself. From what I could hear in the background, it must be quite a show," Flavio murmured as he disconnected.

As soon as Tony and Wade walked through the front doors of the Cashdollar Mortuary, they were hit with the sounds of piano music and hymns being sung with enthusiasm, if not talent. Over all of the musical sounds, Tony could hear agitated, high-pitched voices and one distinctive male voice. It belonged to Mayor Calvin Cashdollar.

"Ladies, please." Tony thought Calvin was begging. "Please, don't do that."

When he and Wade entered the visitation room, Tony was grateful he was considerably taller than most of the mourners. The room was packed, and no one was moving to let him pass. Over the heads of a cluster of weeping women, Tony was able to see the two most elderly Flowers sisters leaning over their sister's coffin. One was scrubbing on the corpse's eyelids with a tissue, spitting on it, and returning to the task. "Sister never wore lavender eye shadow a day in her life. What was Calvin thinking?" Her strident voice cut through the chatter.

The second sister must have pulled a tube of lipstick from her purse, and she began applying it generously to her late sister's lips. "Poor sister. She looks so pale." The amateur makeup artist's aim was poor, and the walker supporting her teetered. In seconds she had painted a scarlet slash across most of the dead woman's face, turning it into a grotesque sight.

Tony exchanged glances with Wade. "Is any of this illegal?"

"Weird? Hell, yes." Wide-eyed, Wade raised one shoulder and let it drop. "Illegal? I don't know."

Calvin waved the men closer. "Can't you stop them?"

"You called about a fight." Tony forced his eyes away from the elderly women and their makeup project.

"Yes, yes. Look at this," Calvin pointed to a trail of broken gladiolas and some overturned memorial potted plants. A porcelain vase had shattered, apparently when it hit the wall behind it. "They are destroying my place of business."

Tony spotted Blossom huddled in the far corner of the room with at least six of her sisters. Her fiancé Kenny was jammed up against the wall, behind some of the Flowers men. Tony strode over and cut her out of the herd. "What happened here?"

Blossom's eyes watered, and she dabbed at them with a tissue. "Our aunts have been out of control ever since Aunt Hydrangea died. Her sisters went wild with grief and now, just minutes ago, we learned Aunt Hydrangea had been hiding a second marriage. I can promise you they were not happy about learning the old lady has — had — two husbands." Blossom nodded toward a pair of elderly men, identical in appearance and attire, and each clutching a bouquet of flowers in one hand and the casket's handle with the other. "That's them, the husbands."

"If it's true, I can't exactly arrest her for bigamy. Since she's dead," Tony muttered to himself. The sounds around him continued to grow. He sent Wade to silence the piano.

In a louder voice, he urged the mourners to all say their farewells and quickly leave the building. As one of the ancient sisters moved past the new widowers, she paused to study them and sniffed, lifting her nose higher. "Quantity not quality."

It took a while to pry the old guys loose, literally, their gnarled hands seemed locked in place. Eventually they managed to clear the room.

Wade and Tony paused at the doorway and looked back. The carpet was soaked with water from overturned vases. Broken flowers littered the room. Calvin sat near the casket, which was askew, one corner almost touching the floor. Calvin was holding his head with both hands.

"What do you think, Wade?" Tony pulled out his notebook. "How do we write a description of this?"

"I'm thinking this has got to be some strange dream. I sure hope I can remember the details when I wake up." Wade gathered a handful of crumpled flowers from the floor and dropped them in a trash can, one almost completely filled with used tissues. "Grace will love it."

Chapter Twenty-Seven

As Tony and Wade walked outside, Tony received a call, telling him where to find Sinclair, Candy's frequent visitor.

"Candy always had cash and was a lot of fun." Sinclair snuffled and turned his face so he could wipe his nose on the back of his hand and cleaned it on the seat of his pants. "She'd slip me a little, you know, gas money, so I could come out and visit."

"Rumor has it you're selling drugs." Tony took a step closer. It put him much closer than he wanted to be to the man. It hadn't taken great detective work to locate the owner of the blue Toyota. He was sitting in it, parked at Kwik Kirk's. "I think Candy was one of your best customers."

"Oh." Sinclair's narrow face developed a bit of a sneer. "You know, rumor ain't the same as proof. I say me and Candy was friends, and you c'aint prove otherwise."

"If I borrow a drug dog, I don't suppose

you'd mind if it paid you a little visit?" Tony raised his palm to stop the inevitable tirade about interfering with personal freedom. "You don't need to answer, just give it some thought." Tony almost laughed at the idea of Sinclair doing much thinking. "Did you and Candy have a spat recently?"

"A spat?" Sinclair seemed not to understand the term.

"An argument."

"Oh, I know what that is."

"And did you?"

"Just a little difference of opinion. I wanted pepperoni on the pizza and she wanted ham and pineapple. Silly girl pizza."

"And did you eat this pizza in her house?"

"Nope. We had us a little moonlight picnic in the yard."

Tony pretended to study the yard across the road. "In Alvin's greenhouse?"

"No way. I ain't traipsing off into the dark." Sinclair looked insulted. "I got better sense than to wander back there even with a flashlight. It's cuz of that boy of hers, Alvin, always digging holes like some damn gopher."

"Did Candy like going back there?"

"Nossir. She was worse than a girl. Always going on like ooh, there might be bugs or snakes, or one night she swore there was an axe murderer back there with a flashlight and a gun."

"Not an axe?" Tony couldn't help himself. To him, Sinclair didn't sound any braver than Candy. It also didn't sound like the couple was likely to be in the greenhouse at night.

Sinclair looked a bit cross-eyed at Tony's jibe. "You got a problem?"

Tony ignored the question. "Did you ever go into the greenhouse in the daylight?"

"Why would I?" Sinclair leaned closer, his breath vile. "There's nothing so great about it. Candy said her boy wouldn't let her grow any weed back there, so I say, what's the point?" His tirade stopped in mid breath. His brain must have finally caught up with his mouth.

Unfortunately, Tony believed him. He seriously doubted Sinclair would walk all the way to the back of the yard without powerful incentive — money or fear. Neither fit the facts as he knew them.

Trapped in her own office, Theo sat next to Martha on the window seat. Tony's aunt kept crying, and all Theo could do was to keep handing her more tissues. "I didn't think you liked Candy Tibbles."

"I didn't." Martha wailed like a toddler.

337

"She was an awful girl, an awful mother, and a general waste of skin."

"So, of course, you're sitting here bawling all over my expensive fabric." Theo didn't understand. "What am I missing?"

"I feel so sorry for Alvin." Martha's sobs became hiccups. "He was just getting used to being emancipated, and now he has to deal with funerals and the property and grief." She wiped the tears from her face with a wad of tissues. "Do you think he'll move back to his house?"

Theo hadn't given the matter any thought. "I guess he could. I'm sure his grandparents paid the house off years ago, and I can't imagine he won't inherit it."

Martha sighed. "So much responsibility for a young man."

"He's a boy." Theo refuted Martha's statement. "I've got shoes older than he is."

"It would be nice if he'd stay in my downstairs." Martha blew into the tissues with a loud honk.

"Aha." Theo felt like the lights had just come on in the tunnel of her confusion. "This isn't about Alvin, it's all about you. You enjoy being a landlady."

"I do." Martha managed a smile. "If, or actually when, Alvin leaves, I think I'll rent again. The space is perfect and private and yet" — she exhaled heavily — "if I should fall and break my leg, maybe I wouldn't have to lie there for weeks before someone would know to come rescue me."

This statement surprised Theo, because Martha was not old. It would have been less shocking if Jane, who was considerably older than her sister, was the one concerned about living alone. Of course, Jane had a very active, if overworked, guardian angel. She could still picture Tony's face when he'd given her a description of Jane and the bear, the wild bear. His reenactment had gone into great detail, including his own part in the melodrama. "I promise we'll check on you if Alvin moves out and you can't find another tenant."

"I'm really curious about how the tools got under the porch." Tony lined up a couple of sheets of paper on the table. "If Alvin shoved them under there, I will jump off the courthouse roof and fly."

"I agree." Wade rocked back on the chair legs. "Alvin would have put them neatly in the shed, and latched it shut. Maybe even locked it. But . . ."

"What?" Tony wondered if his deputy was thinking the same thing he was. "Who would be using them, and why? We didn't find any holes. Of course, someone has been digging out there. It's a garden. Alvin's the only one who can tell us if something has been changed, damaged, or rearranged."

"Maybe someone thought Alvin buried money in the garden. You see it in movies where someone stashes the loot in a coffee can and buries it next to the tomatoes. And, as you say, who but Alvin would be able to tell if someone other than him had been digging in there?"

"Sinclair said he saw a light and heard digging one time when he and Candy were having their picnic. Or did he say they had seen it at another time?" Tony rose to his feet. "Time to get Alvin to give us a tour of his garden. Maybe he'll spot something out of place."

As Tony drove Alvin out to the Tibbles home, he saw no reason he couldn't release the house and its contents to the boy. Nothing they'd found inside it showed any connection with Candy's death. Tony cleared his throat, wondering about the best way to broach the subject to Alvin.

"If you'd like some help with cleaning up the house," Tony mumbled. "There's a group of women from the church who are willing to come out and sort and clean and organize a yard sale for you."

"Why?" Obviously surprised, Alvin jerked forward, making the seat belt tighten across his chest.

"You don't have to." Tony realized he'd been hasty in his suggestion. After all, the boy's mother hadn't even been buried. "It's your call."

"I pay them?" Alvin's voice was only a little louder than a whisper.

"No. It's a volunteer group. It's still all your stuff. Everything belongs to you, and you keep everything you want and all the money it brings in." Tony didn't suppress a chuckle. "There might be a few ladies who would enjoy having the first chance to purchase some item going into the yard sale but it's yours until it's sold."

"You mean I wouldn't have to go through all of my mom's junk and the rotting stuff in the kitchen." Some of the tension in Alvin's face dissipated and was replaced with a modicum of relief from the responsibility he neither wanted nor was prepared for. "I have money. I'd pay."

"No." Tony wanted to be sure Alvin understood. "You don't pay. This is a sympathy gift for you. I've seen those women in action a few times, and to tell you the truth, except for the bio hazards, which they will dispose of, they are extremely efficient and non-judgmental. You still have to decide what goes and what stays."

"In other words, they'll get rid of my mom's drugs and wash things."

"Yes." Not for the first time, Tony admired the matter-of-fact way Alvin approached the subject of his mother's lifestyle.

"It already is *my* house, you know, not Mom's." Alvin spoke after a prolonged silence. "My grandparents left it to me, in some kind of trust. They fixed it so Mom could live in it as long as she wanted to, but it was not hers to sell because they knew she would sell it out from under us and we'd end up living in a car." After delivering his monologue, Alvin paused to breathe.

Tony hated to think of the years of despair it took for Candy's parents to make a decision like that. "Who was the responsible adult for the property before you were emancipated?"

"Mayor Cashdollar." Alvin smiled. "He and my granddad were big fishing buddies."

"I've heard that." Tony did a little mental arithmetic and realized the two men were probably very close in age, or would be if one hadn't died.

Alvin finally relaxed on the seat. "They used to take me along sometimes on their all-day trips, but I didn't love it. Fishing, that is." His eyes gleamed. "I did enjoy the water and the picnic, but I didn't actually like to fish."

"I know the feeling." Tony felt a slight lessening of his own tension; at least Alvin's grandparents had protected him as much as they could from his unstable mother. "Fishing doesn't float my boat either, but my brother Tiberius is a fanatic. He spends more hours in his bass boat than he does on land."

Tony pulled into the driveway at Alvin's house, parking near the garage, and cut the engine. "You don't need to rush your decisions." The expression on Alvin's face as he looked up at the house made Tony sense the boy almost felt obliged to move back into the house, but didn't really want to. "It's your life. Live where you're most comfortable. Rent the house out if you want."

"My garden is here." A look of mingled sorrow and fear passed over his tense face, and his eyes filled with tears.

"Keep your garden. The lease could specify the area as yours." Tony hesitated, not wanting to interfere. "If you decide to, you might be happier if you get Claude or my brother Gus to remove the old greenhouse when it's not needed as evidence any more. You could still commute, like you do now."

"Your aunt's nice." Alvin looked like he was considering Tony's suggestion.

Tony had to laugh. "Yes, she is. I think she enjoys having you residing in her basement." He waited another moment before asking, "Does it feel weird at school? You know, having your English teacher for your landlord?"

Alvin cracked a grin. "I thought it might, but no. I live totally separate. I don't see her often and she doesn't like, you know, come in and pry. I have my own little kitchen area and total privacy." He stared through the windshield at his home. "But I know I can knock on her door and ask for advice, you know, if I'm cooking."

"What about your friends?" Tony sincerely hoped the boy had friends.

"They kinda understand, and it is way better than having them deal with my mom." His face flooded with color, and his focus dropped to the floor mats. "I tried."

Tony couldn't miss the mingling of embarrassment and guilt. "Remember this and believe it, Alvin. You were never responsible for your mom's behavior. You didn't cause it, and you couldn't fix it. You did the best you could."

Alvin nodded but didn't lift his head.

Tony opened his door and climbed out of the Blazer, shocked by the heat after the cool provided by the air-conditioning. He kept his eyes on Alvin's house. After a couple of minutes, he heard Alvin open the door and join him.

Alvin's voice sounded a bit froggy. "I'd like to accept your offer of help with the house and Mom's stuff."

"I'll let the ladies know." Tony wasn't sure why he was so relieved Alvin wouldn't have to be the one to go through all the trash in the house.

Moments later, Wade arrived in his own vehicle and parked behind Tony's Blazer. "Hot enough for you yet?" He laughed as he approached. "Lead on, Alvin."

Tony noticed Alvin, after a couple of glances, was careful not to look at the house, still draped with crime scene tape and with seals on the doors. "We'll clear those off before the ladies arrive." Tony wished there was a way to make this easier for Alvin, but he was the only one who could tell them if something looked different in the garden or the surrounding area. The path to the garden took them through the backyard.

Alvin walked steadily, but his complexion paled considerably and there appeared to be a tremor, barely more than a vibration, surging through his body as he led them up the gravel driveway and past the detached garage. He slowed more as he followed the path between a pair of trees and stepped into the garden clearing. To his left was the garden, to his right the hidden tool shed, and straight before them was the greenhouse. Alvin leaned forward, forcing his head low, his eyes watching his feet.

He stopped and made a half turn to the left, facing the garden. Only then did he straighten, focusing on the plants.

Tony heard a strangled sound. "Alvin?"

"What happened to it?" Alvin's voice rose higher with each word.

To Tony, the garden looked just as it had when he first saw it. They could check the photographs made at the beginning of the investigation, of course, but he remembered thinking how careful his department and the TBI had been not to trample the young man's beautifully tended garden. "I'm sorry if it's damaged."

Alvin turned to look directly at him. "The plant at the far end of the row has been dug up." He walked closer, bent over and studied the dirt. Wade and Tony walked around the outside of the garden and stood quietly watching.

"It was one of the test plants." Alvin's face blanched, then went scarlet. "I've been robbed."

Tony studied the soil at Alvin's feet. "Don't take this the wrong way Alvin, but, would someone have killed to steal it?"

"You mean . . ." He gulped. "You think that's why my mom was killed? You think she was protecting the garden?"

"I have no idea." Tony felt honesty was the only way to find more information. "What was it worth?"

Alvin shook his head. "Maybe nothing. Maybe a lot. It's an experiment I've been working on to develop plants resistant to beetles."

Wade whispered, "The peeper."

Tony nodded. "But he's been seen frequently in the area, even since Candy died."

"So, he was watching and waiting." Wade looked up toward the ridge where the man had been spotted before. "If he didn't kill her, maybe he's our witness."

"Let's talk about your tool shed." Tony, Wade, and Alvin had abandoned the garden for the moment and sat in some sturdy lawn chairs in the shade. Wade had bought them all cold drinks at Kwik Kirk's and they were all pretending things were almost normal.

Alvin bobbed his head as he slurped another big gulp of soda pop. "It was originally a privy; you know, an outhouse, probably a hundred years ago. Someone moved it after the house got plumbing. There's no foundation and there's no hole."

"You keep a padlock on the door." Tony said.

"Yeah, but the key hangs on a hook by the back door into the house. Anyone could unlock it and get to the tools. None of them are valuable."

"Why bother to lock it?" Wade shook the ice in his empty cup and poured some into his mouth.

"Mostly it's to keep the critters out." Alvin gestured widely. "The latch won't stay shut without the lock, and the last thing I want is some skunk or other beastie moving in."

Believing Alvin was calm enough to handle more questions, Tony turned the subject back to the missing plant. "What is different about the missing plant?"

Alvin said, "I've been working to create a strain of beans that's resistant to beetles. Something they don't like to eat."

"Not another kudzu experiment?" Tony

could see a couple of patches of the perni-
cious vine from where he sat. It was working its way up the trunk of a tree. No kudzu
grew on the Tibbles's land. He guessed
Alvin was relentless in his quest to rid the
area of it.

"Oh, no, it's just to keep the beetles from
eating it. It's not poisonous to them or to
people or anything."

"But if you're successful, it could potentially save farmers scads of money they're
currently losing to the bugs."

"Yes."

Alvin seemed pleased Tony understood.
Not only would farmers benefit, Alvin
would probably earn a fair amount of
money.

"If you want to tend your very valuable
garden for a while, go ahead." Tony was
relieved when Alvin wasted no time heading
for it, bucket and weeding tool in hand. "At
least you can check the remaining plants."

When Alvin was out of earshot, Wade said,
"If it's the floppy-hat guy — what's his
name?"

"Erikson," Tony said.

"If he's the thief, why would he wait so
many days before actually digging it up?"

"Maybe he was in the middle of digging it
up and Candy chased him away."

349

"Or she tried to chase him away and he killed her." Wade leaned forward. The excitement lighting his dark blue eyes faded almost immediately. "It was daylight."

"Yes, and it wouldn't make sense if, after he killed her, he returned to the scene of the crime in the moonlight." Tony shook his head. "We're missing something. I believe Candy was too frightened to come out here in the dark, and I don't think it was a gardener she feared."

Theo made the calls to line up the cleaning crew for Alvin's house. She started with Nina. Her best friend sounded as if she'd run to answer the house telephone after she hadn't answered her cell phone.

"Oh, it's you, Theo."

"You sound disappointed." Theo guessed her friend had been expecting a different call. "Sorry I'm not Dr. Looks-so-good. How goes the romance?" The dentist shared a practice with Tony's brother Tiberius in Knoxville. Nina and the dentist had recently started dating, a situation Nina's children had mixed reactions to. The kids thought he was nice, but they still held out some hope their parents would reunite. Nina assured them a reconciliation was not a possibility.

Theo asked, "Does he kiss as good as he looks?"

Nina ignored her question. "What's up?"

"Cleaning the Tibbles house. We get to do our good deed for the year." Theo coughed. "It's going to be all kinds of fun."

"Oh, goodie. There's just nothing I'd rather do." Nina laughed. "I'm thinking we might need hazmat suits, or maybe the fire department can come out and hose us off when we're done."

Theo couldn't disagree with Nina's assumption they'd get dirty. If Candy kept house the way she dressed, they were in for a long, filthy, sweaty day. "Bring your favorite cleaning tools."

CHAPTER TWENTY-EIGHT

"Tony? Sheriff? This is Olivia Hudson." The woman hesitated.

"What did you see this time?" Tony knew the woman had a grand view of the entire valley. Her mountaintop home was both beautiful and private. She also had a telescope.

Merry laughter was his answer. "You must think I have my telescope up here so I can spy on my neighbors."

"I'm sure you have a few other things to do with your days." Olivia was an artist. Her landscape paintings of the area were breathtaking. "So, not just spying. Maybe painting and spying?"

"I think someone else is." She sighed. "More precisely, not painting, but another person is spying."

"What did you see?"

"Binoculars. A man with binoculars has been hanging out near Kwik Kirk's. I might not have noticed, but he drives a car identical to my mother's. It caught my eye."

Tony heard a thread of irritation in Olivia's voice and felt amused. "Afraid your mom was arriving for an unannounced visit?"

"Yes."

Always happy to hear it wasn't just *his* mom who had such an effect on her children, Tony pulled out a notebook. "Tell me about the car."

"It's an off-white Cadillac SUV. The iridescent pearl paint." Olivia talked more slowly. "The driver climbed out and had binoculars and was looking across the road toward Candy's house."

"Can you describe him?"

"Honestly, I can't even swear if it was a him or a her. Wearing the wide-brimmed hat and sunglasses, it could be anyone. Well, anyone of average size. I know it wasn't you, your brother Gus, Wade, or my husband. All four of you are too tall and too muscular."

"Anything else?"

"Yes. Later in the day, I went into town and was on my way home, and I saw the same car in front of me. It turned onto the dirt road on the ridge above the Tibbles house."

Tony found it annoying that everyone had seen the car or the man except the members of his department. "Thank you. Will you call if you see it again?"

"Certainly."

Tony didn't have enough information to satisfy his curiosity. He wanted to have the Cadillac pulled over and the identity of the driver ascertained. He'd ask his deputies to keep an eye out for it. He was sure it was Erikson, but he wanted proof. There were more questions he wanted to ask the botanist as well. Stealing plants was no less illegal than stealing anything else.

Still checking on Candy's blackmail victims, the ones they could identify without the list of her secret codes, Tony and Wade tracked down another name they'd picked up in their interviews. Stan-the-Snakeman. Stan was in his lean, clean-shaven, mid-summer state. Still as jolly as he'd be in a few months when he'd grow out his beard, gain weight, and morph into Santa Stan, he welcomed his visitors. The gap where two of his lower front teeth had been was filled with a wad of chewing gum. Parked in his driveway was his intensely yellow pickup with the snake logo on the side. It was as identifiable from a distance as Theo's SUV.

"Rumor says you drove by Candy's house on the first of every month and stopped by the mailbox." Tony couldn't talk to Stan without remembering his adventure over a year prior. It made his skin crawl a bit just to look at him. He hated snakes. "Blackmail?"

Stan's grin disappeared. He nodded.

"What was your code name?"

"T.S. You know, The Snakeman."

"Other than the reason you were paying blackmail, what was your relationship with Candy? Did you visit?" Tony couldn't picture Stan and Candy as a couple.

Stan shook his head. "No. I paid like I was supposed to, more for the boy's sake than Candy's. I don't believe the boy is mine. I, um, was dumb, but not stupid in my younger years, if you catch my meaning."

Tony did. "Improbable but not impossible for you to have fathered the boy."

"Yep." Stan studied the sky for a moment. "If the boy needs anything . . ."

"I'll let you know."

CHAPTER TWENTY-NINE

Of the possible men paying blackmail, Tony knew only a few by name. Calvin, Stan, and Claude Marmot. The list of blackmail payers was much longer. He really would like to find Candy's little pink code book.

He knew Theo and the rest of the clean-up ladies were already at Alvin's house. They wanted to get as much done before the day's expected high temperatures as they could. He dialed Theo's number and she answered her cell phone, but she sounded exasperated when she did so.

"What?"

Tony needed her help so he apologized. "I hate to bother you when you're having so much fun, but would you do me a favor?"

"That depends." Theo lowered her voice. "If it involves more rotting food, the answer is no, no, and absolutely not. Never. Not ever." She emphasized the "ever."

"You're lucky the hamburger meat is

gone." Tony went on to describe the aroma and the maggots in one of his glorious moments when descriptive words tripped off his tongue.

"Gag," Theo said. "All right, you win. What do you need?"

"A pink notebook about the size of a deck of cards. It has a white kitten on it and I'd be extremely grateful if you should find it."

"Hmm, how grateful are we talking here?"

Thinking Theo sounded a bit reluctant to help, Tony hesitated. What could he offer? "I'd paint your toenails again."

Theo laughed. "I only needed you to paint them once, and that was because I was too pregnant to even see my feet. How do I know you actually put polish on them?"

"I did. Well, whatever you want then." It wasn't until he disconnected the call that the concept of carte blanche kicked in, semi-terrorizing him. He couldn't begin to guess what Theo would make him do, but he wanted the code book badly enough to jump through any size hoop. He just hoped she'd find it.

Theo and the other five members of the clean-up crew had dressed in their grubbiest, and coolest, work clothes. The house stank so bad, the first thing they did was open every window. The stench was much worse than being too hot. Pulling on double industrial-strength gloves, they began. Each team had a box of extra-strong trash bags and a sponge and bucket of bleach mixed with heavy-duty detergent. They covered their noses and mouths with masks. Theo and Nina were a team, Martha and Emily Austin were a team, and two Flowers sisters, cousins of Blossom, Willow and Aspen were the third team. This was not a job for the older members of their group. Jane and her employee, Celeste, were babysitting the twins. The older ladies would step in later and arrange the yard sale.

Anything obviously trash, they tossed. That included every open food item. They carried a special hazardous waste container to collect Candy's drugs and medications. The idea was to scrub everything they didn't throw away. The dishwasher ran constantly, and so did the washing machine, at least after they removed the accumulated garbage from the appliances. Theo couldn't imagine using the dishwasher as a trash can, but maybe Candy should be congratulated for throwing something away, even if improperly. The house was filled with empty boxes, empty bags, and piles of mouse poop.

It gave Theo the creeps.

Added to Candy's junk, after the investigation, there was a fine dusting of fingerprint-powder residue or dirt on every surface in the house. Cleaning it all was not going to be a quick process.

At noon, Ruby's employee, Pinkie Millsaps, roared up on her motorcycle, delivering their lunch. The sixty-year-old grandmother had her gray hair pulled into a ponytail, tattoos of flowers and unicorns covering her arms, and was dressed in her traditional black leather pants and a vest. Like the Pied Piper, Pinkie led the workers up the gravel driveway and past the detached garage into the shade. Pinkie avoided the bags of garbage as she spread a picnic blanket for them and arranged their food. Then she climbed back on her motorcycle and roared away, promising to return to pick up after them.

The women cleaning had already filled numerous bags and put them out on the driveway for Claude. They were feeling proud they had completed cleaning the main level of the house, even if they had worn out a mop and killed the vacuum cleaner found in a closet, hidden behind more boxes. The poor thing had not been built for industrial-strength grime.

The women gathered around the bags of

food and sat outside in the shade, enjoying the fresh air. Even the sweltering temperature couldn't damper their enthusiasm for food.

"Have you found any treasures?" Nina bit into a thick sandwich and chewed enthusiastically.

"There's some nice antique glassware. I'd guess it belonged to Alvin's grandmother, maybe even his great-grandmother. If Alvin decides he wants to put it up for sale, I know several collectors who might be interested," Willow said. "It would probably fetch some decent money for him."

"I've found boxes and wrappings for some expensive items, but only the boxes." Martha examined her empty potato chip bag, her face registering disappointment. "A lot like this."

"I found some of those too." Willow sighed. "It's like she bought things but then forgot about them, or they weren't what she thought she was getting, and she kept the wrapping rather than take the time to throw it away."

"Nina and I found some clothes in the refrigerator." Theo waved a chip before popping it into her mouth. "They still had the store tags on them. Nice things that should sell fairly quickly in the yard sale." She chewed slowly, wondering how to learn about the notebook Tony wanted without giving out more information than necessary. "Have any of you found any personal items, things that might have actually meant something to her or to Alvin? Jewelry? Notebooks? Photographs?"

Five heads shook from side to side.

They finished eating, drank copious amounts of water, and headed inside to clean the upstairs rooms. Theo and Nina were the youngest ones, so they were assigned the attic.

Nina stood in the center of the attic, the only spot where she could straighten up without whacking her head on the ceiling. "Even the dust looks old up here." She pulled her mask back over her nose and mouth. "Let do it."

Theo hauled clothes and junk and boxes down the stairs and trotted up for more while Nina was methodically going through everything, separating it into piles. Keep, toss, and ask Alvin.

"Hmmph." Nina fumbled with an antique tobacco box. It slid out of her hands, crashing onto the floor, barely missing her toes. "Good gravy, that thing weighs a ton."

Intrigued, Theo crawled over and flipped up the latch. Gold coins gleamed through the dusty air. "Oh, my." The metal box was about a foot long and wide and maybe six inches deep. It wasn't full, but there were at least a hundred coins inside, some tiny and some the size of a fifty-cent piece. "Alvin's rich."

Nina picked up one of the tiny coins and read the date. "Eighteen hundred sixty-one. They're old."

"You can bet Candy didn't know about them." Theo pulled out her cell phone and pressed the number to connect her to Tony.

"I'd call that motive in a box, if anyone knew about them." Nina looked at various different-sized coins. Holding them up to the light, one at a time, she whispered, "They're beautiful."

"Tony," Theo began.

He interrupted her before she could say more. "Did you find the notebook?"

"No. Nina and I did find a box of gold coins, though. We're thinking of slipping a few out of the box and taking a trip to a spa, a very nice spa."

"A what?" Tony's voice boomed from the telephone and through the room. And then, "Gold?"

"Alvin's inheritance." Theo reached for a plastic lunch box. It was heavy for its size. "Wait a minute." She flipped the latch on the dark blue box with cartoon figures on the front. Alvin's name was written on the back. "Alvin's old lunch box is loaded with coins too. Will you come get these before Nina and I ditch our friends and family and run off to live in luxury, preferably someplace with no dust?" She sneezed several times in succession, drowning out most of Tony's reply.

Only a few minutes had passed before Tony and Wade arrived and climbed up the narrow stairs and into the low-ceilinged attic room. They paused at the top of the stairs and stared. Theo guessed the sight of the two incredibly dirty, sweaty women surrounded by piles of gleaming gold coins was what made Tony laugh.

"You two look like you've been prospecting for gold." After his initial view of the women, Tony didn't take his eyes from the treasure.

Wade whistled admiringly and reached down and picked a coin off the nearest stack. "That is some pretty coin." He started to straighten up, as if to examine it more closely, and whacked his head on the low ceiling. A muffled oath escaped as he quickly returned to his hunched position. "Oh man, my head hurts."

"Have you counted them?" Tony seemed struck by the beauty of the gold, not the monetary value of it.

Wade's experience made him continue to stay bent over in an uncomfortable stance, staring at the floor. Theo guessed it wouldn't take long before his back started screaming.

"It really is mesmerizing, isn't it?" Wade said.

"Sorry, you two don't get to keep any either. Yes, we've counted it, and we're turning the list over to Alvin." Nina gave the two men a mock frown and waved the paper in the dusty air. "I know neither of you would filch anything, but it's always nice to have a list."

Tony agreed wholeheartedly before he and Wade each grabbed a box and headed down the stairs.

Theo could hear them talking as they left.

"For lack of a better idea, we'll store the coins in the evidence locker until Alvin wants them. Or at least until all the legalities are sorted out," said Tony.

"Where do you suppose they all came from?" Wade's response fit Theo's own question.

Theo couldn't hear Tony's answer, but she did hear a few of the antique lovers on the second floor asking to examine the old tobacco box. It created a stir, but none of them learned what the boxes contained. "If Tony's not telling . . ." Theo looked at Nina.

"I know. Neither are we. Being sworn to secrecy has its drawbacks. I need a friend who gossips more than you do." Nina pulled her dust mask over her nose again. "Back to work."

Chapter Thirty

"You didn't know anything about the coins?" Tony studied Alvin. The boy looked better than he had the previous day, but still had the lost-puppy expression in his eyes. "There are quite a few of them."

"No." Alvin held the old lunch box and its valuable contents on his lap. "Grandpa said something one time about my future being held in the treasures of the past. He made a big deal about it at the time but never mentioned it again." His words trickled away. "Of course, it was years ago when he brought it up."

"That's all he said?" Tony didn't know what else he expected. Maybe for Grandpa to tell Alvin to search the attic in hard times.

"Yeah, I remember my mom coming into the room about then and Grandpa changing the subject."

Tony felt a glimmer of understanding. "So, your mom probably didn't know anything valuable was up in the attic."

Alvin shook his head. "Mom was *not* good with secrets." At his own words, Alvin started laughing. "That's like saying there's water in the ocean."

"I had hoped she might have kept her code book up there, but unless she could fly, she would have left footprints in the dust." Tony sighed. "My wife and her friend didn't find any kind of notebook like you described."

"Sheriff, Mayor Cashdollar is here." The disembodied voice came through the speaker.

"Send him on back, Rex." Tony glanced at Alvin. The boy suddenly looked overwhelmed. "But maybe ask him to walk slow."

A few moments later, Mayor Cashdollar tiptoed through the doorway. "Alvin?"

"We found money." Alvin swallowed hard, and tears glistened in his eyes. "I can pay for Mom to have a proper funeral."

"She was always going to have one of those." The mayor nodded a greeting to Tony, his attention focused on Alvin. "She was my best friend's beloved daughter and deserves to be treated as such."

They all sat in silence for a while, Alvin clutching his lunch box, Mayor Cashdollar leaning forward, his long arms resting on his knees and his hands clasped tightly together. Tony alternated between watching them and wondering how he could diplomatically get them out of his office.

Calvin broke the silence. "Have you thought about when you might want to have her service?"

"Tomorrow? The day after?" Alvin sounded like the lost child he was. "I don't know about these things, but would the day after be okay?"

"Yes, we'll have the funeral the day after tomorrow." Clearly realizing the boy needed advice, Calvin's professional demeanor kicked in. "How's ten o'clock?"

Alvin nodded but said no more, leaving the major decisions up to Calvin.

Theo was beginning to think she would never get enough water to drink. She gulped down three big glasses full almost the moment she made it out of the attic. The upstairs room was spotless, and all of its contents were either under lock and key or spread out in the living room.

Finally rehydrated, she and Nina, having had the smallest area to clean up, trudged back upstairs to help the others.

On the second floor, there were three

bedrooms and a bathroom. Two bedrooms were currently being scrubbed, one crew per room. One of the masked cleaners called out, "You two can either take the other bedroom or the bathroom."

Theo and Nina exchanged glances. "Dust or mildew?" Theo asked.

"What the heck," said Nina as she snapped the wrist opening on her left glove. "Let's go for the bathroom. We've done our share of dust abatement."

"Oh, goodie." Theo pulled her mask back over her face. "Nothing like a little sweat and mildew in the afternoon. Maybe I should go check on Jane."

"Not your baby girls?" Nina shook her head and made a tisking sound. "What kind of mother are you?" Knowing Theo was a devoted mother made it impossible for her to keep a straight face. "I think you're just looking for an excuse to ditch me and our lovely project."

Theo didn't disagree but acted wistful. "Celeste is there for Jane's backup. By the time I can go collect them, the girls will be spoiled rotten, if they're not already." Theo glanced down just in time to move her foot before a giant cockroach scampered up her leg. "Oh, ick. I hate those things."

Nina leaned forward a bit, even as she

took a step backward. "Look, it's wearing a hard hat and a tool belt." Armed with her industrial-sized spray bottle filled with bleach, Nina zapped it. When it paused, she crushed it with her foot. "Keep an eye out for the grieving relatives."

"That's nasty." Theo felt a shiver of disgust run through her. "You know, it's probably only one member of an extended family. I think we'd better have the exterminator pay a visit before anyone moves in here." She reached into the medicine cabinet and began dropping its contents into their biohazard bucket or the trash bag, depending on what it was. "We're going to use a lot of bags. I think some of this stuff belonged to Candy's parents."

Nina's response was muffled.

Theo turned to look and started laughing. Nina had pulled a plastic shower cap over her auburn hair and donned a swim mask and snorkel she'd obviously borrowed from her kids. Behind her, bathroom foam was sliding down the filthy tiles like something escaping from a test tube. It reminded Theo of some grade-D science fiction movies she'd watched. She lowered her voice like a radio announcer. "Tell me, Professor, have you found any signs of life in your underwater laboratory?"

Nina nodded and made swimming motions.

Theo went back to tossing Candy's garbage, including the mildewed shower curtain. She set aside whole bars of soap, an unopened bottle of shampoo, and lotion. Maybe Alvin would want these items, or maybe he'd donate them to the community shelter. They found some more of Candy's drugs stashed in the toilet tank.

By the time they'd tossed the trash and scrubbed every inch of the room, they were well past filthy and sweaty. Towels and linens they took downstairs to the washing machine. Almost everything else not permanently attached to the floor, and lightweight enough to pick up, was headed to the dump. Theo almost felt sorry for Claude. She didn't know how he had things arranged in his domain. The man lived for garbage and was even more fond of recycling, or repurposing. She hoped there was a special area for toxic refuse like this. It was dirtier than dirt.

One of the volunteers, Willow, had brought along a carpet and upholstery cleaning machine. The poor machine slurped sludge for hours, helping remove years of food stains, yard dirt, and spots no one wanted to get near or examine very carefully. While its owner worked in the first two bedrooms, the extra woman, Aspen, joined Theo and Nina in the third bedroom.

Looking at its contents, Theo guessed the room had been Alvin's while he lived here. They carefully cleaned and then set aside all of the old toys and games. A bookcase filled with early readers, a trophy from a spelling contest, toys from kid-meal boxes. Typical, normal stuff. Theo checked everything carefully. No pink notebook.

Under the bed, they found another stash of pills. "Pretty brazen, hiding them in Alvin's room."

Theo glanced out the now spotless window and saw Alvin's old truck slip into a parking space at Kwik Kirk's. He headed across the highway toward the house on foot. For a moment, Theo was confused. She laughed at herself when she realized their mountain of garbage was taking up a fair amount of the front yard. Alvin couldn't even park on his own driveway. Time to call Claude.

Theo hurried down the stairs to intercept Alvin. She wanted a chance to talk to him before he walked into a house he might no longer recognize. They arrived at the front porch at the same time. Theo said, "Hey, Alvin."

"M— Theo," he hesitated. "Your husband told me about the coins."

"I'm sure they'll make your future plans easier." Theo couldn't tell from his expression what he might be thinking. "Your grandparents had to be collecting them for quite a while."

"I probably would never have looked inside those boxes." Alvin chewed on the corner of his lip. He looked dazed and lost. "Thank you. Thank all of you for doing this."

"You're welcome." Theo remained in the doorway. "We've pretty well torn up the place but it's your house, do you want to come inside?"

Alvin watched one of the ladies dumping a bucket of water, thickened with dirt, onto some old rose bushes. "I think I'll wait and let it be a surprise."

"Are you going to work in your garden?"

"No, ma'am. I just wanted to thank you for cleaning the inside of the house." A faint twinkle lit his eyes. "I'm sure I won't recognize it. My mom wasn't much for washing things."

"Orvan's almost back to his normal irritating self." Ruth Ann slipped the brush back into the tiny bottle of sky-blue fingernail polish.

"What's Doc Grace have to say?" Tony had almost forgotten the old man's collapse. Out of sight, out of mind. With everything else happening in the county, Orvan was definitely out of mind.

"Grace says he needs to eat every day, and drink some clean water before he sucks down any of his moonshine." Ruth Ann gestured to some papers neatly stacked on her desk. "Do you realize how many of our county's citizens, particularly children and old folks, aren't eating every day?"

"I do on some level, but I'm not sure I understand why they don't. There are all kinds of meal programs, right?" Disturbed by the idea of anyone going hungry, Tony massaged the back of his neck. "I'm always seeing the volunteers carrying containers of food to be delivered out of the community kitchen, and I've seen what is served at the senior center. It's free, or all but, depending on your ability to pay."

Ruth Ann nodded. "The programs are available, but you have to sign up for the deliveries or come into town. Maybe we could become a stop for the mobile pantry. Our parking lot could handle it." She gently blew on her fingernails. "I'll bet there is even a program to have someone come to your house and do light housekeeping or help you shower or take you to see the doctor, if you need help. If you know where to look."

Tony knew of some counties with programs organizing volunteers to check in with designated seniors or other residents who lived alone. They provided a safety check and some social interaction. He'd been toying with the idea of starting something similar here in Park County, but it needed a coordinator from his department. "Do you know where to look?" He held his breath. Waiting and watching.

"Yes." Ruth Ann gave him a happy smile. "Are you asking me if I could or if I would like to coordinate the program?"

"Both." Tony mentally ran through his office's budget. There was not a spare dime. "It would mean lots more work for you and no more pay. We simply don't have the resources." He sat down on the chair next to Ruth Ann's desk, feeling an odd combination of hope and defeat. "It could seriously cut into your manicures, but with your law degree and the inside information you glean here, you might be able to save, or at the very least improve, any number of lives."

"One class I took should have been called

'red tape and bureaucracy,' because we dealt with it constantly. I earned an A," Ruth Ann said. "I've gotten tired of watching people like Orvan slide into the cracks."

"Did you know he was in such bad shape?" Tony hated to think someone had known and ignored the situation.

"No. If I had, I'd have told you or one of the doctors." Tears welled in her dark eyes. "He's a rotten old buzzard, but I love him. He's my biggest fan."

Tony believed her. "It sounds like you've been planning this for a while. Why didn't you mention it?"

"I would have." She sighed. "But until recently, when Walter began improving, it gave me something to think about besides him, his health, and us and our own problems. And, to be honest, for a while I thought we might have to move away from here. It's only in just the last few weeks that I felt confident of our situation and our ability to remain here."

"And with Walter better, his mama went back to her home." As Tony remembered it, Ruth Ann had celebrated her mother-in-law's departure by bringing in cookies and cupcakes for a party.

"That too." Ruth Ann's dark eyes sparkled.

"I'd love to give you the volunteer organization assignment." Tony laughed. "I'm game if you're game. It will take a while for word to get around, and it will require time to recruit volunteers and contact the residents in need. It's your program. You set it up however you think will work the best."

Her smile lit up the room and lifted some of the weight off his shoulders. "Tell me what you need, and I'll try to get it."

Ruth Ann ignored her single remaining unpainted fingernail, screwed the lid on the polish jar, and dropped it into the trash can. "Let's get started and see what we can do."

Blossom arrived at the Law Enforcement Center with a fresh, warm apple pie, a gift-wrapped box, and a shopping bag filled with homemade caramel corn. She stood in front of Tony's desk and stared at the floor, her lower lip jutted forward. "I'm sorry."

Tony's stomach rumbled. He was hungry, and the smell of the pie was tantalizing. He wasn't prepared to forgive her for the gossip firestorm yet, but it was inevitable that he would. "What does Kenny think about your bringing me pies? And now, what do you have, packages and caramel corn? It has to stop, Blossom."

"Kenny says he'd prefer I not cook so

much for you and so I'll take the corn and the gift back." Her head moved slowly side to side. "Won't you keep the pie?"

"You know I can't resist." Tony took the offered pie and put it on his desk. "I get plenty to eat at home, and I can buy a pie you bake at Ruby's. Don't you think that's a better way for me to eat your cooking?"

"I guess." Blossom's shoulders rose slightly. Tears filled her bulbous eyes and overflowed, streaming down her face and dripping onto her blouse. She made no attempt to stop them or wipe her face. She groped behind her until she located the chair and collapsed onto it.

Glad the chair hadn't broken, Tony handed her a wad of tissues. He thought she was acting like an oversized three-year-old. "Mop up." He glanced through the doorway. Ruth Ann stared openly, her mouth ajar. He gestured for Ruth Ann to join them. "This is not about pie, is it?"

Blossom shook her head and blew her nose. Ignoring the trash can he offered, she placed the used tissue on her lap and used another one. By the time she seemed calm enough to talk, she had five tissues lined up in a tidy row.

"I hate her." Blossom's entire body shuddered with the force of her statement.

"Her who?" Tony sincerely hoped she wasn't going to say "Theo."

She didn't.

"That ex-wife of Kenny's. She's awful!" Blossom blew her nose again. "She don't want me near her girls or Kenny or even Miss Cotton."

Hearing the problem had to do with her love life, Tony was relieved as well as concerned. "Isn't Miss Cotton *your* dog?"

Blossom's head bobbed. "But 'cause Kenny's little girls love her so much, she wants my dog." The sobs morphed into a wail. "She says she's getting a lawyer to stop me from — what'd she call it? Alien affection. And I said to Kenny she's won and we can't get married, and I gave him back his ring." She began crying again even harder.

Ruth Ann delivered another handful of tissues, pressing them into Blossom's hand. Keeping a tissue for herself, she carefully cleaned the used ones from Blossom's lap and tossed them into the trash can.

Tony frowned. "Don't let her run your life." He floundered in the face of her obvious heartbreak.

"Blossom." Ruth Ann stepped forward and patted the larger woman's shoulder. "She can't sue you for alienation of affection. Kenny divorced her long before you

379

two became an item, didn't he?"

Blossom managed a nod.

Ruth Ann said, "Do you love Kenny?"

Blossom nodded vigorously.

"Then you need to talk to Kenny." Ruth Ann had Blossom up on her feet and headed for the doorway. "Tell him exactly why you gave him the ring back and kiss and make up. Kenny's a good man. He'll understand your side of this."

Tony waited until the women were out of sight before taking the pie to the kitchen. He cut a big slab, slapped it on a plate, and shoveled a bite into his mouth. Instead of the normal exquisite flavor, all he could taste was salt. He spat it into the sink and washed his mouth out with water. "That's nasty."

In her heartbroken state, Blossom must have switched the salt and sugar measurements. He called Ruby to suggest she check the café's pies for edibility.

Theo had days where no one seemed aware of her relationship to the county sheriff. This was not one of them. Every person she'd seen since she left the house had a comment or a question about Tony, his job, the recent rash of crimes, and if Theo was withholding information they'd be interested to hear. She was heartily tired of it. When timid Deirdre tapped on her work-room door, Theo almost yelled at her.

"Theo?" Deirdre whispered. "Can I talk to you?"

Theo sighed. It wasn't like Deirdre to invade her space. The woman was usually so quiet it was easy to forget she was in the building. She was younger than the senior group and older than the new quilters. "Come in."

Deirdre sidled in, glancing from side to side and barely opening the door wide enough for her to pass through. "I'm sorry to bother you, but I hope you can help me."

"Let's sit down." Theo herded her to the window seat. She did not offer her anything to drink or sit down herself.

"It's about my husband's cousin." Deirdre exhaled loudly as if getting a load off her mind.

Theo waited. Silence. "What about him?"

"He's been acting weirder than usual. I mean, there's always been something wrong with him, if you know what I'm saying, but it's getting worse." Deirdre's hands floated in the air and waved about like they were pushed by a gentle breeze, but no words ac-companied their movement.

Theo blinked, waiting for the meaning of

Deirdre's story to become clear. "And?" She wanted Deirdre to leave.

"Well, you're the sheriff's wife. Don't you think he should know?" The mouse snapped at Theo. "Honestly?"

"What *are* you talking about?" Defeated and curious, Theo sat down next to her.

Deirdre studied the floor in silence. After a couple of moments, she exhaled sharply. "Oh, I guess I didn't tell you, did I?"

Theo shook her head. "Try again."

"He — that is my husband's cousin — has been staying in the tool shed on the back of our property ever since his wife ran off with a man named Bob. I've never liked him but, honestly, he's gotten way worse lately than he ever was before. I know he does drugs, but I don't know what kind. And then just the other day, I saw him drinking gasoline out of the mower can. Who drinks gasoline?" Her voice rose to a near wail.

Theo knew enough of the Bob/Not Bob story to realize this truly was something Tony should know. She called him on her cell phone, gave him the gist of what she had learned, and handed Deirdre the phone so she could answer his questions. Her recitation to Tony was a duplicate of the one she'd given Theo. She still seemed more impressed by his beverage choice of gasoline than his probable vicious bashing of total strangers.

Because Deirdre was so timid, Theo made sure she didn't run home to try to smooth out any family rift and get hurt herself.

As the two women waited for news, Theo's good manners broke her down, and soon she gave her visitor something to drink and threw in a mini-demonstration on the easiest way to quickly cut lots of the same-sized squares.

About a half hour passed before Tony called Theo back. "We've found him, thanks to you and Deirdre. He was passed out on his cot, and the hammer and wrench are in plain sight. It won't take very long to transport him to the jail. Your friend can return home whenever she wants to."

"That was quick." Theo was surprised, but pleased.

Tony laughed. "It isn't every day my wife calls with the solution to a puzzle like this. Thank you, sweetheart."

Theo thought a box of good chocolates would be a nice reward, but she'd settle for some good old-fashioned gratitude. Moments later she had shepherded Deirdre out of her office and gone back to work.

In a good mood after arresting one of the

county's problems, Tony escorted Ruth Ann to the senior center. They wanted to survey the citizens who participated in the center's activities and food service. Lunch was over, but there was a cluster of women at a table waiting to have their fingernails and toenails cared for.

Across the room three elderly men sat playing a board game. Each of them had a walker parked nearby.

A spry-looking silver-haired man came from the kitchen area, attracting the attention of the women in the room. He shied sideways a bit and kept his eyes trained on the floor.

"Have you ever seen him before?" Ruth Ann whispered to Tony.

"No." Tony watched the women watching the older man. It was the way Daisy looked when her food bowl came out of the pantry. "The way the ladies are acting, I'd guess he's someone they want to meet, up close and personal."

Ruth Ann whispered. "I've decided to start with him."

"Why?" Tony didn't care where the work began.

"Because he is clearly here by himself and is new to the community." Ruth Ann stepped closer to the new man. "What's your name, and have you got a minute?"

The man's gaze flickered from Ruth Ann, to Tony's chest and badge, and moved back to the floor. "Sure, I'm Cecil."

While Ruth Ann began her questions about what he thought would improve the seniors' overall lifestyle and condition, Tony watched the elderly women, all of whom were keeping tabs on the new guy. They reminded him of sharks he'd seen one time, swimming in circles, checking out a piece of bait. Tony leaned forward and whispered, "Cecil, would you prefer to talk outside?"

"Yessir. I think you've got a dandy idea." He led Ruth Ann and Tony into the fresh air. Once on the sidewalk, he straightened his spine and smiled more naturally. "The ladies are lonely."

A pleasant-looking woman stopped her car near them, almost parking on the side-walk. She climbed from it carrying a plate of cookies. "Oh, Cecil, these are for you."

"Thank you, but I can't accept." Cecil smiled but shoved his hands into the back pockets of his jeans. In a voice barely audible to Tony, who was only a couple of feet away, he said, "Never, ever, accept food from a widow if you're single."

"Really?" Tony hadn't heard of the rule. To be frank, he hoped he would never have to find out for himself. He liked being married.

"Yessir. I did back in Kansas. It was just one time, and then I like to never got rid of my admirer." Cecil glanced up, meeting Tony's eyes. "She tracked me to my house. Knocked on my windows. Sent me notes. Put boxes of cookies by my door." He glanced over his shoulder. "I moved here to be closer to my daughter, but mostly to get away from all that attention."

Tony was surprised by the gentleman's intensity. "You don't enjoy socializing?"

"Oh, yes, I do. I like to play cards. I even like to dance a bit, but I ain't lookin' for a woman who'll likely as not yammer at me twelve hours a day. Life's too short."

At the request of Mayor Cashdollar, Tony and Wade attended the very private funeral of Hydrangea Flowers Jackson, in uniform. After the debacle at the visitation, only immediate family was invited to the service in the funeral home chapel. It was a subdued group — a couple of older attendees sported bruised faces and arms, probably due more to the fragile skin of the elderly than the violence of the fight.

The procession to the cemetery grew larger as it traveled through the gates. Once on public ground, it was suddenly well attended. Hordes of curious, some mourning, citizens joined in. The true mourners sniffled and stayed fairly quiet until the last amen. Then, chattering like small birds, they headed for the home belonging to one of the remaining sisters, Gladiola and Tulip, for the post-funeral party.

Tony watched as Calvin politely held the limousine door open for the sisters. Each woman paused before climbing in and offered the mayor a sincere apology. Calvin merely nodded his acceptance. All watching might assume he had come to terms with the fiasco in his place of business, but Tony had seen a copy of the bill. Words were not going to replace cold hard cash.

The twin husbands lagged behind the sisters but did not climb into the limousine. They walked side by side, moving slowly, leaning on each other. They paused near the group of women surrounding Calvin. Tony thought they might not have been invited to the post-funeral party. When Calvin reached into his pocket and handed one of the old gents a small pink notebook with a white cat on the front, Tony's attention became totally focused on them. He stepped toward the men but encountered a pack of anxious women.

"My sister had two husbands," Tulip shrieked. "And I've got none. Do you think that's fair?" The feisty woman was so frail she wobbled in spite of her walker.

"If you hurry, maybe you can snag one or both of them."

"What's the hurry?"

"You're not getting any younger and neither are they." Her elderly companion laughed. "I always thought her husband had a bad memory — not that he was two people."

Before Tony could extricate himself from the ladies and reach the twins, they had slipped through the cemetery gates and vanished, hidden by a stream of antique vehicles rattling down the road.

Tony decided to give the elderly widowers a few hours to themselves. Now that he knew they possessed Candy's code book, he could let them grieve for a bit. He'd be surprised if the twins knew as much about it as he did.

Mystery Quilt
Putting it all together

Layout — place the two Block One's on design wall or flat surface, one above the other. Place one Block Two on both sides of each Block One. Arrange a row of three Block Two's (yes, it does sound funny but that's what it is) above and another row of Block Two's below the center. Sew together into rows and the rows into finished quilt center.

Measure through the center, length and width. Cut 2 of the 2 1/2" wide border strips (B) the lengthwise measurement. Sew one on each side of the quilt top. Press to (B).

Cut 2 of the 2 1/2" border strips (B) the width (before border added). Sew 2 1/2" square of (A) on each end of both border strips. Sew one on top and bottom of quilt. Press to border.

Repeat process with 5" strips of (A) and 5' squares of (B)

Quilt as desired.

Bind with remaining 2 1/2" strips of (B).

Chapter Thirty-One

"Sheriff Abernathy, this is Deputy Sheriff O'Brien." The county's name was lost in transmission. "I think we've got a little problem."

The voice came through the receiver along with some howling wind and static, making Tony think O'Brien was calling outdoors using his radio or cell phone. "What's up?"

"You know a Kenny Baines?"

"Yes." There was more static, but Tony was sure he understood the words "woman killed" and "Blossom." He couldn't help feeling alarmed. "What's happening there, O'Brien?" Tony tried to visualize where O'Brien's county might be. It was not any of their immediate neighbors because he knew, or thought he did, all of the nearby law enforcement officers. "Where are you, and what is Blossom doing there?" He spoke his thoughts out loud.

"She's not with me." O'Brien said. "We've

got a traffic fatality here, a Mrs. Baines, and there is a note in the car from your Ms. Flowers addressed to the Baines woman. Ms. Flowers sounds royally upset in her note about someone trying to steal the affections of Kenny Baines. While there is not a direct threat mentioned, it sure sounds like one to me. I presume both of these Baineses are connected?"

"Divorced." Tony couldn't say for sure that Blossom would never kill someone, but he found it hard to believe she would be able to engineer a car accident. "How'd you know Blossom belongs here?"

"Return address on the letter. It's not like a thirteen-year-old sending anonymous letters. Ms. Flowers is not hiding out."

"What happened to your woman?" Tony could imagine Blossom being angry and pushing Kenny's ex-wife, but he couldn't picture Blossom intentionally killing anyone.

"She lost control of her vehicle. Crashed into a guard rail, spun around, and hit it again." O'Brien sighed. "It could be a simple accident, but I don't usually find hate mail at accident sites. The woman was not wearing her seat belt and appeared to be clutching her cell phone. Maybe a telephone threat led to an accident or even suicide. Maybe I'm watching too much late-night television."

Tony considered a car crash probably accidental. It would be impossible for Blossom to be two places at one time, but he felt bad nonetheless. Kenny's ex-wife might have been nine kinds of trouble for Kenny and Blossom, but she was the mother of two small girls. "Can you tell who she was talking with?"

There was a pause while O'Brien checked the cell phone. "According to the call log, she sent a text message to your Ms. Flowers about the same time as she hit the rail."

"Texting while driving sounds like an accident looking for a place to happen."

"I agree." O'Brien's voice was sour. "Unless something else turns up to change my mind, I'm going with stupid accident, but you might want to chat with Ms. Flowers about making threats."

Tony was relieved. He was even more pleased that the accident had not occurred in Park County. It was not his department's responsibility to investigate. He had more than enough to fill his time.

He'd barely completed the call when the next one came in. This one he had expected. The TBI lab. Mike had driven the wrench and hammer removed from their suspected attacker to the lab and begged them to squeeze in a bit of testing on the tool surfaces. In spite of the existing heavy workload, their newest technician, Kiefer, had agreed. Tony suspected the man was as curious as he was.

Kiefer began talking almost the instant their phones were in contact. "Sheriff, I do have some positive news. Positive in that the results are positive, not that you'll necessarily like them. I really don't have any information about what you want."

"It's okay." Tony laughed, enjoying the man's enthusiasm. "Quit tap dancing around the news, Kiefer, I'm very interested in what you've learned."

"Well, these are preliminary results but some of the blood and skin and hairs on the wrench and hammer appear to be positive matches to samples you had labeled with full names and secondary identifiers, 'Not Bob' and 'hitchhiker.' I can tell you they were not the only blood and skin specimens we found on the items." Kiefer paused to breathe. "However, we'll keep the results on file, so if you find more victims, we might be able to have more matches."

Tony was very pleased the evidence matched the presumed attacker, currently waiting in the jail, to their victims.

Tony was not as pleased with the news of

additional blood types and hair and tissue samples. Somewhere out there, whether in Park County or somewhere else, other people had been attacked by the same man with perhaps the same level of ferocity. Tony considered the possibility of searching for other victims, maybe still alive but not reported missing, to be the stuff of nightmares. He made a note to himself. "Find out if there are others."

Kiefer sounded like he was prepared to chatter all afternoon.

Tony interrupted him. "Did you find anything on either item matching our other case?"

"No, sir. Not a hair, fiber, or spot on them belonged to either of the Tibbles, mother or son." Kiefer spoke with assurance. "And there are no signs that any attempt to clean either tool was made, ever."

"A man can dream." Tony wasn't surprised. "Thank you for your help."

"I'm serving tea at four, Sheriff. I expect you to be here and bring the good-looking deputy. Not the girl." Mrs. Fairfield's voice boomed through the receiver.

Tony did not recall having made a date to visit the woman. "I'm sorry." He turned it

394

into a question. "Why are you expecting me?"

Mrs. Fairfield's voice lowered fractionally. "You said you'd like to meet my husband. He'll be joining us for tea."

"What's the address?" Tony didn't expect to share food with a dead man, but the woman did know how to pique a man's curiosity. He was positive he'd have to fire Wade or lock him in a cell to keep him from coming along if he got wind of the invitation.

The morning roll call was just about to start when Tony had received the invitation, or more precisely, a summons, to tea. "Have you all paid a professional visit to Mrs. Fairfield's home?"

Everyone nodded.

"And, *is* her husband in a glass coffin?"

His question was met with shaking heads, lifted eyebrows, obvious curiosity, or disapproval. But one face suddenly glowed with discovery. Sheila whispered almost to herself. "I'll bet that's what it was."

"What?" More voices than just Tony's asked the question.

"She's got this long box on table legs sitting along one wall in the living room. It looks really top-heavy for furniture, and there's a floral cloth, like a scarf, edged with long fringe covering the top." Sheila whispered, "I can't wait to hear more about it."

Tony watched as Ruth Ann took on her new responsibility with charm, dedication, and the enthusiasm of a professional matchmaker. She might even describe the task in the same terms. One at a time, she planned to match a person with a volunteer. The two needed to be compatible. It was especially important to be sure each party would feel comfortable sharing time and personal information with the other.

Ruth Ann notified the senior center and encouraged them to help with the project. Most of those needing a volunteer were not people who could, or would, go to the center, but many of those who did would be able to help her make lists. She put out the call to churches, clubs, and civic organizations, asking not only for volunteers, but for recommendations of neighbors or individuals in need. And money. She hoped to be able to supply old cell phones to those who could not afford them. Simple phones, no bells or whistles, but ones that could connect to 911 and possibly save a life.

Tony wasn't surprised when Orvan Lundy became Ruth Ann's first project. He was very surprised when she matched Orvan with her own husband, Walter. "Is it wise to have your husband and boyfriend comparing notes?"

Ruth Ann winked at him. "I was thinking they'll always have something, or someone, wonderful to talk about."

"I won't allow dueling in my county." Tony tried to look stern.

"Oh, please." Ruth Ann couldn't suppress a chuckle. "Can't you just see it? Orvan and Walter, dueling pistols at dawn in dense fog, under the giant magnolia tree in the park. Spanish moss." She sighed. "How romantic."

Tony relaxed back in his chair and closed his eyes, picturing tiny, wizened, and gray Orvan in his ragged overalls facing off against Walter, who was twice Orvan's height, half his age, and had skin the color of caramels. "We don't have Spanish moss."

"It was an entertaining vision while it lasted." Ruth Ann rose to leave. "For your information, Walter and Orvan get along fine. It was a little difficult to find a match, because Orvan doesn't have telephone service, but Walter said he wouldn't mind, and I quote, 'Taking food up to the old buzzard's roost.' "

Tony smiled. One down. Tony hadn't realized the level of concern he had been experiencing and was ashamed he hadn't fully recognized the tenuous condition of some of their citizens until it looked like help had arrived.

Tony and Wade stopped by the Fairfield home a few hours before their tea-time invitation had suggested. In case Mr. O'Hara was interested in meeting Mrs. Fairfield, Tony was going to offer to supply the pig farmer with her contact information.

"It's rude to come early." Their hostess frowned as she opened her front door to them.

Mrs. Fairfield had her hair wrapped into old-fashioned pin curls nailed to her scalp with bobby pins. If Tony's mom didn't do the same with hers, he'd have had no idea what she'd done to her head. It looked painful. "I apologize. We can't come later."

Wade smiled gallantly. "So sorry."

The sight of the handsome young man giving her his very best smile melted the ice in Mrs. Fairfield's attitude. "Come in then."

The moment they entered the living room, Tony realized Sheila had been right. Except the furniture in question did not sit along the wall, but had been moved into the middle of the room, and the fringed shawl was turned back to expose the dearly departed's face. A white damask tablecloth was spread on the bottom half of the coffin and was set for a formal tea with an antique silver service.

Wade gulped several times before vanishing outside for a few moments.

Tony couldn't think what to say. His mind went blank and he forgot why he stopped by her home. He backed toward the open door.

Speaking wasn't necessary. Mrs. Fairfield chattered about everything going on in town. Then she patted the coffin, about where the gentleman's chest would be. "He never was much of a talker. So really, it's not much different since he passed."

Leaving Mrs. Fairfield complaining about their manners, Tony drove out to the Jackson house with Wade as his passenger. They turned off the highway a little beyond Kwik Kirk's, drove past the pig farm and the Mc-Mahon place, and just about dead-ended into a mountain. The house, the earthly residence of the late Hydrangea Flowers Jackson, was over a hundred years old but in pretty good condition. It had a new roof and the ladder-back chairs on the front porch were in pristine condition. Three of the chairs sat in a row. An old man sat in each of the end chairs, leaving the center chair empty. Hydrangea's chair.

"Tell me about your wedding." Tony had already extended his formal sympathy speech.

"I married Hydrangea when she was seventeen." Tears welled in the old man's eyes. "The purtiest woman I ever saw."

Tony couldn't help thinking about his twin girls. He certainly didn't want them sharing a spouse. "And your name is?"

"U.Z." His voice trembled. "Ulysses Zebulon."

"We're twins." The other brother spoke. "I'm also called U.Z. for Ulysses Zacharias, and I married her on the same day. We all eloped. Went to two counties and had two ceremonies." He smiled. "It was a glorious day. We got home and wrote all the names in the family Bible."

"It would be harder for you to get away with that these days. Computers, more questions of identification. Passports." Tony fell silent. He wasn't going to ask why, but he wanted to know.

Wade studied the empty chair. "No one knew?"

"No," U.Z. the first replied. "When we married, this was the end of the road. We used horses and wagons to get up here, and there was no pavement. We farmed a bit, growing tobacco and corn, kept a few hogs, and lived a quiet, simple life."

U.Z. the second picked up the story. "Hydrangea spent at least one day a week with her sisters, riding a mule down the hill, and later drove herself in an automobile. The cousins canned fruit together and sewed or just sat and talked, but Hydrangea never told them about the two of us. We knew it was not right, what we were doing."

"And no children?"

U.Z. the second shook his head. "She lost several before they was born. Doctor said there weren't anything she could do different, but she did spread love on her nephews and nieces."

"How did no one know?"

"I worked in town and U.Z. the second worked the farm."

"But everyone knew you." Wade mumbled. "Well, thought they did. Saw you at events, at church."

"We alternated Sunday's at church." U.Z. the first broke in. "Religion's important, you know. And all them massive Flowers family gatherings, it was a relief for us not to have to attend but half of them."

U.Z. the second nodded vigorously. "You seen the way they was at the funeral home?

401

Lawsy, the older women are a tough bunch. Our Hydrangea was a gentle soul."

"What about the pink book?" Tony saw nothing but grief and devotion to their shared spouse on the old men's faces. "The one Calvin Cashdollar handed you."

"She come home with it one afternoon, just days before her death." U.Z. number one reached into his shirt and retrieved it. "Said she took it from a neighbor's burn pile and hid it in her treasure bag. Rescued it."

"She wouldn't put it down." U.Z. number two ran a shaking hand over his face, wiping away the tears. "So we thought if it was so dear to her, maybe she should carry it with her to beyond, along with her Bible."

"Mr. Cashdollar was powerful mad after the viewing." U.Z. number one cut in. "He said he did keep her Bible with her and later he said he'd bury her and we could have a private service, but there was no way he was going to allow the family to destroy his business." The old man wheezed as he finished his statement.

"So we had a few people at the church and the burial." U.Z. number two picked up the story. "Mr. Cashdollar handed us the pink book because it got knocked out of the casket and onto the floor during the fight, and he didn't find it until later."

"I was there. I don't believe I've ever witnessed a fight quite like it before. May I see the book?" A gnarled, shaking hand held it where he could take it. Tony flipped through the pink book, feeling his heart beat faster as he read through the names. It was the solution to their puzzle. Candy was smarter than anyone had given her credit for. "Thank you for this."

Tony looked at Wade. "Let's have another little conversation with Kirk. I'll drop you off so you can get your car. Meet me at the convenience store in ten minutes."

It was closer to eighteen minutes by the time Wade walked into the store by his side. The antique cars were headed back to wherever they'd come from and created a traffic snag when they all stopped for gasoline and snacks on their way.

Tony watched Kirk handing a credit card receipt to his customer even as he checked the movements of others nearby. "If he didn't kill her himself, I'll bet he saw the killer, whether he realizes it or not."

Wade nodded. "I agree. Kirk keeps a close eye on his customers and his store. He has to know when someone leaves a vehicle at the store and walks across the road to visit

Candy."

"It's quieter out here in the winter, but I don't think I've ever seen it without a customer." Tony absently tugged on the neck of the protective vest under his shirt, hoping to let in a little cooler air. It didn't help much. At least the store was air-conditioned. Kirk was expecting them and had a pair of security recordings set up for them to watch.

They joined Kirk in his office. The two screens were a bit fuzzy, but it was possible to identify features and license plates. People coming and going. In and out of cars, shopping, pumping gas. "Wait a minute." Tony leaned forward. "If you didn't see the mustache and beard on that guy," he said, pointing to a ponytailed customer walking out the door, "From the back would you immediately think male or female?"

"Depends on the body shape." Wade's eyes sparkled. "Although my first thought would probably be female."

Tony nodded. "Both genders. All shapes and sizes. Did we just double our suspect pool?"

Wade said, "I remember when I took the law enforcement aptitude test, there was a series of sketches, and the object was to recognize people from an assortment of pictures using different hairstyles and glasses or no glasses. It's tricky to look past the features easily changed by something like a mustache."

Feeling like they were onto something important, Tony studied the people in the store and wandering outside. "So, maybe you're an older person or have poor vision, or just get a glance at a person, you might get it wrong." Tony glanced at Wade.

Wade pushed his sunglasses onto the top of his head. "I'm thinking I've seen quite a few bodies from the rear that could belong to either gender and not all of them had a ponytail, but longish hair."

"A woman carrying some extra weight, a ponytail, and tattoos. Like Pinkie Millsaps or Santhe Flowers."

"Or a man who sometimes wears his hair in a ponytail, and sometimes doesn't." Wade smiled and paused the playback. "And is married to this woman."

Tony smiled. "Duke McMahon."

CHAPTER THIRTY-TWO

"How much did you know about the coins?" Tony guessed they were the catalyst and decided to ask Duke about them in an informal setting, Duke's family hardware store, but first he determined the man was unarmed.

Duke McMahon frowned, twitched, then sagged, leaning against the counter. He looked defeated. "My dad and Candy's dad were friends. They went through a period where they were all into investing in the future. Gold and other coins were something they felt strongly about." Duke snuffled into his handkerchief. "I went along once on their buying trip. They'd drive all the way into the city, buy a gold coin with their whole cash-stash, and take it home and lock it up somewhere safe." He stuck his lower lip out in a pout. "We didn't even stop for lunch."

"Does your dad still have his coin collection?" Wade stood between Duke and the door.

"Yeah, as far as I know." Duke narrowed his eyes and managed to look insulted, like someone else was guiltier than he was. "Would you steal from your folks when some junky has more than plenty enough money? After blackmailing me all these years, she could afford to miss a few coins and payments."

"Did you ask Candy for the coins?" Tony tried to connect the dots in his head.

"Oh, yeah, and she acted all confused and claimed she didn't know nothin' about them." Duke leaned forward. "There's nothin' worse than a liar, is there?"

"A killer," Tony wanted to say, but forced himself to tamp down the angry words straining to jump from his throat. Somehow, he was sure Duke would believe his reason for killing was justified.

Tony kept his eyes on Duke, and when he saw the man realize what was about to happen, he said, "Wade, I want you to use your handcuffs now."

Wade turned Duke away from the door. "Place your hands on the counter. Palms down. Feet back here."

Duke followed instructions, almost as if he didn't believe it was happening.

"What if she wasn't telling a lie?" Tony's question brought Duke's head around just as Wade locked the second wrist to the first behind his back. The muscles in Duke's shoulders showed the strain created by the uncomfortable position.

"No way." Duke shook his head. "She had to know."

"We, or more precisely, the church ladies, found some coins while they were cleaning." Tony paused, letting the information hang in the air.

"See? I told you." Duke lifted his handcuffed hands slightly and smiled in triumph. "I knew she had them. I'll bet they were in her bedroom."

Tony was fascinated by the hole the man was digging so deeply and putting himself into. "No. They were in the attic, sitting in a dusty box I'm sure Candy never knew about."

Duke stared at Tony. "So what was worth so much out in the garden that she begged me to leave it alone? I had to whack her just to make her quit screeching at me."

"What was she saying?" Tony felt uneasy. He hated the violence and unwarranted pain. He wasn't sure he wanted to hear the details of what Duke had done.

" 'Leave Alvin's plants alone!' " Duke

shouted. "She screamed the words at me, and so I knew he had buried them in the garden. Isn't that what people do with treasure? If she had just given me the coins, none of this would have happened. It was all her fault."

The bell over the door rang, signaling the arrival of a customer. Tony glanced toward the open door. "Sorry, the store's closed for a while." When the door shut again, Tony said, "Let's lock up and go to my office, shall we?"

"This better not take long." Duke frowned. "I'm losing business every minute I'm closed. You want my vote in the coming election?"

Tony ignored him.

The transfer to the Law Enforcement Center didn't take long. They ushered Duke into the interrogation room, ironically in this case, nicknamed the greenhouse, and turned on all their electronic recording devices. Tony thought there were a fair number of double meanings connecting the murder site greenhouse and their confessional.

Wade unlocked the handcuffs and settled their suspect on a chair facing the table, then stood near the door. He waited.

Tony settled onto the chair facing Duke.

"You sure you don't want a lawyer?"

Duke snapped at him, "Quit asking me. The answer's still no." Duke had refused an attorney no fewer than six times, on video-tape and in a voice recording.

"Okay then, just tell me exactly what happened." Tony glanced at Wade and tipped his head, indicating Wade should join them and sit at the table. His deputy's fingers were wrapped tightly around the pen and edge of his notebook.

"It's not like it matters, not now." Duke sneered in the direction of the video camera. "She got what was coming to her."

"And how did her death come about?" Tony hoped his expression merely showed his curiosity and not his revulsion.

"I went over there the night before," Duke said. "We talked about the money thing. I said since the brat probably wasn't mine and wasn't even living with her any more, I wasn't paying her another dime. Next thing you know, she threw me out of the house." Duke's eyes narrowed. "Nobody tells me what to do."

"But you left." Tony let the statement hang.

"Yeah, well, I decided I'd come back in the morning, in the daylight, so it would be easier to find things out in the garden. I knew better than to dig in the dark. Even the moon can't light up her backyard, not with all those trees." He jutted his chin out like a belligerent child refusing to admit being afraid of the dark. "I told her I'd be back and I left."

"What time did you return in the morning?" Tony felt his tension in the strength of his grip on his pen. He was surprised the thing hadn't broken in half. It did seem a bit curved in the center though. He carefully stretched his fingers.

"It was maybe ten-thirty. I went to the store and opened up first. There wasn't much going on, so I told my part-time employee I was going out for coffee. I grabbed a bolt cutter off its hook on my way out, drove by, and picked up the wife."

"You took your wife to visit your girlfriend?" Wade's voice raised in apparent disbelief.

"Bolt cutter?" Tony frowned. "What was that for?"

"Incentive." Duke gave Tony the "how dumb can you be" look. "What do you use when your woman doesn't obey?"

Tony was positive Theo had never promised to obey him. He found the whole concept of obedience of a spouse close to absurd, except with Duke, it became hor-

411

rifying. He thought he'd change the direction of their chat for the moment. "Why take your wife?"

"It was her idea, sort of, because she said she was sick to death of her and the kids paying for my sinful ways." Duke leaned forward and narrowed his eyes. Spittle filled the corners of his lips.

"Okay," Tony said. "Let's go back to your story. You grabbed your bolt cutter and picked up your wife and then headed out to Candy's house? Is that correct?"

"Yeah, yeah, yeah." Duke slouched back further onto his spine. "Are we about done here? I got things to do."

"True, so true." Tony couldn't keep himself from thinking about the arrest and booking procedures that would accompany Duke's intake in the jail. He might have smiled if he wasn't so angry. It would take his staff some time to process their newest resident. Paperwork. Fingerprints. Photographs. They'd switch Duke's personal work clothes for an ill-fitting orange pair of pants and a shirt stenciled with Park County Jail, Inmate. Take away his fancy cowboy boots and give him some shower shoes to wear. He'd be issued a blanket, but the blanket was most likely not up to Duke's normal standards. Explain the rules.

Tony didn't think Duke was going to be a compliant prisoner. "Let's go on. What happened at Candy's?"

"We went out to the garden. She showed me Alvin's tool shed, and I picked out a couple of things to dig with." His expression displayed true aggravation. "Good thing I was wearing gloves. Some of those old handles were more splinters than wood."

Tony was rather hoping Duke would succumb to blood poisoning or tetanus. He considered it rather bold of the felon to be so cranky about the situation. "What was Candy doing and what did you do next?"

"Candy was no help. None at all. She kept yammering on and on about Alvin not liking people in his garden and how she might not be much of a mother, but the least she could do was stay out of his garden. She tried to squeeze past me so she could slip away. Like she could get away from me. Dumb cow." Duke was bristling with anger and self-assuredness. "Hell, I whacked the back of her head with the bolt cutter, just to get her attention."

"Why didn't she fall forward then?" Tony didn't want any holes in the confession. While they had been talking, Archie Campbell, their prosecutor, had arrived and was silently watching the show.

"I don't guess it matters now." Duke's words slowed as the problem he'd created for himself began to sink in. "She started to fall, so I grabbed her hair and yanked it good and hard and kinda jerked her backwards. She fell on her back in that stack of garbage Alvin called a greenhouse. Stupid. It was all her fault. She brought it on herself." Duke glared at each of them in turn. "Bet you would have done the same."

"And?" Tony wasn't going to argue with Duke, but he certainly was not going to agree with him either. "So really, why *did* you bring the bolt cutter?"

"To open the padlock."

Tony wanted everything to be cleared up, neat and tidy. "The padlock on the tool shed?"

"Yeah."

"Was it locked?"

"No." Duke leaned forward on his chair. "But I had already looked all over her house and couldn't find the notebook or the money." He swallowed hard. "She was bleeding me dry."

"Did you try explaining your financial situation to her?"

"Explain?" A sound that could have been called a laugh escaped Duke's mouth. "For a dumb chick, she was mule stubborn. You could talk all day and never convince her of anything."

Tony wondered if Duke had ever heard the old saying about not speaking ill of the dead. If he had, it hadn't impressed him. "So after looking in the house, you headed for the garden and shed, or did you do something else first?"

"I went to the shed and the key was in the lock." Duke shook his handcuffed hands for emphasis. "I pulled out a few tools and asked her where to dig. The cow ignored me. Just lay there in the greenhouse, staring at me. I pulled some of the tarp off the roof, thinking maybe with some more light, I'd see some sign of something being buried."

"And then?" Tony saw no signs of remorse in him, no acceptance of guilt.

"And nothing. I dug in a few places but Candy wouldn't talk to me, you know, like tell me where it was buried." He pouted. "I dumped the yard tools under the steps and told her I was through paying her. Then I threw one of those flip-flops she was always falling out of at her. She couldn't walk two steps without having to stop and put them back on, but she just blinked a few times and then stared at the sky and ignored me. Can you believe that? Dumb, stupid cow."

"What happened to the flip-flop later?"

Tony managed to act conversational, but he was totally revolted by the true nature of this man.

"I should have just tossed it on the ground, but I thought it'd be funny to shove it in the mailbox like I did all that money over the years. Payback. She deserved payback." He clenched his hands and shook his head, swinging his long mane of hair across his face.

Tony gently placed the sealed evidence bag containing a powder-pink notebook about the size of a deck of cards on the table. Carefully noted on the bag was the case number. The victim's name, Candy Tibbles, and the suspect's full name, Duke Michael McMahon, were printed on the bag. "I expect you can guess whose fingerprints we found on this besides Candy's." Tony smiled. "It has your thumbprint on the front and three identifiable prints of yours on the back."

What he didn't mention was it also had McMahon's wife's fingerprints on it. Some they couldn't identify, but he guessed they belonged to Hydrangea Flowers Jackson. They were not digging her up to check.

"I don't guess I'm getting the money I'm due, am I? Alvin gets to keep it all?" Duke sat there in front of witnesses and continued to spout angry words maligning the woman he'd killed, the elderly woman who'd rescued the pink book, and his own wife who'd let someone steal the book from her fire.

Tony was afraid to move. Afraid of himself. And what he might do to the man. He motioned to his deputy. "Wade? Get him out of here."

"Yessir." But Wade sat still, looking almost as paralyzed as Tony. "I'm on it."

After a second, the spell broke and they both rose to their feet and escorted the most blatantly stupid criminal in the world to the jail.

Then they went to talk with Mrs. McMahon, who was delivered to his office by Sheila and Mike. Her story matched Duke's except for one notable difference. She was sobbing, apologizing for everything she'd thought and encouraged Duke to do. "I never, ever, thought he'd kill Candy. I just wanted him to spend the money on his family. I even told him I wouldn't care if Candy put the information about them being a couple on the front page of the newspaper." She lifted tear-drenched eyes, "I'm so sorry."

"How did Hydrangea get the pink book?" Tony asked.

"The old lady saw it and reached into the

burn pile and grabbed it before the fire reached it. She had quick hands for a senior citizen. What was I supposed to do, knock her down and take it away?" Mrs. McMahon's hands fluttered helplessly. "She stopped by our yard a lot to chat, always dragging this old cloth tote filled with strings and newspaper clippings and things she found by the side of the road. I thought it was safe enough."

"Until it showed up again." Tony handed her a wad of tissues. "Did you see a couple of cell phones in her bag or a key on a chain?"

"No." She laughed, a bitter hollow sound. "No phones anywhere, but, I saw Duke pull a key and chain over Candy's head. I guess he pulled so hard they flew out of his hand and vanished into the shrubbery."

"Did you search?

"No. We ran."

Tony wasn't sure what Archie might charge her with. "I'll get your mom to watch your kids until we know what's going to happen."

"Thank you, Sheriff." The brokenhearted woman sat staring at her hands. "I knew you'd find out. I saw the woman next door standing in her window. She must have seen it all."

CHAPTER THIRTY-THREE

"So what do you think?" Tony stared at his ceiling.

Wade's attitude was subdued. He spoke softly, slowly. "I think he killed her just like he said and looked around but couldn't find the gold. So he took his bolt cutter and went back to his store like nothing had happened. I'll bet he put it back right where it had been."

Tony agreed. "Let's get a search warrant. I think we'd better go check those tools in the store for blood and fingerprints. We certainly don't want to miss something and let Duke get away with murder." His musing was interrupted by a call from the head jailer.

"Sheriff, sir, did you promise Duke he could go home?"

"I did not." The question made Tony smile. "I promised not to waste any more time than necessary listening to his whining, and I read him his rights captured on video, and then I said he wouldn't have to worry about clothing."

"I suspected it was something like that. We've got a real cranky prisoner." There was amusement in the jailer's voice. "He doesn't approve of his new clothes."

"That's too bad. Why don't you give him the scratchiest blanket in your inventory."

"Sir?" Sheila stood in his office doorway. For what seemed like the first time in weeks, when he looked at her, she was clean and dry and her normal well-groomed professional self. Her hair was neatly combed. She wasn't sweating or covered with blood. He liked it. Maybe something in his county was returning to normal.

"Do you have a minute?" Sheila's fingers toyed with her watch.

"Come in." Tony thought she seemed almost tentative, which was not her style at all. Of all of his deputies, Sheila usually struck him as the most steady and self-contained. He'd always supposed it had something to do with her continuing sniper training. She exercised, ran for miles, climbed trees, always carrying heavy things, and then she had to turn around and be motionless, sometimes for hours. He'd never seen her fidget. Ever. If anything, her stillness often made him want to move around. "Is there a problem?"

"It's personal." Sheila gently closed the office door before approaching his desk.

Tony waited, a touch of apprehension growing within him. He found himself thinking, *please, please don't let her quit.*

Sheila stopped in front of his desk and ignored his gesture toward a chair. She paused, then exhaled. "Not Bob has asked me out to dinner."

"He has good taste in women." Tony pretended there was not a problem. He couldn't even begin to measure his personal relief. "What was your answer?"

"I told him I'd have to check with you. He's a victim. I'm one of the investigating officers." She stared into Tony's eyes. "Is it ethical?"

"Not exactly." Tony laced his fingers, placed them on his desk, and leaned forward. "What do you think of him?"

"Not Bob has nice eyes and nice feet." A flush of pink touched her cheeks. "If I wasn't staring at his life leaking through my fingers, I might have noticed more." She swallowed hard. "I keep thinking, what if I'd let him die?"

Tony knew Not Bob's life hadn't been

completely under her control. "You did all you could. Luckily it was enough." They were words he'd heard himself and hadn't agreed with. Sometimes the truth sounded like claptrap, a word his late father had loved. Tony supposed there were worse things than starting to sound his old man, as long as he didn't succumb to the temptation to refer to anyone as "the old dear."

"He sent me flowers along with the invitation to dinner."

Sheila's words pulled him back from his mental wandering. "Roses?"

"Worse. Tulips and daisies." The corners of her lips pulled down. "My favorites. How did he know?"

Tony guessed it was a case of blind good luck on Not Bob's part. Tony didn't know Theo's favorites, but was pretty sure she liked the ones printed on fabric better than cut ones in a vase. He hoped so. "Maybe they were the only ones available." He laced his fingers, tapping his desk with his thumbs. "Officially, in this case, I don't consider you dating him a problem. He's a grown man. You've never dated another victim?" He turned it into a question, and was relieved when she said no. "This is a small town. You obviously knew about him before the incident because you saw him

422

working and knew what he did for a living. What did you think about him then?"

She smiled and her eyes sparkled. "I thought he handled a shovel well, and it gave him nice broad shoulders."

Tony laughed at her comment. "Okay, there is every reason for me to believe you two would have met without the matchmaking abilities of a nut job with a hammer and wrench."

Sheila relaxed a bit. "Do I hear a but?"

"A small one." Tony considered his next words with care. "Take it slow. He's been severely traumatized, and you're his guardian angel, the woman who saved his life, literally preventing him from dying with your bare hands."

"I'll leave my halo at home. I promise." Sheila poked a loose tendril back into her braid. "What's going to happen with the botany spy?"

"I'll bet he doesn't get the award for producing a beetle resistant strain of plants. I don't know if his Ph.D. can be revoked, but I'll bet he has trouble getting university work. They tend to be a little picky about hiring known thieves."

"Sheriff?" Rex's voice interrupted the discussion.

Tony thought he detected amusement in

Rex's voice and mentally braced himself. At least it was probably not too serious. "What is it?"

"You are *not* going to believe this." Rex paused a moment. "Mrs. Emily Austin just drove to the front door, climbed out, and came inside to lodge a complaint. She says she loaned someone a mink coat and she wants it back."

"Does she know what the temperature is today?"

"Probably not." Rex laughed. "Mike said he followed her all the way to the door and charged her with driving under the influence and driving on a suspended license and couldn't believe it when she led him here. He tried to pull her over, but she just kept driving."

Tony was yanked into real time. "Wait, when you say drove to the door . . . ?"

"Yessir. The car is on parked on the front sidewalk, wedged pretty tightly against those yellow safety poles. Someone from Thomas Brothers is coming to lock it in the impound lot."

"Her family is going to have to take away her key; alcohol isn't mixing well with her medications." Tony shook his head, both relieved and concerned. He didn't want Emily to live out her last days in his jail.

"Sounds like we're back to business as usual. I'll bet your next call involves squirrels stealing seeds from the bird feeders."

ABOUT THE AUTHOR

Barbara Graham began making up stories in the third grade and immediately quit learning to multiply and divide. Her motto is "every story needs a dead body and every bed needs a quilt." She writes because she cannot "not write." Barbara continues to be intrigued by the problems and situations her imaginary friends manage to get themselves into. She refuses to accept any blame for their misfortunes and actions.

A prize-winning quilter, she enjoys combining her fabric addiction with her predilection for telling tall tales.

Married to a man who can do math in his head (very useful to a quilter), she has two perfect sons, one perfect grandson, and "is not the worst mother-in-law in history."

CPSIA information can be obtained
at www.ICGtesting.com
Printed in the USA
FFOW04n1914310114